By the Same Author

Day Shift Werewolf (3-Day Books)
winner of the 2005 International 3-Day Novel Contest

A thorough delight that will make you laugh out loud.
—*Bay Area Reporter*

Underwood's winning entry is a series of interlocking stories exploring the existential crises of monsters living and working in the same small Northwest town...Reading it, you find yourself stopping several times to admire that anyone could write like this in such a short amount of time.
—*The Oregonian*

Each character is brilliantly drawn, with never a thought or action that doesn't ring true. First-time novelist Jan Underwood has written an eminently readable, often hilarious, book.
—*Broken Pencil magazine*

Jan Underwood brings us a first novel that is just stunning. This fun little book has less than 100 pages and I raced through it in less than a day...A wickedly fun and entertaining book.
—*The Literary Word*

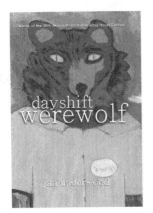

The most endearing bunch of misfits you could ever hope to meet...The writing is so zestful and funny that it clearly is a winner.
—*The Bookmonger*

These funny and believable characters sparkle without being obvious or overwritten and their individual tales remind us of the value of all creatures.
—*Geist magazine*

for Maddie

Utterly Heartless

Is giving you a copy of my book like making a gift of a framed photo of myself ??

Jan Underwood

Underwood

summer 2013

for my wonderful parents

Chapter One

BONUS, MELIOR, OPTIMUS

The waters were high tonight, so before she set out for work, Alice pulled on her hip waders. Wading made the going slow. Usually she arrived early so she could place arch supports inside her shoes and swipe the pole with disinfectant, but by the time she reached the club, there was no time. Alice slid into the dressing room and changed. The club was throbbing with music and with the white noise of patrons. Alice scooted onto the floor, careful to avoid eye contact with the Larries, who were already sucking their drinks at the bar.

She hooked her leg over the pole and swung herself up, arching backward and then pulling herself upright. Her white nurse's orthotics could hardly be less sexy, but that was part of the visual joke. Still wrapped about the pole, she drew one knee at a time to herself so she could unlace the shoes and fling them to the side of the stage, then wiggled her feet in their white stockings. Wednesdays were costume night at the club, and they were her favorite nights. Stripping was, after all, a form of acting.

Alice had a four-hour shift, then calculus homework. She should try to make it to bed by 2 a.m. because she had Latin in the morning. She dry-humped the pole a few times, stroking the brass with one hand and wishing for a change of music. Band practice at 4 tomorrow. She should finish up her scholarship application, too. She was applying for the Millicent Vena Cava Award for humanities students, and she figured she had a pretty good shot at it.

Alice started to dance a little faster, then pulled back. Her technique was to ratchet up and back off to build tension. She'd written her essay but still needed to ask three profs for letters of recommendation. And she might need to dig up her tax records. She should make a checklist. Alice danced freestyle for a few minutes. Then she shimmied back and forth across the stage, smiling and winking at the patrons, pulled herself up onto the pole one last time and did an inverted snake for her finale as the music ended.

Alice gave her nurse's cap a tug in a salute to her patrons, then glided to the tip rail. She approached a zitty young man whose expression betrayed his newness to the strip club scene. His friends elbowed and razzed him as Alice smiled his way.

"That was great," the young man told her, flustered. "You were great."

Alice leaned way forward toward him. If he'd wanted to, he could have nested his nose into her décolletage, but she knew he wouldn't. It was always a judgment call, how close she could get to the patrons. Some patrons she needed to keep beyond arm's length. Others, like this one, were safe to within a millimeter. City statutes said four inches. Alice told the young man she was glad he enjoyed the show and asked him what he liked to do when he wasn't at Cootchie-Coo.

"Uh, play World of Warcraft," he said, flummoxed.

"Oh, you play WoW? What class do you play?"

A stripper who played WoW: Alice may as well have been an angel just descended from the heavens. "Uh, oh, uh, a level 85 mage," the young man told her.

"Awesome," Alice said in a silky, flattering voice. Alice was not actually a gamer, but she'd learned enough about RPGs, model airplanes, pro hockey and league bowling to keep her tips high. She lingered. The mage's friends nudged him and he fumbled with his wallet and pulled out a five.

"Um," he said.

"Just slide it right in here," Alice said, proffering one gartered thigh.

She moved on in accordance with her personal guidelines for collecting tips: always leave the patrons wanting more, and never stay so long with one that the others think you've lost interest in them.

She had twenty minutes between now and her next set, so in the dressing room she set her timer, pulled her Latin textbook out of her backpack and started in on Chapter 23: Comparatives and Superlatives. They seemed pretty straightforward. *Longus* became *longior, longius* in the comparative, *longissimus, -a, -um* in the superlative. *Brevis, brevior, brevius; brevissimus, -a, -um.* One reason Alice could appreciate this job was that Renee didn't mind if she did homework between sets. Some places wouldn't let you do that—you might get distracted and miss your cue. In those clubs, the dancers just sat in the back, smoking and messing with their makeup. Of course, Renee had a one-strike-and-you're-out rule. But Alice wasn't going to screw up.

When her timer went off, she stepped back out on stage, dancing without imagination. Adjectives ending in *-er*, Alice said to herself, have a superlative in *-errimus*. She rubbed her ass on the pole, the brass cool between her butt cheeks.

Pulcher, pulcherrimus; celer, celerrimus; miser, miserrimus; acer, acerrimus.

Alice did a kick-up invert and wound herself with syrupy slowness around the pole. Irregular adjectives: *Bonus, -a, -um, melior, melius, optimus, -a, -um. Magnus, -a, -um, maior, maius, maximus, -a, -um.* Upside down, she watched the knees and pant legs of her patrons and the club's black walls spiral in and out of her field of vision. Alice couldn't call to mind the rule regarding adjectives whose stem ended in a vowel. She'd have to review on her next break.

She didn't tally her tips until the end of the night. She'd done okay, even forgoing the dollar bills of the men named Larry, who sat front and center most nights. The Larries weren't good at honoring the no-touchy rule, and the house wasn't good at enforcing it. She pulled a couple hundred dollars from her earnings for her stage fee, then drew tip-outs for the bus boy and Renee. She'd netted $190. Now she'd be able to pay the balance on her bookstore tab.

Though she lived just eight blocks from the club, Alice knew better than to walk home at night after a shift. She treated cab fare, on nights when she didn't bike, as a business expense.

The door of the house Alice shared with three other students was swollen shut with winter weather. Alice waited until the cab pulled away and then swung one leg high over the   living room windowsill and pulled herself up and in through the window.

Her housemates Amy and Jillian were studying. Tad was in the basement with his guitar. Alice went straight to the bathroom and dumped the contents of her bag into the sink to soak in a dilute solution of white vinegar. There was nothing else like that skin club smell, at once fleshy and metallic—a venomous potage of sweat, booze, cigarettes, ass, cologne,

Pine Sol, French fry grease, jism, isobutyl nitrite, urine, vinyl, pussy and air freshener. She jumped in the shower to scrub the club off her skin, reciting irregular comparatives and superlatives as she did so.

Alice did one more thing before she went to bed. She pulled out her Latin notebook and flipped it open to the back inside cover. There she made a single hatch mark next to 362 others. 363 down; 446 to go. That was the exact number of nights of stripping she had left before graduation.

Chapter Two

LOSING HEART

It was rush hour and the bus was very crowded. Commute-weary workers squeezed two to a seat and formed a rumpled line down the center aisle, hanging onto their rubber handles and lurching with each stop. Linnea knew the route well—she was on Bus 9, rumbling up Poe Avenue—but she didn't remember leaving campus or boarding the bus. It was as though she'd been deep in thought and had gotten herself here without noticing. Now she awoke from her reflections with a start.

A man, tiny and papery with age, occupied the seat next to her. He wore a pea coat and held a canvas bag of groceries on his lap. Despite his frail appearance, he had a sharp eye and seemed to take an interest in Linnea, glancing at her with curiosity. Linnea made a prim little half-smile in his direction, not wanting to be rude, but not wanting to engage in conversation. She had things to figure out.

She hugged her arms to herself, a posture that fended off human interaction and the blasts of cold air that came in with the commuters at each stop. She really could not remember how she'd gotten here. Images flashed through her mind. They were violent and unclear, involving blood and fear and physical pain. Images of struggle and tiled floors. Given her memory problem and the curious way the stranger with the groceries was eyeing her, it seemed likely that she'd suffered some kind of head trauma. She probably ought to get herself to a hospital.

Linnea strained to remember her day. She had taught; she had gone home and packed her bags for the Classical Studies conference; she'd gone to the Splash to speak at a union-organizing meeting. Here was a spot of the barbeque sauce she'd spilled on her skirt. She was still dressed in the clothes she'd worn to the meeting.

She remembered laying out for the other organizers what she'd learned of the deans' plans for budget cuts. She remembered the determined, earnest faces of her colleagues—Isabelle Grenouille from French; Ian Elf, an English prof; Bleistift from Physics and a few others. They were close to having enough support for a union. "If we push," Linnea had told them, "I think we're going to be able to call an election before the term ends."

All right; what then? Linnea narrowed her eyes. She'd returned to campus at about 9 to wrap up some odious paperwork for her department. What had happened after that? She concentrated but could not remember finishing the documents or leaving Middlebridge.

Buses stopped running at midnight, so she would expect it to be around 11 now. But the bus was crammed full of people as though they were on their way home from work, with briefcases and umbrellas and high-end raincoats. Had Linnea lost a day somewhere? Was she waking from amnesia?

The old man next to Linnea was shrunken and bent, his

face a dust-bowl landscape of cracks and fissures, but his eyes were oddly bright. He tilted his head and looked at her. Embarrassed, Linnea looked away. The window beside her was opaque with condensation. Between the blasting heat and the warmth of all those commuting bodies, it was plenty warm, in a damp way, on the bus, but everyone else wore a coat and Linnea did not. Her blouse gaped between buttons over a torso that had expanded a size or two in the last year. As she tried tugging it back into modesty, she felt a tear in the fabric. She looked down. Her blouse was stiff with what appeared to be dried blood. Linnea turned away from her seatmate toward the dark window of the bus to continue her inspection. She slipped two fingers into the tear and found a wound in her chest, ragged scraps of flesh around its edges. She prodded, amazed to feel no pain. It was a great gaping hole of a wound, she discovered with hypnotic awe. A hole where her heart should have been.

"Crap," she said aloud.

Linnea looked up and saw the image, in the bus window, of her little old seat-mate. Their eyes met in the reflection.

"What's wrong, dear heart?" he asked.

Linnea sat back in her seat. "I think I'm dead," she said.

The old man held her gaze, searching her face with those piercing bright eyes. "I think you are, too," he told her. "But let's be certain. May I?"

He took her wrist in his bony hands, his knuckles big with arthritis, and felt for her pulse. "Nothing," he said after a moment. "May I touch your carotid artery?"

Linnea nodded, frightened and fascinated. The elderly little man pressed two fingers against her throat.

"*Tabula rasa*," he said. "Dead you are, my dear." The old man patted her knee and told her, "There's an information booth about three blocks up. I'd go with you, but this is my stop."

"An information booth?" Linnea knew there was no such thing on this stretch of Poe Avenue. Her fellow passenger was struggling to get up. Linnea held his canvas bag for him while he pulled himself to standing. "What do I ask at the booth?" she said, but the old man, who was perhaps hard of hearing and who needed all his concentration to negotiate the trip to the exit, disappeared into the crowd. Linnea heard the heavy thunk of the bus door opening and closing.

The bus rumbled forward, and Linnea yanked the stop pull. She had doubts about what to do next, but she could think of no good reason to stay on Bus 9. She disembarked in the rain and looked up and down the street. It was dark. Headlights and brake lights flashed in the shiny blackness. A hundred yards ahead, where no information booth had ever been before, sat a good-sized green kiosk. Linnea hurried over to it.

The kiosk was staffed by a thick, unsmiling woman in uniform. Her name tag read "Esme." "Date of birth," she barked as Linnea approached. She turned to her computer terminal, waiting.

"8-19-68," Linnea told her, surprised but relieved that the other woman had taken the lead.

Esme tap-tapped without commentary, her eyes scanning her monitor. "Linnea E. Nil?"

"Yes."

"I need to see photo I.D."

Linnea rummaged in her bag and produced a driver's license.

Esme continued to look through Linnea's file. "It says you are unaffiliated."

"Unaffiliated …?"

"Religiously. No membership in any known congregation,

past or present."

"That's correct," Linnea said, mystified.

Esme scrolled down. "And you subscribe to no particular spiritual beliefs."

Linnea concurred.

"Your only brush with religious thought," said Esme as she squinted at the screen, "has come in the form of an undergraduate course in comparative world religions in the fall of 1986. And," she continued, tap-tapping, "a certain affinity for the practices of the ancient Romans during the era of the Republic."

Linnea said, "I wouldn't call it an affinity, exactly. I've done some scholarly work—"

"Immaterial," Esme barked.

"All right, well, what do I do now?"

"Go to Hades, obviously. I advise against delay." She gave Linnea a look of warning from beneath her stern brow as though she expected dilly-dallying from the dead professor.

"Hades? What do you mean?"

Esme read again from the screen, "A certain affinity for the practices of the ancient Romans during the era of the Republic."

"I have to spend eternity in Hades on the basis of two essays I published in the *Antiquities Studies Journal*?"

"You haven't given us anything else to work with."

"But that's ridiculous," Linnea protested. "Can't I just go to Heaven?"

Esme's stout bosom rose and fell as she snorted with impatience. "You should have worked all this out before now, shouldn't you?"

"There's been some misunderstanding," Linnea said. "Isn't there someone I could talk to?"

Esme pulled a paper map from beneath the counter. "You

are here," she said, circling an icon of a kiosk on Poe Avenue. "Here," she said, drawing an X, "there's a public square called Puddle Place."

"I know," said Linnea. "I've lived in Bridges for 12 years."

"Well you've never *died* here before, have you?" Esme snapped. "Now. You're going to walk north—" she drew a straight line up 17th Avenue with a magic marker "—and bear left at the square. Here," she continued, circling a spot, "you will find the entrance to Hades. Once you descend, follow the directional signs." She folded the map and handed it to Linnea with a briskness that indicated their conversation was finished.

Chapter Three

FEES AND NOTIONS

Thursday Alice went to the library to study her notes from the previous day's Latin class. "Purpose clauses with the adverb *nē*," Dr. Nil had told the students, without cracking a smile, "exist so that students of Latin might grace their translations with the English word 'lest.'" Whenever Dr. Nil made these sly statements about language, Alice recognized her professor as a kindred spirit. *Bonōs librōs nōbīs dent nē malōs legāmus!* May they give us good books, *lest* we read bad ones! Delighted, Alice had copied the Latin sentence and its translations from the board and written "Lest!!" in the margin of her notebook with a big star around it.

After a year of shopping around in the humanities for a major, Alice had discovered Latin in the first semester of her sophomore year. She was lovestruck. She declared herself a Classics major and outfitted her bike helmet accordingly, affixing to it a headdress, fashioned from a push-broom, like that of a Roman centurion.

Wednesday her favorite professor had been looking a little weary, but Alice was undeterred: they were studying the uses of the subjunctive, which was delectable. Alice had long mourned the passing of the subjunctive from the English language. She made a practice of clipping examples of English verb mood abuse from newspapers and magazines, sentences where reporters had erroneously used an indicative where a subjunctive was called for: "It is important that you are here on time," for example, in the place of "It is important that you *be* here on time." She and her friends from Latin class gathered these clippings and, once or twice a semester, made a bonfire of them and observed a moment of silence.

These friends included her best buddies Brian and Mick, who were the strongest students in Latin 102. After they'd met in the fall, they had started a punk band called Watery Discharge. Alice played bass, Mick drums, Brian lead guitar, and when Alice and Tad had gotten together, Tad had jumped in and started playing rhythm.

Alice and her band buddies were among a crop of students who had formed what seemed to be a nationwide Latin cult. Thanks to them, Latin was becoming the new knitting: an endeavor so geeky that to master it was deeply cool. These were the learners who fell in love with proviso clauses and deponent verbs, who adored the passive periphrastic and revered the ablative of means and who fist-bumped each other when they nailed the conjugation of *eō*.

Now in the library, Alice turned a page in her notebook and looked over her recent work. In the previous class session, Dr. Nil had had the students puzzle out translations in pairs, and Alice had gotten saddled with a certain classmate, Dexter Beet, who was in a constant state of befuddlement. She didn't know how Dexter had escaped Latin 101 alive. He was pale and clammy, and whenever he was paired with Alice he broke into a cold sweat. Alice had no patience for him.

"Okay," Alice had said, preparing to read from the text. "'We will not sing, lest they throw boots at us.'" She had paused. Dexter, breathing audibly, had looked around the room and at the clock.

"You look up 'boots' while I look up 'to sing.'" Maybe she could prod Dexter by giving him a specific task. "Okay. *Nōn cantābimus*, obviously," Alice had said. "*Nē...* Did you find 'boots'?" Dexter hadn't stirred. "Oh, give me that." Alice had grabbed their Latin textbook and flipped to the glossary at the back. "*Nē caligās nōs...* 'to throw at' is *adiciō*, third conjugation, so the third-person plural subjunctive would be *adiciant*. *Nōn cantābimus nē caligās nōs adiciant*. Right?"

Dexter was almost trembling. He'd looked at the clock again and said, "I gotta go." To Alice's surprise he'd grabbed his backpack and more or less fled the room. The students who had been sitting near them all looked at Alice. She'd shrugged. "I think *nē* clauses freak him out," she'd said.

Crammed with pizza places, used bookstores, second-hand clothing boutiques and tattoo shops, the pleasant side streets adjacent to the Middlebridge campus hosted an agreeable jumble of businesses catering to the tastes of college students. After leaving the library, Alice headed to her personal favorite, a tiny notions shop on the corner of 16th and Poe. It housed barrels of buttons, rows and rows of knitting needles, and a whole wall of thread spools in every color imaginable and some colors not imaginable. Alice liked to design and make her own clothes out of found objects, and this shop was the best place in town to look for a length of ribbon or a needle of a certain size. It was hard to imagine how a store where everything cost so little could stay in business, but the notions shop did a brisk trade. It was, after all, the job of college students to pick and choose from a lot of notions.

Case in point: all through middle school and high school, Alice had had the idea that her teeth were too big for her mouth. They were big and a bit outsplayed, those teeth, and they lent her face a swollen and faintly simian look. Throughout her adolescence Alice had hated them, and never smiled with her mouth open. She had begged her parents for braces they couldn't afford.

Then she'd come to Middlebridge and discovered the notions shop. Early in the first semester of freshman year she'd wandered in, curious, and had picked up the notion "conventional prettiness is not very interesting." She wasn't sure it suited her, but it was on sale, so she'd bought it and taken it home.

Within a week or two, she'd met Tad. On their very first date he said to her, "You have a really big mouth."

Alice had frowned at this forthrightness.

"I feel like you could swallow me whole."

Alice was about to tell him what a jerk he was when he'd added, "It's extremely hot." And within seconds they'd had their mouths all over each other.

So with a little help from her boyfriend and the tiny shop on Poe Avenue, Alice had swapped out an old notion for its opposite, and the shop became one of her favorite places in Bridges.

Today the notions shop had a two-for-one special going. Flipping through the M-N section, Alice considered "Microwave ovens make you sterile" and lingered over "No one can take advantage of you without your permission." In V-Z, she perused "Vaccinations give babies autism" and "Western medicine causes more illness than it cures," wondering if she should pick them up for her pregnant housemate Jillian. She decided against that impulse; Jillian already had more notions than she had space for.

"Hey, Alice."

Alice looked up. A guy from her Western Civ class had just come in the door. All the hairs on his head seemed to have been fused together in a single piece, like the thatch on the roof of some peasant cottage. He had explained to her that he was conducting an experiment to see what would happen if he simply stopped combing his hair. It had been six or eight months now.

"Hey Guppy," said Alice. "What's up?"

Guppy shrugged. "Not much. I need to get some money together. I brought in some dialectical materialism I thought I might unload."

"Oh, yeah?"

"Yeah, well, we'll see. They probably have a surplus here."

"You could put it on Craig's List," Alice suggested. She continued browsing. Guppy began to poke through a sale bin at the end of the aisle.

"I might do that. Hey, do we have a quiz Tuesday?"

"Yup. Robespierre and the French Revolution."

Guppy said, "The French Revolution is so bad-ass. So what about you? You looking for anything special?"

Alice shook her head. She moved to the next rack. "I just like browsing."

Guppy said, "You going to the game Friday night?"

Alice had to stop and think about what game that might be. She was not a sports fan. "Hunh-uh."

"The Marmots're favored in the regional championships," Guppy said.

The Middlebridge Marmots had had a strong basketball team for quite a few years in a row, and there was a kind of frenzied enthusiasm for them on campus that Alice regarded as noisy and lowbrow.

"I've always thought ball games were kind of pointless," Alice said. She spoke with conviction, but a look of disappointment crossed Guppy's face, and Alice felt bad. She liked Guppy; she had no reason to demean his personal interests.

"Dude, no. They're, like, a nexus of sociological activity. There's music and audience-participation games and dance performances." Guppy set his backpack on the wooden floor of the notions shop and knelt to unzip it. "Somebody always comes out and throws free T-shirts into the crowd. Plus watching the crazy fans is a spectator sport all unto itself."

The mention of dance performances got Alice's attention.

"You don't know about them?" Guppy turned his face up toward Alice. "The Marmettes. They're awesome."

"Wow. I thought ball games were just a bunch of guys shoving each other around for a couple hours," Alice said. Staged to satisfy the public's blood lust, she added in her mind. She had always considered team sports a kind of choreographed violence, the natural evolution of the ancient Romans' gladiatorial games and animal tortures. Guppy was pulling stuff out of his crowded backpack and setting it on the floor. "They don't have a very dignified name," she couldn't help pointing out. "Marmettes."

"That's true," Guppy said. "And they don't get scholarship money, either. They should, though."

Alice had never thought about it before.

Guppy found what he was looking for and began placing items back into his pack. He smiled at her. Alice knew she had been forgiven her trespasses against basketball, and she was embarrassed.

"I gotta get going," said Guppy. He slung his backpack

on, saluted her, and turned away. Alice watched as her classmate took his second-hand Marxism to the front counter to see what he could get for it.

Before dinner, Alice sprawled on the floor of the living room and flipped through images. "I'm getting a new tattoo," she told her housemates. "Wanna see?"

"You just got one," said Jillian from the kitchen. She was pulling pots and pans from the cupboards with loud sighs, pausing to put her hands on her kidneys in a long-suffering show of lower back pain.

"I did not 'just' get one. That was last semester," Alice said. In November, after she'd declared herself a Classics major, she'd marked the occasion by having a quote from Hannibal tattooed in a spiral around her calf. *Aut viam inveniam aut faciam*: Either I shall find a way, or I shall make one. "Come look."

Amy peered over Alice's shoulder at the musical instrument catalog Alice held. Alice flipped to a page displaying a handsome electric bass similar to the one she played.

"Sweet," said Amy.

"Would you like it better outlined in red or black?" Alice asked her, musing.

"Mmmm," said Amy. "I think black."

"Yeah, I think so, too."

"Doesn't it hurt?" Amy asked. She asked that every time the subject of tattoos came up.

"Of course it does," Alice told her.

Amy shuddered. "I couldn't do it."

"I thought you said you didn't have money for 'non-essentials,'" said Jillian from the kitchen, a bag of carrots in her hands.

"Music is not a non-essential," Alice retorted. "Art is not a non-essential. My identity is essential to me, thank you very much, and the guitar is part of my identity. Besides," she said, a little more loudly, to intercept any more snide remarks coming from the other room, "Watery Discharge just got its first paid gig."

"Seriously?" Amy said. "Where?"

"A pub called the Splash," Alice said. "On the west side. Next Thursday night."

"Cool," said Amy.

Alice expected Amy to say she'd come to the performance, out of loyalty to her if not out of love for the art, but Amy was silent.

Jillian said, "Can I get some help in here?" It was her turn to make dinner for the household with Alice's help.

"Be right there." Alice took one last greedy look at the image she wanted to have etched onto her thigh and then tucked the music catalog into her Latin textbook and went to the kitchen to help Jillian.

"I'll do the washing and the chopping," Jillian told her. "You'll need to do the actual cooking, because the smell makes me sick."

"Okay." Alice rummaged in the cupboards for oil and whatever seasonings they had on hand.

"How much will you get paid?" Jillian asked with just a touch of derision, implying that not many people would shell out money to hear Alice's band.

Alice shrugged. "Depends on how many people show," she said. "But we're guaranteed $200, plus a percentage of whatever they bring in in cover charges. So however it works out, I'll have enough to cover a tattoo. A little one."

Jillian scraped peppers and celery from a cutting board into the wok.

"That's a good thing, with the first of the month coming up."

"Rent is a big bite," Alice concurred.

"You still owe a balance on your spring semester tuition, don't you?" Jillian said. Alice wished Jillian didn't know so much about her finances. "You know you pay more if you pay in installments." Jillian had adopted that tone she used when she imagined she possessed superior knowledge.

"Yes, of course I know. I don't have a choice," Alice said, irritated. Jillian was able to pay a full year's tuition up-front because she'd gotten an advance for the surrogate baby she was carrying. She had it all worked out: she planned to deliver four babies, one for each year of college. With the smug satisfaction of a healthy young woman with no fertility issues, she was timing her conceptions to coincide with tuition due dates.

Alice measured out a cup of brown rice and two cups of water. Her parents kicked in a chunk of the cost of college, and her earnings from Cootchie-Coo took care of the rest, just. She was taking a full load of classes and working half-time. It was that or graduate, like so many of her peers, tens of thousands of dollars in debt.

"That's too bad," said Jillian blithely. "What will you do about the new fee increase?"

"What new fee increase?" Alice stopped pouring.

"Didn't you hear?" Alice could see in Jillian's face how Jillian loved being privy to information. "Uh-oooh!"

"Hear what?"

"Some dean came out with a big announcement Monday morning. They're instituting a 20 percent increase in existing fees and adding some new ones."

"Oh, God," said Alice. "Seriously?" She set the measuring cup down and leaned against the sink.

Fees had become a clever way for colleges to raise revenue without appearing to increase tuition. The list of fees to be included in each semester's payments at Middlebridge went on for pages and threatened to someday overtake the money spent on credit hours. In spring term Alice had been charged a bike parking fee, a sump-pump fee, a fee for enrolling in an odd number of credits, an ivy-clearing fee, a scholarship collection fee, a financial aid distribution fee, a final grades posting fee, a registrar's birthday fee, a Wi-Fi fee, a student loan application fee, and a marmot fee.

"When does it start?" Alice asked. "Fall term?"

"They want to make it retroactive to the beginning of this school year," Jillian said, "and collect it right away. They're not going to allow faculty to release our midterms to us until our fees are paid." Jillian swept the remaining vegetables from the cutting board into the wok and said, "Looks like our prep work is all done. Can you handle the stir-frying on your own?"

Alice's mind was sprinting. She tried to imagine what she could cut from her budget, but there was very little left to cut. Room and board did not get skinnier than this anywhere; her only real expenses came from Middlebridge. If she worked more hours, she'd have to take fewer classes, and that would extend the number of semesters she'd need to stay in school. Plus she already had the most desirable work shifts, the nighttime ones. Except for the lunch hour, Cootchie-Coo's business was sluggish during the day. "I feel sick," Alice told Jillian.

Jillian said, "Maybe you should start taking vitamins," and left the room.

Chapter Four

LA PLUME DE MA TANTE

Dori Amore had dean troubles.

The Dean of Allocations had summoned Dori to her office that morning, saying she had an "idea" for the French department. Dori's heart sank to hear it. Dean Eleanor Fiercey's (six-figure) post was a new one—created to help the college trim its budget—and Fiercey had earned admiration in some circles for her unflinching willingness, in her phrase, to "cook off the fat."

When Dori arrived at the dean's suite, Fiercey exclaimed, *"La plume de ma tante est sur le bureau de mon oncle!"* Evidently Fiercey had studied French forty years before, and she trilled this pointless phrase every time she laid eyes on Dori, who chaired the departments of French and Italian. *"La plume de ma tante,"* she repeated, and then she gushed, "Tapes! I learned so much French from tapes! Now we can have it all again, using the current technologies!"

Dean Fiercey, built like a Buick and fond of houndstooth

suits, closed the door behind them and offered Dori coffee and cream. She took a seat beside Dori, where she could nudge the French professor with her elbow in a conspiratorial way as she laid out her vision. French as a discipline, she explained, would become a strictly distance-learning program. Students would access the disembodied voices of Frenchmen on-line. They would practice repeating and responding at home and then record and upload their best efforts to the system. By means of voice-recognition software, computers could even grade students' work. Dori felt queasy as Dean Fiercey leaned in toward her, describing with an oily smile an instructional method that eliminated both instructors and instruction.

She was willing to devote resources to the foreign languages, Fiercey said in a cozy tone, including a fleet of powerful new computers. Dori might even be in for a promotion; perhaps she would become Associate Dean of the new program. All Fiercey wanted from Dori, the dean said, were the names of French professors who could be "thinned" from the department.

Fiercey slid a list of faculty members and a highlighter marker across her desk. Dori thought the dean wanted her to start highlighting names then and there, and she grew bilious. Then Fiercey said with a smile, "Take your time with this, and return it to me at your convenience."

To shake off her thoughts, Dori went from Fiercey's office to the gym. (Dori continued to call it the gym, though to the college it was the Facility for Educationally Athletic Recreation, or FEAR.) Her fencing partner, Jaspar Kensington, was always happy to leave the stacks of the library for a few bouts.

The gymnasium sat on the west edge of campus,

overlooking the shabbier neighborhood beyond. From the basketball court (which Dori and Jaspar referred to as their fencing *salle*), Dori could see students and homeless people lining up outside the plasma donation center, and, just beyond campus, a payday advance business, a pawnshop and a skin club.

The friends suited up and set about fencing, their silence broken only by grunts of effort. At 5'2" and 103 lbs., Dori enjoyed the strength she felt while fencing. Fencing was a sport in which being a muscled hulk was no particular help. Cleverness, agility and lightness on one's feet were much greater assets. She had a passion for the concentration fencing took—the way the world fell away and there was nothing but the match, jockeying for advantage, looking for openings, feinting—all with as much speed and dexterity and cunning as she could muster. She thought only of the move at hand, loving the challenge, the way it forced her to stay in the moment, the *tic tac tic tac* of the blades.

Dori and Jaspar fenced for thirty or forty minutes, until they were hot and breathing hard. They took a water break, and then Dori told Jaspar she'd like to move on to saber work. She wanted to be well-rounded for the upcoming regional fencing tournament, and she wanted to be ready to face her longtime rival, the odious saber champion Aldous Adipose.

They began to bout. Despite her strong start, Dori's balance and timing were poor in this round. The saber was the most difficult of the three fencing weapons—saber fencing was fast and aggressive—and Dori had a tendency to get a bit wild with it.

Cut, parry, cut, parry, feint, thrust, riposte, retreat, bend your knees, loosen your grip, cut, parry, cut, no leaning, advance, don't let your free arm flop—Jaspar scored his fifth point against her and they both stopped, panting. Dori removed her helmet. She was disgusted with herself. Now that she'd hit her 40s, she'd noticed, she wasn't as precise as she'd once been. With waning estrogen came a clumsy impulsivity that was new to her.

They saluted and began again. Advance. *Tic, tac, tic, tac*, clash, *tic, tac.* Too much arm, not enough wrist. Retreat. Loosen your grip, Dori. Use technique, not strength. Jaspar retreated, and Dori used the distance between them to execute a beautiful *flèche*, a smooth run that propelled her forward like an arrow in flight, sword arm outstretched to score.

"Whoa!" said Jaspar. "What's that about?" No running attacks were permitted in saber fencing. Dori had gotten carried away.

"I'm sorry," Dori said. She paused to collect herself. They began again. Jaspar scored on Dori twice. Then he moved in for another attack. Dori met his blade with hers but, excited, she jerked her arm and sent his saber flying off to one side, where it clattered on the polished gymnasium floor.

"Ouch," said Jaspar.

"Oh, God, I'm sorry."

"Do you want to call it a day?"

After practice they stood in the hall with their helmets under their arms. "So, do you feel ready?" Jaspar asked. The tournament, Pacific Northwest Blades of Lightning Championship, was just ten days away. "I am looking forward to the gloating."

"Now, now," said Dori. "Gloating isn't sportsmanlike."

"Oh, I wouldn't gloat about my own victories," Jaspar told her. "Only about yours."

"Well, we'll see what happens," said Dori. She and Jaspar both hoped she would triumph over the widely despised Aldous Adipose, with his cheetah's speed, his gazelle's grace, and his mountain gorilla's ego.

Dori accepted that Adipose was the better fencer. But he had a habit of taunting and belittling his opponents, and always in a way that wasn't quite a cardable offense. He knew Dori spoke French, and he liked to needle her with francophone insults no one else could understand. At last year's tournament he had soundly defeated Dori, then leaned in toward her and said, smirking, *Qui s'y frotte s'y pique*: She who rubs there gets stung there. Dori itched to put him in his place. She'd been training hard in preparation.

"I'm not feeling all that ready," Dori told Jaspar. "I certainly didn't fence well today." She stretched each of her quads in turn.

"You'll do great."

Dori knew why she was off her game, and it wasn't her feeble hormones. She told Jaspar about her visit with the Dean of Allocations and about Fiercey's plan for the departments of French and Italian.

"But that's crazy," Jaspar said.

"Fiercey doesn't care. There's a lot of potential profit in distance learning. Imagine! Putting up one of those fun little websites where people can learn to say '*Où est la toilette?*' and offering college credit for it."

"How can Middlebridge go down that road and not lose its accreditation?" Jaspar said.

"She doesn't care about that, either," Dori said. She crossed one leg over the other and squatted, stretching her piriformis. "Middlebridge is just a stepping-stone in her career. She'll be on her way to the next college before we're in real trouble, and she'll use her track record of 'budget savings' to get there. Linnea is right. This is exactly why we need to be unionized."

"Just be careful," Jaspar said. "Fiercey isn't going to take kindly to anyone getting in her way."

They lingered, shaking their heads over the current state of affairs for students and staff alike: the increasing numbers of students carrying a load of 21 credit hours to try to finish their degrees faster, for example, and the absence of health benefits for domestic partners of college employees.

"Antoine needs a root canal," Jaspar said of his boyfriend. "Thirteen hundred dollars. We said to each other last night, 'There goes our summer trip to Catalina Island.'"

Dori stretched her calves while she empathized.

"But it'll be good to get him out of pain," Jaspar continued. He clapped a hand to his jaw to indicate toothache. "He's been mewling like a baby."

Back in her office, Dori stood with her hands on her hips, considering the room's lone window. Ivy grew over it—as it grew over everything on campus—leaving the office darkened. Linnea, her office mate, hated the ivy and the way it oppressed their workspace. Dori thought she'd do Linnea a kindness and clear some of it away. She opened the window, grabbed a handful of the vines and yanked them free.

Dori looked out through the porthole she'd made among the creepers. The sky was the color of wool. A few crows brooded on the bare branches of campus trees. The south end of campus, beyond the registration building, was under water. Students were wading in fishing boots to the curb to wait for the public water taxi.

Dori checked the windowsill for the mysteriously regenerating treasure-trove that was often there. Today a crow feather, a green marble and a Canadian quarter lay on the sill. How these items could have gotten there, on the second floor of the massive old building, she couldn't imagine. The quarters had begun appearing in the fall, sometimes two or more at a time. Dori and Linnea often split the quarters between them, joking but puzzled about them. And now here were these other tidbits too. She left the feather but scooped up the other things in her free hand.

Maybe a crow had collected this miscellany. Corvids were known to be fond of shiny things, Dori thought, and a certain crow had taken to passing its afternoons on that windowsill. She and Linnea could often hear it out there, cackling and carrying on. It liked to nudge ivy leaves out of its way with its clever beak and press its shiny black eye to the window glass, watching the women at work.

Dori wondered if Linnea would be in soon. She was eager to tell Linnea about her encounter with Fiercey. She thought of the conversation she'd had the day before with her office mate about Linnea's own dean difficulties. Linnea had scurried into the office, shut the door behind her and said, "Budgie nearly caught me."

"What do you mean?" Dori asked.

"He's after me for the MADCAP."

"You haven't done it yet?" Dori had turned in *her* department's Midyear Assessment of Demonstrable Continuous Academic Progress weeks earlier.

"No," Linnea said wretchedly. In spite of their nickname for it, the document was anything but zany and fun-loving. It had to address 34 points in prose and provide substantiating data in the form of charts and graphs. As Linnea was Department Chair of Classics this year, it was her turn to write up the MADCAP, and she'd been avoiding it for ages. Dori lifted one eyebrow at her friend.

"I was here until after midnight last night, pulling together all the data," Linnea continued. She set her oversized bag on her desk and started pulling papers out. "I'm giving a paper at the Classics conference at the end of the week. I have midterms to prep. And the Textbook Review Committee. And the U."

The "U" was the union-organizing committee that Linnea headed. She never spoke of it openly on campus.

"You have too many clichés in the fire," Dori told her.

"I have too many irons in the cliché."

"So what happened with Budgie?"

"I saw him in the hall, frowning my way," Linnea explained. "In that yellow suit of his. I knew he was going to demand the MADCAP. As soon as he turned his head, I hid behind a pop dispenser."

Dori ran one hand through her hair. She had hair like soap bubbles, curly, pale and disheveled. "You didn't feel foolish?"

"I suppose so," Linnea conceded. "But when I caught sight of that oversized bird coming after me for the deplorable MADCAP, I just wanted to disappear."

Though she didn't think her friend's disappearing act would serve her well at Middlebridge, Dori couldn't help smiling. The aptly named Budgie often wore a suit that, in some lights, could be construed as yellow. Taken together with his beakish nose and chinlessness, it did make him somewhat resemble an enormous parakeet.

"At least I've got all the facts and figures for the MADCAP now. I think I'll come in and write it up after the U meeting Thursday night." Linnea flumped into her chair. "The MADCAP has become a real workload issue."

Remembering their conversation now, Dori thought she should jot down a few notes on her exchange with Fiercey. Linnea would want to let the other union organizers know what Fiercey was up to, and she would probably add Dori's notes to that flowered notebook where she kept records of all that sort of thing. Dori glanced around for the notebook, but of course Linnea wouldn't have left it lying around in the open.

Dori took out the list that Fiercey had given her. It named everyone in the department in ascending order of seniority, starting with part-time faculty, then full-timers who didn't have tenure, then everyone else. Fiercey was looking for anyone who wouldn't, or couldn't, put up a fight.

Dori grabbed her sudsy blonde hair in both fists. These cuts were a theme that was beginning to repeat itself at the college. Dean Fiercey had halved campus security, even though a Middlebridge student had recently disappeared from campus under suspicious circumstances. She had canceled plans to alleviate asbestos hazards. Now it looked as though she'd turned her roving eye to academic programs. French would be the first to fall. But Dori knew this was just the beginning.

She wondered if anything could be done to appease Fiercey. She remembered that she had advised Linnea to take some pastel mints with her when she turned her MADCAP in to Dean Budgie. He loved those things.

"A sop to Cerberus," Linnea had murmured.

"Cerberus. Remind me?" Dori said.

"The three-headed dog that guards the gates to Hades."

"Oh, that's right," Dori said. "He lets you in, but he won't let you back out unless you offer him a treat."

Budgie might relax a little if a faculty member offered him candy. But Dori had a notion that Fiercey, if she would negotiate at all, would demand a much higher price.

Chapter Five

HEART OF GOLD

A wet wind slapped Linnea across the cheeks. I suppose this could all be a dream, she thought. I might wake up any minute now. I've probably dozed off in the airplane on my way to the conference.

The rain across her face felt unpleasantly real, and Poe Avenue looked just as it did in waking life. Linnea saw nothing at all out of the ordinary, just a clot of cars on their weary evening commute, streetlights shimmering and wobbly in the watery darkness. She walked the five blocks to the central square called Puddle Place and saw only the central post office, a credit union, a farmers' market closed for the season, and, spouting away—redundantly, in this weather—a fountain. She drew the map Esme had given her from the front pouch of her briefcase and frowned at it. According to Esme's directions, the entrance to Hades lay in a parking strip in front of the credit union. Linnea approached the building, looking up and down. In the parking strip were two *daphne odora* shrubs and, between them, there it was—a subway entrance, or something like it, where, the last time Linnea had deposited a check, there'd been nothing but grass. Linnea narrowed her eyes and stepped closer. A stair led down into the darkness. Linnea looked around. She saw no one. She tapped down the steps, which led to an empty hallway, fluorescent lights flickering above. Some fifteen or twenty feet down the hall a grate had been pulled shut and locked. A placard on the wall showed Hell's operating hours: Tuesday-Friday 11 a.m.-6 p.m., Saturday 1-5 p.m., closed Sundays and Mondays. Underneath, the sign read, "Please call again!"

Linnea turned, stomped up the stairs and marched the five blocks back to the corner of 17th and Poe. She steeled herself to face down the taciturn Esme and to demand to know what her options were. They couldn't just leave people out in the rain. If she didn't like the answers she got, she was prepared to put up a fight. But when she got to the corner where Bus 9 had dropped her off, the green information kiosk was nowhere to be seen.

"Crap," Linnea said aloud. "Now what?"

"Now," said the little old man with the bright eyes, "you confer with me about your next move."

"Oh!" Linnea said. Her bus seatmate was standing at her elbow. "It's you. I'm so glad to see you again."

"I had an idea you might not find what you were looking for," said the tiny man, pointing his chin in the direction of the plaza, "it being Friday night and all. I went home and unpacked my groceries, and then I thought, that poor dear is out there in the cold without so much as a ferry ticket across the Acheron. I'd better go see if I can be of service."

"Oh, thank you so much," Linnea told him. "It's all so confusing. I don't even think I'm supposed to go to Hades, and I don't know where to turn."

"Why don't you come to my apartment for a cup of tea?"

said the old man, "and we'll try to get it sorted out."

"That's very kind of you. My name is Linnea, by the way." She offered her hand.

"Vergil," said the wizened little man. "It's this way. Not far at all."

Linnea moved her oversized briefcase to her opposite shoulder so the old man could hook his arm under hers. Vergil seemed unsteady on his feet, so Linnea helped him down a curb and they crossed Poe together. They moved down the block without conversing, since Vergil appeared to be concentrating on his steps. After they turned down a narrow residential street lined with horse-chestnut trees, Vergil led them to a brick apartment building.

"This is my place," Vergil told her. He held his key, tied to a length of twine, in a trembling hand. "Would you mind doing the honors? This gets a bit tricky for me."

Linnea took the key from him and opened the door.

"I'm on the second floor," Vergil said. "It's something of a journey."

They went upstairs very slowly, Vergil gripping the banister with one hand and Linnea's arm with the other. Twice he stopped to catch his breath. Linnea wondered how he managed on his own.

"This is a lot for you," she told him in a gentle voice. "Have you thought about getting a first-floor apartment?" She was actually thinking he was a candidate for assisted living, but she felt she didn't know him well enough to say so.

Vergil didn't answer. Linnea didn't know if she'd offended him or if he was just too out of breath to respond.

At the top of the stairs she unlocked Vergil's apartment door and pushed it open.

The air smelled of burning dust. "Ah, I see I forgot to turn off the space heater again," Vergil clucked.

"That'll run up your utility bill in a hurry," Linnea said.

"Yes," Vergil agreed cheerfully, "and reduce the place to ashes one of these days." He brushed his hands together in a gesture of being rid of something. "Might be a relief to see all these manuscripts go up in smoke."

Linnea saw stacks of notebooks and loose sheets of paper on the floor and more strewn on the kitchen counters. Vergil's lone bookcase was crammed with books, shelved two rows thick and with additional volumes stacked on top. More books and papers were piled on two small end tables.

"Make yourself comfortable," Vergil told Linnea, waving a gnarled hand in the direction of the apartment's only chair, a frayed La-Z-Boy.

Linnea guessed the building dated to the 1920s and had once been grand, with arched doorways, beveled-glass windows, built-in cabinetry. It was now decrepit and drafty. Vergil's apartment was a studio, an irregularly shaped single room that might once have been a servant's quarters or a master bath. The space had a single window and was mainly lit by what appeared to be 40-watt bulbs. There's hardly enough space in here to swing a cliché, Linnea thought.

Vergil looked worn out. "Are you all right?" Linnea asked him.

"I do like a bit of a rest after an outing."

"You sit. I'll make the tea," Linnea said. The kitchen area was divided from the living space by a counter. Linnea set her bag on the floor by the door and took a look around to see where she might find teacups. She pulled open a cabinet door, but the cabinets were full of shoes. She looked at her diminutive host.

Vergil shrugged. "There's nowhere else to put them," he said.

Linnea pulled open another cabinet door, then another,

only to find that Vergil had dedicated all his cabinet space to a collection of women's footwear.

Vergil waved a hand in the direction of his bookshelves, where Linnea found a pair of mugs from the Hard Rock Café in Bangkok. She emptied them of pencils, scrubbed them, filled them with tap water and popped them into Vergil's microwave. She allowed her eyes to float over some of the hand-written pages lying on the kitchen counter. Here were lines of poetry, some scribbled out and rewritten, others with question marks beside them in the margin. Under a thesaurus lay a rhyming dictionary and a copy of *The Elements of Style*.

"Are you working on a writing project?" she asked him.

"Always," the old man said with closed lids. "I've been working on the same manuscript for a long time. Can't seem to finish it. I'm afraid I have a bit of a writer's block." Vergil's tone was dejected, and Linnea didn't want to press him on the matter.

"Are you from Bridges originally?"

"Oh, no, dear girl," Vergil said. "I was born in Italy."

"You hardly have an accent," Linnea observed.

"It's been a very long time," he told her. Vergil lifted his skinny old arms in a gesture that said, who knows? "I lose track."

"Well, how is it that you came here?" Linnea found a box of Lipton by the microwave and fished out two teabags.

"One wants to see the world," Vergil said simply.

"Yes. I love to travel. I love Italy dearly." Linnea carried the two mugs to Vergil's side.

"Oh, you've been?"

Since there was no other chair in the apartment, Linnea settled on a footstool at Vergil's feet. "Mostly Rome," she told him. "I teach Latin, so I've visited a number of times for my professional development. I need to get back there soon."

Linnea had momentarily forgotten that she was dead, and that her traveling days were probably over.

"Rome," Vergil sighed. "I too am a great aficionado. In fact, my last name—Maro—is an anagram of both 'Roma' and 'amor.' Isn't that wonderful? Now, about your situation," Vergil went on. Linnea sat up straight, remembering that she indeed had a situation. "You say you've been assigned to Hades, but you think there's been an error."

Linnea nodded.

"Well. You can request a transfer, if you truly believe they're sending you to the wrong place."

"Really?"

"Oh, yes, it happens all the time. Between you and me," Vergil lowered his voice and leaned toward Linnea, "I think they're a little sloppy about where they send you. People end up in the wrong afterlife all the time. Full of gods they've never heard of, punishments for things they didn't do. It's rather disconcerting."

"That's outrageous!" The union-organizer in Linnea was incensed. For an instant she was tempted to take on the battle on behalf of the wronged deceased. But she had her own immediate troubles to attend to. "What do I have to do to get a transfer?" she asked.

"Lots of paperwork," Vergil told her. "You'll have to face up to Esme." He threw Linnea a knowing look. "But you can do it. You're made of tough enough stuff, I think."

Linnea's main concern was not so much the bureaucracy as the decision about where to go. On what basis does one choose an afterlife? She was worried about the language barrier. "I'm not sure where I might fit in," she admitted. "I don't think I'd fare so well in a place where everyone was speaking Athabascan or Zulu. With my background I could probably manage one of the Romance languages."

"Well, that shouldn't be an issue in the Roman Catholic Paradise," Vergil said.

"I doubt they'd have me," Linnea told him. "I think the entrance requirements are awfully stiff."

"Oh, you're not—you're not Catholic?"

Linnea shook her head.

"I apologize for making assumptions," Vergil said. "The last fellow who sought my advice was more Catholic than the Pope, the Bishops and Mel Gibson put together. What are you, then?"

Linnea shook her head. "I don't know. I'm not anything. Can't I just pick something?"

"Oh, my, no." Vergil looked surprised and a little scandalized. "There has to be some demonstrable basis for your placement. You can't fabricate a religious background." Vergil tsk-tsked, and Linnea blushed. "But since you aren't a follower of the Roman gods, you must have some other attachments, no?"

"Not really," Linnea told him. "Where do atheists go?"

Vergil twisted his lips together and gazed at his wide ceiling beams for a moment. "Atheists," he mused. "I couldn't say."

"Oh."

"I am remiss!" said Vergil. "Do you take sugar and milk in your tea?"

"No, I'm fine. If I might ask—" Linnea said, "—what would happen if I just stayed here on Earth?"

Vergil shook his head. "You have a grace period of two weeks. If you're not registered in an afterlife of some kind by then, they come get you. They have a nasty goon squad that rounds up deserters." He shuddered. "The only place I know of to hide is in your own body, and that, as you can imagine, isn't very pretty over time."

"I'd have to stay there forever?"

"Yes, though of course eventually you'd be compost."

"That doesn't sound so bad," Linnea said.

Vergil shook his head. "A bright young woman like you, I would think you'd be frustrated. There's very little intellectual stimulation in living as a pile of dirt."

Vergil leaned forward, fixing Linnea with his bright eyes. "Understand that if you let the grace period lapse, you forfeit your shot at a happy afterlife. If they have to chase you down, they'll punish you, and you won't ever get to go to the right place."

"The problem is, I don't know what place that would be," Linnea told him. She considered how much research she could conduct in 14 days. "You said I needed to be registered to keep the goon squad away, right? If I could get down there and sign up for Hades, and then somehow find a way to slip back out—do you think they would notice?"

Vergil frowned in thought. "It's true that they're much more concerned with facts and figures than with the reality on the ground. I don't think they care much what happens to you, as long as they can show documentation that makes their head counts look good." He stroked his chin, pondering Linnea's options. "The tricky part would be leaving. You know about Cerberus, right?"

"Yes."

"He's terribly ferocious, I'm afraid." Vergil stroked his chin. "There may be another way for you. Maybe. You might be able to get redeemed."

Linnea's eyes widened. The old worshiper of Jupiter and Dido was sounding like a revival tent preacher. "What do you mean?"

"A deed of sufficient worth is redeemable for a human soul," Vergil told her. "It can be given in exchange for the spiritual freedom of another."

"I don't understand."

"Love, loyalty, perseverance, *pietas*. These things can redeem a soul," Vergil said, "if the redeemer is pure of intention."

Linnea repeated the words, trying to apply them to her situation, without result.

"Someone in your life must love you greatly," Vergil said. "Your mother, perhaps? A husband, a child?"

Linnea shook her head.

"Well, you seem very lovable, you know." He patted her hand again. "*Cygnus inter anatēs.*"

"A swan among ducks." Linnea smiled.

"Someone who loves you might be willing to do a deed on your behalf, a gesture of such devotion and purity that it measures up to the size of your soul itself."

"But how would the authorities know ...?"

"Deeds are collected by the registrar," Vergil explained, "and taken down to the Forum and weighed. A really good deed weighs something like a quarter of a drachma, which is about the same heft as a human soul, depending on the final tally of your rights and wrongs. They keep all that stuff in a database."

Linnea cringed to think of Esme at the information kiosk, pulling up some spreadsheet that showed the sum of Linnea's life's worth. "Could you give me some examples of deeds?"

"Let's see now," Vergil said, petting his lap blanket and thinking. "Have you heard of Castor and Pollux?"

"Sons of Zeus."

"That's right. Pollux was immortal, and Castor was not. So when Castor was killed, Pollux asked to be allowed to go to the underworld with him."

"That *is* very loyal."

"Zeus was so impressed by Pollux's devotion that he let them both go to Heaven."

"Oh." Linnea was discouraged. It seemed unlikely any of her friends and acquaintances would volunteer to do the same for her.

"And then there was Damon and Phintias," Vergil said.

"I'm not familiar with them."

"They were great friends. Phintias plotted against the tyrant Dionysius I. He was caught, tried, and sentenced to death."

"Oh dear."

"Yes. But he had to put his affairs in order. So Damon offered to stand bail for him. The deal was that if Phintias didn't return in time, Damon would be executed in his stead."

"Did Phintias return?"

"He did. And Dionysius was so impressed by their friendship that he granted Phintias a reprieve, and asked if he could be friends with them, too. It was very sweet."

Linnea unbuttoned and rebuttoned the cuff of her blouse, thinking. "So what you're saying is that if I have a friend who is willing to die with me or for me, then I have a shot at redemption."

Vergil stroked his chin. "I'm sure there must be other deeds of friendship," he said. "My memory's not what it used to be. I'd warrant that an adequate deed has to involve risk, but not necessarily death, for the doer."

Linnea felt no closer to an answer.

Vergil yawned. "There's a Murphy bed on the wall there." He pointed. "Would you mind, dear?"

Linnea pulled the wall bed down for him and helped him into it. Her eyes drifted over the titles on Vergil's nearby bookshelf.

Vergil had eclectic and wide-ranging taste, she saw, and

his library included a solid collection of classical Greek and Roman work. She had a sudden, startled thought.

"Vergil Maro," she said. "Publius Vergilius Maro. Are you the poet? The author of the *Aeneid*?"

"That's me, I'm afraid," Vergil said, smiling.

"Oh!" Linnea was stunned. "I'm your biggest fan!" Linnea had taught passages of the *Aeneid* herself in advanced Latin classes.

"If I—" said Linnea, suddenly shy and bumbling "—if I brought you my copy of the book, would you be willing to sign it?"

Vergil opened his eyes and said with mock gravity, "I never autograph anything. Too many of my so-called fans hock my signature on eBay." He gave Linnea a broad wink and settled his head back on his pillow. And then he was sound asleep.

Chapter Six

HEARTSICK

Dori subscribed to several dating websites, and tonight she had a date with a man from one of them. After she got home from work, she went to the computer and reread his description to refresh her memory.

The personals were written in code, and she couldn't decipher them without the key, which appeared in a drop-down menu. She scrolled down, looking for the simple words that had attracted her attention a week or two earlier.

DABiMAnist, sens dmer, frt adv, w2mt. (Divorced Asian bisexual male anarchist, sensitive dreamer, ferret advocate, wants to mate.)

SWLibSagFTM tg rwfdst pnk seeks M/W for h/g, xtrm spts, cdling. (Single white libertarian Sagittarius female-to-male transgender raw foodist punk seeks man or woman for hunting/gathering, extreme sports, cuddling.)

Dori skimmed through the ads until she came upon "SLaM"—"Single Latino Male, 45, loves trees, music, film, food"—who was hoping to meet a woman with similar interests. The guy looked nice enough in his picture, if a little tame.

Dori remembered with irritation having told Linnea, a few days earlier, about SLaM, 45. Linnea had tried to arrange her features into an expression of interest, but she couldn't hide her discomfort. Dori even detected a twitch of disapproval at the corner of Linnea's mouth. Linnea would never venture on a blind date or try to meet someone over the Internet. She claimed to be old-fashioned that way—she wanted to find someone in person, get to know him slowly without the pressure of expectations, and have things unfold in a natural, organic way. It sounded good, but the truth was, Linnea hardly went anywhere, and though she seemed permanently grumpy about it, she didn't make any changes to her life.

All right, Amore, Dori said to herself. You're being kinda grumpy yourself. After all, Linnea is one of your closest friends.

The two did enjoy a kind of twinship. In outward appearance they were nothing alike. Linnea was dark and tallish and heavy, and Dori fair, thin as a whip and so petite she had to shop for clothes in the children's department. Linnea had the fashion sense of a teacher—she favored high-waisted pants, flowered blouses and heinously sensible shoes—while Dori knew what went with what and could find clothes that were spunky and fun. But they shared similar upbringings in hometowns of the same size; similar university experiences at different women's colleges; dual passions for the Romance languages; and mutually reinforcing perspectives on life at Middlebridge.

They also had in common the absence of a love life, and they shared the small secret sadness of approaching middle age alone. But Dori made a point of keeping herself in circulation, while Linnea more often buried herself in work.

"Do you think you might need to get out more?" Dori sometimes asked her friend, shaking her head at Linnea's habit of staying at the office until the tiny hours of the night. "Do you feel like you have much of a life outside of Middlebridge?"

"I have a rich inner life."

"Meaning …?"

"Well," Linnea had told her once, "Truthfully, a lot of my mental energy is devoted to the workings of Latin. And I think about ancient Rome a lot." Linnea hadn't been to Italy since before she'd landed her position at Middlebridge—she told Dori there always seemed to be too much work to do—but, she said, she was often there in her mind.

To Dori, Linnea's attitude was a little worrisome. Linnea worked devotedly, but it didn't seem to make her happy: on the contrary, she nursed a chronic low-level resentment and growing weariness about her job. Dori, by contrast, kept fewer hours and on the whole felt good about her work. Dori found she was mostly able to take the stresses of college life in stride, while Linnea tended to take them to heart.

Be that as it may, both women considered it fantastic luck to have landed each other as workplace roomies. They had laughed, cried, and comforted each other through uncounted dramas at Middlebridge, from affairs between colleagues to student pranks to the increasing commodification of learning. They compared notes on the politics of certain college committees; on the historical development of various diphthongs; on skincare for forty-somethings. They policed clichés together. They leaned on each other during times of worry, like the previous fall when that student had disappeared. Dori enormously admired and rooted for Linnea's union-organizing efforts. Linnea envied Dori her fashion sense (she'd dubbed Dori's all-purpose black blazer the Stylin' Jacket), and told Dori she didn't think she could bear to share an office with anyone else at Middlebridge. From her academic credentials to the merry way she always waved goodbye when her workday was finally over, Linnea was one of Dori's nearest and dearest. I shouldn't be impatient with her, Dori thought now. I don't know what I'd do without her.

After re-reading the personal ad, Dori put on some music and tidied. Not much tidying got done during the workweek, and the condo was heaped with laundry and unopened mail. It took the better part of an hour to get through it, and then, feeling stiff, Dori thought she'd work on some fencing moves to try to redeem the afternoon's dreadful workout. She pushed her nubby yellow loveseat back into a corner to give herself some room, and set about passing—advancing and retreating by crossing one foot in front of the other—concentrating on keeping her steps quick and even and her posture upright. Afterward she went through some conventional exercises, twenty *doubles*, twenty *coulées*, twenty *coupés*, twenty *dégagés*. Then she was hungry, so she made herself some toast while she contemplated her mistakes on the fencing strip.

The sound of a siren rose from inside Dori's purse. Due to a technological glitch, Dori's cell would produce only one tone, that of a police siren. Dori pulled her phone out, looked at the screen, and flushed. She'd forgotten all about her date.

She grabbed her soap-bubble hair in her other fist. "Amore, what's the matter with you?" she said aloud. She hit "answer" with her thumb and groveled as best she could.

SLaM, 45, whose name was Pablo, had a soft, warm voice. "Oh, hey," he said. "These things happen. Please don't feel bad."

His sweetness made her feel even worse.

"Can we reschedule?" he asked.

"If you're willing to take another chance on me," Dori said.

Oh, the first day of one's period!—that blessed time in which the suffering of all beings, past, present and future, is compressed and tucked into one's own small tender breast, and one grieves every drop of it.

Dori spent the better part of the morning in a very hot bath with a back issue of the Sierra Club magazine, silent tears slipping down her cheeks as she flipped through photographs of endangered tropical birds. Luckily she didn't have an early class on Fridays. She stayed in her condo and let herself be miserable for a while.

In the late morning, fragile and out of sorts, she pulled herself together as best she could and took a public boat in the rain up to campus. She was still annoyed at herself for her forgetfulness of the night before, cringing at how gracious Pablo had been in the face of getting stood up.

Dori must still have been red and puffy around the eyes when she got to her office building, because a colleague from the French department, Isabelle Grenouille, looked stricken when they ran across each other near the Pepsi machines. She cried out, "Oh, Dori! Are you all right?" and unexpectedly hugged her.

"I've been better," Dori admitted. "I must look worse than I thought."

"Of course. You poor thing," Isabelle said. "It's dreadful."

"It *is* dreadful. The things women have to face sometimes! I feel so vulnerable." Dori shook her head at her own pathetic state.

"It is natural. I do, too; we all do, of course," Isabelle said.

The features of her small, pointy French face were all drawn together in sympathy. "We must look out for one another."

"Yes," Dori said, heartened but rather surprised at this sudden outburst of female solidarity from the part-time instructor, whom she only slightly knew.

"I am frightened for the future," Isabelle continued. "We are all struggling, of course, in our different ways. But it is so much harder for you than for me. I can't even imagine, Dori."

It was true that Dori, who was 41, had entered the anovulatory years, when the menstrual cycle begins to spin out of control and all the indignities of inhabiting a female body multiply. Still, she wasn't that much more ancient than her co-worker. Dori was annoyed. "It *is* going to get harder," she said, a bit vengefully. Isabelle might as well face facts. "But," she brightened, "it's nothing a little chocolate won't improve."

"What?" The sympathy all dropped out of Isabelle's face.

"Chocolate—you know—" Dori wondered if she had stumbled into some kind of intercultural miscommunication.

They looked at one another in confused and uncomfortable silence.

"What have you been talking about all this time?" Isabelle asked finally.

"PMS," Dori said.

"Then you don't know."

"What?"

The color drained out of Isabelle's small face. "Oh, no," she murmured. "Oh, no, no, no, no."

Chapter Seven

CARPĀMUS DULCIA

Alice was lying in bed listening to music, her chin nodding out the beat of the bass. Other instruments might provide the flesh and blood of music, she thought, but bass provides the bones. Without bass, rock would be limp, shapeless, a rag doll. Alice smiled, pleased with her metaphor, and kept listening, sometimes fingering a riff in the air.

It was Friday morning and normally she'd be in Latin class, but class was canceled today because Dr. Nil was attending some conference. Alice thought fondly of Wednesday's class and how she'd nailed a translation from Persius: *Carpāmus dulcia, post enim mortem cinis et fābula fīēs*: "Let us seize sweetness, for after death, ashes and fables you will be." Alice hated that they had to go even one day without Latin, but since she was only able to catch up on sleep about once every six weeks, she was taking advantage this morning. She would lounge around until she had to get ready for Art History at 11.

Alice picked up her iPod and thumbed the scroll wheel,

looking for something else juicy to be the soundtrack to her morning, when she heard a knock. She crawled out of bed in her flannel pajamas and went to the living room window. Mick, the drummer for Watery Discharge, was standing in the wet mud below. Alice pushed the window up for him and said, "Hey." Mick set his big hands on the sill and made a nimble hop into the living room.

Alice saw Mick nearly every day, and it had only been a few hours since they'd been together last. They had had something of an adventure the night before involving their instruments and the overtaxed electrical system in the basement of the old humanities building. They'd been chagrined and amused by the mishap, and Mick was probably here to relive it with her or give her an update from the fire department.

But Mick did not look amused. He wore a haggard expression. The nasolabial folds in his face—which generally lent him a Robert Downey, Jr. kind of handsomeness— seemed deeper and more famine-induced than usual.

"You look miserable," Alice observed cheerfully.

Mick sized her up and said, "You haven't heard."

Then he told her a thing she didn't want to know, a horrible, incomprehensible thing. It was a moment Alice would remember the rest of her life, a moment when the world broke into two chunks, the time before she knew and the time afterward. One minute she'd been blissfully ignorant, enjoying her sleep-in and her robust bass, and the next minute she knew, and she could never go back to not knowing. Always afterward, whenever she remembered her difficult sophomore year of college, Alice would think of the moment that cleaved everything in two.

Alice spent the next several days just going through the

motions. She rose, did her homework, put in her time at the library and worked at Cootchie-Coo, but she didn't feel anything. Whenever her attention was not fully engaged by something else, she would remember that Dr. Nil was dead. Every ten minutes or so her thoughts were interrupted by remembering. It was like sleeping and waking, again and again, all day long. Alice found herself adrift in feelings she had no names for. Sometimes an urgent drive stirred in her to move forward with her life and her dreams—her Latin studies, her music—because of a heightened awareness of mortality. Other times she wondered what the point was of doing anything at all. Everybody just died sooner or later anyway.

Without any discussion, Watery Discharge had abruptly stopped practicing. No one wanted to be reminded of the scenario that had started with band practice and had ended with news of Linnea Nil's death. Linnea's students were sick with grief and confusion. Mr. Callow, who appeared Wednesday morning to take Dr. Nil's place, didn't teach them anything, although that was a relief. Alice couldn't think anyway, couldn't take in new information or even call to mind what they'd been learning before. Eventually, she and the rest of the class would grow angry about Mr. Callow's non-lessons. But for the moment, it was all Alice could do to keep showing up and occupying a desk.

Alice had never known anyone who'd died before. Her four grandparents were hale and hearty, and no one else in her world was even nearing the age of expiring of natural causes. She had heard about the death in a car accident of someone who had attended her middle school, but it was someone she'd never known personally. Death was something that happened far away, long ago, in some theoretical far-off future or only to strangers. Even now, days later, Alice couldn't stretch her comprehension to fit around the news of Linnea Nil's murder. She kept expecting an announcement that authorities had been wrong, that the body hadn't been Dr. Nil's after all, or that it had been hers but she'd been revived; or perhaps it was all a disturbing dream Alice would awaken from. Some of the other girls in her class were afraid to go to campus, and others had even been pulled out of school by their parents, but Alice wasn't afraid, because she couldn't bring herself to feel it was real. Murder occurred only in mystery novels and on television, and only as a form of entertainment. Alice was sensible about not walking alone at night—she always took a cab home from the skin club, for instance—but she simply could not conceive of herself as a murder victim. So she was not afraid. But she was terribly confused.

And then there were her new money woes. At work, Alice's body danced, but her mind was forever calculating what it would take to stay in school. Could she handle a three-quarter-time work schedule? That would be physically daunting and gobble up study time. She didn't even want to think about how she'd have to give up the band. Alice tallied up her hourly wage, subtracted her stage fee and tip-outs, taxes, tuition, books, school fees. She did the arithmetic four or five times, but however she added it up, she could see that she was going to have to work more hours and take fewer classes to stay in school. That would be grueling. Well, so what, Alice thought, squaring her jaw. I can do grueling. *Aut viam inveniam.*

Alice was not the only housemate worried about rent.

"I am so broke," Amy said to Alice one afternoon as the two housemates walked across campus on their way to class. "Oh, my God."

Amy had gotten a hundred dollars from a wig company the previous week when she cut off her long, flaxen Nordic-goddess hair. But she didn't have regular work and was having trouble finding any.

"You could dance," Alice wise-cracked. "You've got the gams for it." Amy had tremendous legs, slender gazelle legs that seemed to go all the way up to her neck.

"I would never do that!" cried Amy, and then, as though realizing she might have insulted her stripper friend, she faltered, "I don't know how to dance."

"You don't need to know how," Alice told her.

"Right."

"Amy, all you need to be a stripper is a willingness to move around naked and get stared at." Alice was taking note of the way the male heads swiveled Amy's way and followed her with a star-struck gaze as the two young women crossed the campus. "You get stared at all the time anyway. You might as well get paid for it."

"I don't believe you," Amy said. "*You* can dance."

"I *can* dance," Alice admitted. "There's no rule that says you *can't* be a good dancer. I'm just saying it's not strictly a job requirement." She pulled open the door to the student union building. "Anyway I'm just kidding," she told her housemate. Alice had found that Amy, a freshman from Missouri, was easily scandalized.

In the student union, tablers from every sort of organization offered pamphlets and free information. Temp agencies, environmental groups, cults, vendors of handmade crafts, voter registration supporters, hemp activists, second-hand clothing swappers and many others lined the wide passages and lobby of the main campus center. Today as Alice and Amy cut through the building, they passed an egg-donor information table and next to it a military recruiter: makers and takers of life, side by side.

"What do you think about egg donation?" Amy asked Alice.

Alice rolled her eyes.

"But did you see that poster?" Amy said. "'Up to $8,373 per egg.'"

"Exactly a semester's tuition," Alice noted. "What a coincidence."

Amy's eyebrows sprang, and Alice saw with relish that she had punctured another little balloon of innocence.

"Still," Amy said, "it's got to be easier than surrogate motherhood."

Alice had to concur. Jillian, the other woman in their household, had been so very pregnant lately.

Amy waited until they'd entered the stairwell and then asked, "So, does Tad mind?"

"Does Tad mind what?" Alice already knew, but she wanted to make Amy lay bare her unspoken assumptions.

"What you do. For a job."

"Of course not. Why would he mind?"

"Well, I mean … having his girlfriend strip for other men … it just seems like …" Amy trailed off, embarrassed.

Amy obviously embraced the conventional notion that a woman was a kind of possession, a thing to be hoarded and not shared, and Alice refused to validate those beliefs. "Seems like what?" she persisted.

"Like he might get jealous."

"Jealousy is a byproduct of the capitalist economy," Alice said. "When everything becomes a commodity, our emotional lives become beholden to an arrangement where, by design, there are always haves and have-nots." Amy was very conventional, Alice thought; she had a lot to learn. "Jealousy is an artificial feeling manufactured by market forces to fuel the insatiable desire for *more* that perpetuates the materialist system." She felt herself getting worked up now. "Tad and I refuse to participate in the hijacking of our inner lives by an inherently unequal and unjust distribution of the tangible goods of the external world." She blew her breath out her nostrils like a horse.

The call from the landlord came that evening.

"He's raising the rent," Tad intoned when he hung up the phone. "He's raising the rent. He's raising the rent."

"What? No!" Alice cried.

"Are you kidding me?" said Jillian.

Amy looked frightened. "By how much?"

"You don't want to know."

They stayed up late into the night, Alice, Tad, Amy and Jillian, trying to figure out what to do. None of them wanted to squeeze another soul into their rental. The rain-swollen clapboard house on Baudelaire Street had limited common space and only two real bedrooms. The single bathroom with its cracked and peeling linoleum was a stretch for four people, especially when one of them was pregnant. (As a concession to the women, Tad always peed outside.) But the reality was they would no longer be able to afford to split the cost of the house four ways.

Of the four of them, Amy and Jillian were the two who each had a real bedroom, one on either side of the upstairs bathroom. Tad's "room" was the landing. His clothes were inside the window seat and his sleeping bag on top. His books, papers, toiletries, guitar and mountain bike filled the landing itself, so that anyone wanting to go upstairs had to navigate his stuff. (Jillian was particularly bitter about this, but not bitter enough to give up her space.)

"Obviously, Amy and Jillian need to share one of the bedrooms," Alice said.

Jillian said, "I get up no fewer than eight times a night to pee. That wouldn't be fair to Amy."

"You've got to be kidding me." Alice's bedroom was what had once been a breakfast nook off the kitchen with an area rug slung over a wooden dowel rod for a door. The nook was exactly the width of her futon. She had lined one wall—atop her bedding—with cardboard boxes for her belongings. "Where do you propose we put the new housemate?"

Jillian draped a long, derisive look over Alice and Tad. "You two already practically share a liver," Jillian told the couple. "There's only one workable solution here."

"Oh, no. No," Alice said.

In truth she didn't feel much objection to the idea of sharing her living space with Tad, as little would change. They always spent the night together. They walked or biked to class together, ate three meals a day together, did their homework together, cooked and cleaned—to the extent they did either—in one another's company, and spent most weekends pretzeled around each other on the cast-off couch while they studied. But Jillian's prim sense of entitlement rattled Alice. "No," she repeated.

"I don't mind," Tad said.

"It's the only workable solution," Jillian said, and began to push her chair away from the table as though the discussion were over.

"That's not very creative thinking," Alice retorted. "There must be a dozen workable solutions."

"What about if one of us moves into the living room?" Amy said.

"Then we have zero common space," Jillian snapped. "Where would we even eat?" It was true the kitchen was dinky. The living room was the only place all of them could fit at the same time.

Cowed, Amy said, "The basement?"

Tad made a noise of doubt. "The basement is nasty," he said. "I'm not that picky, but it's a mold plantation down there."

Tad suggested they offer to do handyman jobs around the house for the landlord in lieu of extra rent money. Alice loved this idea. It was her ideal to live entirely by barter, stepping out of the cash economy altogether, outside the exploitative capitalist system and beyond the roving eye of Uncle Sam.

"Do any of you guys have handyman skills? I don't," Amy said.

The four housemates looked at each other. "Not so much," Tad said.

"I'm already doing all the work I can handle," Jillian said, patting her pregnant belly.

Alice gave a little snort. It was the wrong thing to do. Jillian turned her wrath on Alice. "*You* might be able to make the landlord an offer."

"What's that supposed to mean?"

"Hey, now," said Tad gently.

"You obviously don't mind certain kinds of … activity," said Jillian.

"What exactly are you suggesting?" Alice knew exactly what Jillian was suggesting. But she wanted Jillian to say it out loud.

Jillian was silent.

"Here's a proposal," Alice said, "to make use of your talents. Why don't you offer to wet-nurse the landlord's little son?"

Jillian flushed and opened her mouth to retaliate.

"Come on, you guys," Amy pleaded. She and Tad had

been exchanging looks, eager to diffuse the tension. "We'll come up with something."

Alice and Jillian glowered at each other, but both sat back in their chairs. Tad drummed a rhythm on the table with a spoon. Amy twisted a strand of her shorn golden hair around one finger. Alice folded a cigarette paper into a tiny origami crane.

"I have an idea!" Tad said. "*I* could move in with Amy." He said it with a little imp-face, a kind of cocked-head, wide-eyed look that said both 'I was just kidding' and 'I would if you'd let me.'

Alice laughed to show everyone she wasn't threatened. After a little more discussion, they all agreed that Tad would move into the breakfast-nook with Alice in order to accommodate a fifth housemate, if they could find one willing to live on the landing. They cleared the table and went their separate ways, Jillian to her room to study, Tad to play guitar, Amy to curl up on the couch writing in her journal. The sound of her own laughter rang in Alice's ears.

Chapter Eight

HEARTBREAK

Dori laid a hand on Isabelle Grenouille's shoulder and steered her into her office. The younger woman sat and began to weep. Between her sobs and her heavy accent, she hardly managed to get her point across. Dori didn't understand the particulars. She grasped only a singular, terrible truth: Linnea was dead.

Classes were canceled and students sent home. Faculty and staff were called to a meeting in the General Electric auditorium, where a police inspector and Dean Budgie had grim news for Middlebridge.

Linnea had been murdered. She'd been killed by an unknown assailant who had cut out her heart and left it in the sink of the women's restroom on the second floor of Verizon Wireless Hall. The whole morning had been one of chaos on the Middlebridge campus. Dori only pieced it together afterward, hearing details over the course of the day from various students, colleagues and police reports. First, in an apparently unrelated incident, an electrical fire had broken out in Verizon Wireless Hall. A fire brigade had had to come in the middle of the night to deal with the blaze. Then, on Friday morning, the heart had been discovered by a group of students, and later an art instructor had found the body itself stuffed into a kiln in the ceramics lab. The whole campus was now being cordoned off for investigation. When classes resumed, new security measures would be put into place, including the presence of additional safety patrol officers and a 9 p.m. curfew. Anyone with any pertinent information should come forward to help the investigation. Deans recommended that employees seek counseling for feelings of stress and agitation. One of the school counselors, Tim Fimbria, would be available extra hours during the coming weeks.

Dori couldn't move. She remained glued to her velveteen auditorium seat, unable to imagine what to do next. Finally her fencing partner, Jaspar, found her and said, "You're coming home with me." He gathered Dori up and walked her out to his canoe, stopping only to insist she pull his Wellingtons over her shoes so she could stay dry as they waded through calf-deep water to the parking lot *qua* marina. "I've already called Antoine and asked him to take the afternoon off work," Jaspar told her. "He's picking up some Chinese takeout on his way home."

Dori didn't think she'd ever be able to eat again. She let Jaspar take her to his place, where she sat on a chaise longue and alternately grieved, raged, shook with fear and tried to puzzle out what had happened.

Jaspar was shocked, too, but his was a generalized reaction to having a colleague brutally murdered in the workplace, as he hadn't known Linnea well. He called a few people from the college, but no one knew anything more than what the friends had heard at the gathering in the auditorium.

"I just saw her a few hours ago." Dori's voice trailed off as she realized what a common, almost clichéd reaction that was. Linnea might have said, "I just saw her a few clichés ago."

Antoine brought Dori a pot of tea and wrapped her in a blanket. He was a big man, shaped like a Pooh bear, and he tended to evoke feelings of cuddliness and affection in everyone who met him. Later the three of them listened to the evening news on the local public radio station. The only additional information they gleaned was that Linnea did not appear to have been robbed or sexually assaulted, and that she appeared to have been killed the previous night sometime before midnight.

"It probably didn't happen early in the evening," Dori said, "because she had a union meeting. Unless she never made it. The other organizers would know." Dori's best guess was that Linnea had gone back to campus after the meeting to do school work. She recalled that Linnea had wanted to finish the MADCAP before leaving for her conference the next morning. She winced, remembering the pleasure Linnea used to take in those Classical Studies conferences.

"You'll probably want to tell the police that," Antoine said.

Dori considered what else the police would want to know from her. They would probably ask her if Linnea had any enemies. "Do you think it could have been someone from the college?" she asked her friends. She didn't know which prospect was worse: a mad anonymous killer on the loose or a murderer who actually knew Linnea personally.

"Who would kill a Latin professor?" Jaspar said.

Dori flashed on a conversation she and Linnea had had a week or two before. The two women had both been at their desks, grading. "Listen to this," Linnea had said. She was going through essays from her Roman Civilization course, and quoted one: "'Before being conquered by the Romans, England was settled by the Angles, the Saxons, and the Jews.'"

Dori had been looking over a stack of French quizzes at the time. "I have a good one," she'd told Linnea. A student had evidently confused the name of the famous French chanteuse Edith Piaf, also known as "the little sparrow," with *pilaf.* Under "identify the following," the student had defined the singer as "a traditional French dish made of rice and sparrow meat."

"Oh, dear," Linnea had said. "Well, I guess this is why people come to college."

"Do you think we're too hard on them?"

"I don't know. I do have this morbid fantasy that when my time comes it will be at the hands of an enraged student. Someone driven to violence by the treacheries of Latin syntax."

"Rendered mad by direct and indirect object pronouns," Dori had said.

"Induced to murder by gerunds and gerundives."

"Pushed over the edge by the imperfect subjunctive."

Now Dori wondered—was it possible a student could grow so bedeviled by schoolwork that he'd cut his teacher's heart out? Linnea *did* have some very stressed students. Latin *was* a murderous subject.

Dori strained to remember more details of that conversation. "Poor fellow," Linnea had said of her Roman Civilization student. "Struggling with Latin I can understand. But he's failing *two* of my classes."

Dori tried to think if Linnea had mentioned the student's name.

"What about a colleague?" Antoine said, startling Dori back to the present.

"I can't think of what motive a colleague could have," Dori said. Linnea got along fine with the other instructors and threatened no one's job security or pet project. Dean Budgie? If he killed Linnea, he'd *never* get the MADCAP from Classics. What about Dean Fiercey? The Dean of Allocations did seem to want to cut out the heart of the foreign languages departments, but she needn't resort to murder; a simple pink slip would do. Were there any other administrators who had it in for Linnea? Someone who wanted to prevent her unionizing efforts, perhaps? That might be a long list, Dori reflected. It could include all of upper management and the Board of Regents.

Antoine looked weary and dejected, his kind round face lined with concern. "I suppose it could have been a random act by a stranger, someone mentally ill. Or maybe it was a gang-initiation thing."

"Maybe it was a fraternity-initiation thing," Jaspar said. "Hazing, taken too far."

Antoine shot Jaspar a look that said his was a joke in poor taste taken too far. "All this speculation probably isn't good for us," he said.

But Dori, who had begun the conversation mystified that anyone could do harm to her friend, was now beginning to feel that potential murderers lurked everywhere. Linnea had been in the humanities building long past the hour of the last classes of the day. Who else was around at that time?

Lots of people, in truth. It was one of the things Dori had always appreciated about Middlebridge: even in these times of market-driven education, the college was still a place where students could do what students were meant to do— stay up all night on campus arguing philosophy, identifying constellations, reading until dawn. Whether the administrators of Middlebridge deliberately cultivated this atmosphere or whether it had simply escaped their attention, Dori was grateful for it. Campus buildings remained open all night, and students were free to use the space to study, wander, curl up with books, doze in armchairs.

Dori personally knew at least one such student, a French major named Mary Ellen, who was prone to staying in Verizon Wireless Hall until all hours. According to Linnea, who often worked very late, Mary Ellen could usually be found in the student lounge after everyone else had gone home for the night, snuggled up with the poetry of François Villon or Christine de Pisan. Linnea had told Dori that she'd once walked in on Mary Ellen in the second-floor women's room, bra-clad, washing her armpits at 2 in the morning. Now the thought of the eclectic young woman gave Dori pause.

Dori chose to sleep on Antoine and Jaspar's chaise longue. In the morning she visited the police department to share what little she knew, and she didn't go home until Saturday afternoon. Her condo was horribly quiet. She crept all around when she first got there, checking for bad men hiding in closets, behind doors, under her bed. She checked and double-checked her locks. She checked her landline and made sure her cell was charged.

Dori needed to plan for the following week's classes, but she couldn't think. Grief had hijacked her brain, and she wandered from room to room, picking up objects and putting them down again, unable to find a sense of purpose.

After making a useless attack on her third-year French textbook—planning three-quarters of a lesson, only to realize she was working with the wrong chapter—Dori gave up. She needed to talk to someone. Jaspar and Antoine would take her call any time night or day, but what she really craved was the company of someone else who had known Linnea.

Dori tried to make a mental list of Linnea's other buddies. Linnea had worked with Ian Elf and Isabelle Grenouille on the unionizing committee, but Dori had the impression their connection was mainly professional. She had never seen Linnea fraternizing with other classics profs. As she ran through names in her head, it occurred to Dori that Linnea might have only had one close friend at Middlebridge, and Dori was it.

What about outside the college? Linnea had worked long hours and didn't get out much. She didn't belong to organizations or clubs that Dori knew of. Oh, she was surely acquainted with a lot of people and was on friendly terms with many, but Linnea had not been close to anyone else Dori could think of. A sadness seeped into her. Dori remembered Linnea speaking warmly of friends in Italy, but that was no help. Men she'd dated? There'd been no one special. Family? Linnea's parents were dead and she had just one sibling, an estranged brother. Dori felt worse and worse the longer she dwelt on the matter.

As an alternative to having a heart-to-heart with someone who'd known Linnea, Dori settled on someone who knew her, Dori, to the marrow—her sister, Kristin.

"Krizzle?" Dori's voice broke as soon as Kristin answered the phone, and she told the whole terrible story of Linnea's murder.

Kristin was patient, and Dori simply talked until the dreadful ice-block of pain inside her began to break up.

Yet on a scale of 1 to 10, Kristin earned a 6, Dori thought, as a listener. To her credit, she had stopped doing whatever she'd been doing and sat still while Dori talked. It was hard for Kristin to sit still. But Kristin didn't do feelings very well. She focused, with businesslike briskness, on the practical. "Are you safe on campus?" she asked. "What security precautions have you taken?"

And so after a little while, Dori said good-bye. She was reminded that having another person close by is a consolation in grief, and that no one human being can replace another.

Dori was stirring sugar into a cup of decaf when a voice at her ear, very clear and calm, spoke her name.

She jumped at the sound, and when she turned and saw Linnea standing at the kitchen sink, she knocked her hot coffee over. "Fuck!" she said.

"Don't be alarmed. I need to ask you a favor," said Linnea.

"Fuck!"

"I need you to get my heart back for me."

"You're not here," Dori said in a firm, almost angry voice, gesturing at the apparition with her spoon. "You're dead. This is a dream, and I'm going to wake up now."

"I need to be reunited with my heart," Linnea insisted.

Dori was disappointed that she didn't seem to be able to will herself into waking. "Linnea. How can you be here?"

"I'm sorry for the imposition. I'd explain, but—" Linnea wavered out of view. She was gone long enough that Dori began to think the conversation had been a vivid fantasy, and she started to recover her *sang-froid*. Then the vision reappeared. "Oops," Linnea said. "I didn't mean to do that. There's one more thing."

"Wait a minute," Dori began.

"This is important. I need it by February 25 at the latest. That's an absolute deadline."

Coffee had begun to drip onto the kitchen floor.

Paralyzed by a thousand questions, Dori glanced at a thin line of mahogany liquid streaming over the side of the kitchen counter. "Who murdered you?" she cried. "Who did that to you, and why?"

Dori looked up, but Linnea had disappeared on her.

Chapter Nine

AN EXCURSION

Now that she had visited Dori, Linnea was relieved. The matter was out of her hands. She just had to wait for Dori to carry out the deed.

Linnea had no idea how the visit had come about. She'd merely been thinking of approaching Dori about the whole redemption business when suddenly she was in Dori's kitchen. Then right after she'd told Dori the all-important deadline, she'd blinked and found herself in the imported-cheese section of a 24-hour Safeway. Thoroughly confused and completely exhausted, Linnea had walked down the street to a Mattress Planet and slept on one of the display beds until the following morning.

Her sudden appearance in Dori's kitchen was not the first such incident Linnea had experienced since her death. She seemed to be suffering from blackouts or amnesia of some kind. She had come and gone on herself several times after she'd left Vergil's apartment Friday night. The first time her awareness disappeared, she woke up in a Barnes and Noble.

On another occasion, she found herself, with no warning, riding the elevator in an insurance company building. This flittering awareness must account for the gap between the time she'd been butchered in Verizon Wireless Hall late Thursday night and the time she had come to consciousness on Bus 9 at rush hour the next evening. Linnea wondered what she'd been up to in the meantime.

The one good thing that came of spotty awareness was finding herself in warm clothes. All Linnea had really wanted when she'd left Vergil's apartment was someplace to stay out of the rain. She'd disappeared on herself shortly after thinking this thought, wearing only her torn blouse and skirt, and reappeared somewhere downtown bundled up in fleece and rain gear and waterproof boots. She'd looked down at herself in bewilderment and cringed to think that, in an altered state, she might have gone shoplifting. But gratitude outweighed guilt. Finally she was warm enough.

Very much in need of his continued guidance, Linnea went to see Vergil on Sunday at the earliest hour that could be considered civilized. He was waiting for her at the head of the stairs, diminutive and cute in a blue wool cardigan. "Come on up, come on up!" he called in his tissue-paper voice. "I was hoping you'd visit."

Linnea asked Vergil right away about her blackouts. They not only inconvenienced her but were a source of worry. What if she used poor judgment during one of these periods of absence? What if she was absent from herself when the time came for her to receive her heart from Dori?

"Oh, you're just wefting," Vergil said. "That's a good thing. It saves a lot of time."

"But what is it?"

"It's a method of travel that takes you from one locale to

another without having to cross the whole distance between. You can also use it to make yourself temporarily visible to the living. It's very handy. I used to do it all the time. Unfortunately, I just don't have the energy for it any more."

"But it doesn't seem to be in my control," said Linnea.

"It's all just a matter of practice, dear heart," said Vergil. "Some part of your mind thinks of a place and takes you there before the rest of you has even noticed." Vergil raised a finger. "The instant you get an idea about going somewhere," he said, "make a decision. Then concentrate for a moment— and there you have it. It's all in the concentration."

Linnea told Vergil all about her inadvertent trip to Dori's house and about the redemptive deed she had asked of her office mate.

Vergil seemed pleased. "Nevertheless," he told her, "you might want to have a backup plan. Not that I doubt your friend, but..." Vergil trailed off, afraid of hurting Linnea's feelings, perhaps.

If Linnea had had a heart, it would have sunk. She could see that he was right. What if Dori failed to get the heart? What if—what if she didn't even try? Maybe their friendship was not up to that kind of test. Linnea might have been acting in haste when, upon finding herself in Dori's kitchen, she blurted out her request. She probably should have thought it through. Maybe she was asking too much.

"I've been thinking," Vergil continued. "I can't speak to the other afterlives, but Hades isn't all that bad. You haven't given it a fair shake."

"It doesn't have a wonderful reputation," Linnea said, dubious. "In Roman literature, Hades always appears as a gloomy place full of depressed people."

Vergil pursed his lips in thought. "It is rather foggy," he conceded. "Now that I think of it, it has a climate similar to that of Bridges."

Ugh, thought Linnea. One of her hopes for the afterlife had been that she could escape the dreary drizzles of the Pacific Northwest. In Bridges she was perpetually damp, and no number of wool sweaters and long johns kept the chill off. During the winter Linnea always felt as though someone had siphoned out her brain and filled her head cavity with shredded newspaper or wet sheepdog hair. Just last week she had been saying to herself that it was a wonder her Latin students could even manage first-declension nouns in such weather, much less the tortured grammatical complications that came with the second semester of study.

"Hades is divided into zones," Vergil was saying. "Tartarus, now, that's a place you wouldn't want to land. But you wouldn't, I'm sure; that's for wicked people."

"And the Elysian Fields are reserved for the VIPs, correct?" Linnea said.

"That's right. The Asphodel Meadows are where they put folks of ordinary goodness." Vergil turned his bright eyes to Linnea. "Is that an accurate description of you, do you think? A person of ordinary goodness?"

"I suppose so," Linnea said. "And Asphodel Meadows— what's that like?" It sounded like a ski resort.

"The meadows are really rather lovely," said Vergil. "Are you familiar with asphodel? It's a perennial herb with an affinity for acidic soils that flowers abundantly in the spring."

Linnea, who liked large cities and busy urban life, did not feel drawn to this description. Hades was sounding like a pretty sorry back-up plan for Redemption.

"There'd be lots of interesting company," said Vergil. "Most people, naturally, being neither particularly wicked nor particularly heroic, end up over there. I could take you to see it myself, you know. I'm an experienced tour guide."

"Oh, that's right. You took Dante through Hell."

"I did indeed. He said such nice things about me in his book. He was a fine lad." Vergil pushed himself to standing and shuffled over to his bookcase. He pulled a volume off the shelf, opened it and pulled out a laminated card he'd stashed there. "You see? I've kept my certification up."

He showed the card to Linnea, who saw that Vergil had been granted access to all of Hades, including the Asphodel Meadows, Tartarus, the Elysian Fields, and even the Catholic Hell, Purgatory and Limbo, when accompanied by pre-approved visitors.

"We could take a little tour so you can get a sense of the place," Vergil said. "You might like it, you know, and then your problem will be solved." Vergil set to wiping the dust off the laminated card with a corner of his sweater.

It was obvious to Linnea that Vergil felt some pride in his status as a certified guide. She wondered, though, whether the old man was really up to the task. He could hardly get up the steps to his apartment. Linnea couldn't imagine how he could lead the two of them through the back country of the Roman afterlife.

"So, what's the writing project you're working on?" Linnea asked.

Vergil sighed. "I've been trying to finish my epic poem for many years now."

"Oh!" said Linnea, another truth abruptly dawning on her. Publius Vergilius Maro had died young, leaving his famous poem incomplete. Some scholars did assert that the poem's sudden, dark ending and broken bits of dactylic hexameter were intentional, but Linnea found this interpretation altogether too postmodern. "You mean the *Aeneid*?" she asked the poet now, just to be sure.

"Yes, of course."

I knew it! she thought. She'd always agreed with those critics who argued that Vergil had died without tying up the loose ends of his story and before he got a chance to do a final edit of his lines.

Vergil did not seem to want to talk about his book. "Now, come over here a minute. I have something to show you," he said. He hobbled to the kitchen counter and opened his laptop. After some minutes of hunting and pecking, he pulled up a document and, with a look of triumph, turned the computer so Linnea could see the screen. Vergil had applied for, and received, permission to take a guest into Hades and back out again. "Do you want to go right now?" he asked her, his eyes bright.

"My goodness," Linnea said, amazed. "Are you sure you're up for it?"

"Oh, indeed!" Vergil said. "We'll have to take sack lunches. I wonder what I have around here." He began to poke around in his refrigerator. "It's been a very long time since I paid a visit, you know. Ah, here we are!" Vergil plucked a jar of Skippy from the fridge.

They made peanut butter and banana sandwiches together, and then they set out. It seemed a long, breathless trip down the stairs, and they had to pause on the stoop so Vergil could recuperate.

"All right," he said, patting Linnea's arm. "I'm ready. Now, I think we should march straight down Poe, don't you?"

"That's the quickest way," Linnea agreed. They did not exactly march, though. It was more like shuffling, with pauses here and there for Vergil to catch his breath.

They walked north, slowly, toward the plaza, Vergil laying out his plans for their journey. "We'll take the ferry," he told her. "Maybe we can have a little picnic on the shores of the Acheron."

"Really?" said Linnea. "It's not too gloomy?"

"Well, you may be right," Vergil conceded. "There are sometimes a lot of ghosts hanging around the near shore, especially of people who had nowhere to go and no one to love them."

A shiver ran through Linnea. "Why is that?"

"Well, that's where they have to stay, if they were unloved in life. They're not allowed to cross over."

Linnea's stomach tied itself into a half-hitch. What if *she* were one of those ghosts? She had been feeling quite unloved since she'd died. In her hollow wanderings of the past two and a half days, no one on the street had made eye contact with her; no one had nodded or smiled. She'd had to remind herself several times that they weren't shunning her on purpose—they simply couldn't see her—and that loneliness was not an existential state but a side effect of invisibility.

Prompted by Vergil's offhand remark, Linnea found herself wondering again whether Dori would come through for her. Did Linnea's death represent a tangible loss for Dori? Or, she thought with an inner pout, would Dori's life simply go on? It was at least plausible that the administrators of Hades would consider Linnea one of the friendless and would condemn her to haunting the dismal near shore of the Acheron forever.

"Other ghosts don't have the fare to make the crossing," Vergil continued, unaware of Linnea's internal struggles. "Come to think of it, the last time I spent time on the near shore, we got panhandled."

"What's on the far shore?" Linnea asked, wanting to think of something besides the fate of the unloved.

"The far shore is where Judgment occurs. First we'll have to go through the Darkling Wood. That's a bit of a hike." Vergil sighed; he looked weary, thinking of it. "It might involve a little route-finding. Do you know how to use a compass?"

They had come to the crosswalk at 17^h and Poe and stopped to wait for the light to change.

"Don't you know the way?" she said. You're the certified guide, she was thinking, but she didn't say so. She recognized the reference to the wood from the *Inferno*, but it had been two decades since she'd read that book, and she couldn't conjure up any images. She wished she could confer with Dori about it. Dori would know.

"It's easy to lose your bearings in the Darkling Wood," Vergil told her. "It's full of wild beasts representing sins—the Leopard of Malice, the Lion of Ambition and so on. But you said you'd been more or less a good person in life, didn't you?"

Linnea had no way of calculating how her sinfulness might be measured in Dantean terms, but she did not relish a close-hand experience with any kind of wild animal. "Won't the beasts leave me alone if you're with me?"

"I'm a tour guide, not a body guard," the old man said. He noticed the look on Linnea's face and added, "Oh, they won't hurt you. It's just that all that allegory can get a bit wearisome."

The light changed, and they began to cross the street.

Vergil said, "From the wood we'll go past Judgment and swing by the Elysian Fields. Oh, would you look at those!" Vergil stopped short, clutching Linnea's arm.

They were in the heart of Bridges' commercial district, and Vergil had just laid eyes on a pair of ankle boots in a shoe store window.

"Aren't they fine?" he said. The shoes were dark green velvet lace-ups with pointy toes. "Could we go in for just a minute?"

Since no one could see them, Linnea and Vergil went inside and stepped right up onto the platform where shoes were displayed.

"I wonder how much they are?" Vergil said breathily.

Linnea had to ask, "Do you wear the shoes in your collection?"

"Oh, no. I have bunions," Vergil said. "I just like to look at them. No, no, I mustn't. I told myself just last month: no more shoes. There's no place to put them. I can't have a new pair unless I part with an old one."

Linnea helped the old man down out of the window display and they went on their way, Vergil casting one last longing glance behind him.

"Anyway, the Elysian Fields," Linnea prompted him.

"Oh, yes. We can pop into the castle where the heroes live. It's pretty swanky."

Vergil and Linnea had to dodge shoppers, who of course could not see them, so their path zigzagged and their progress down the sidewalk was slow. When they came to a bus stop bench, Vergil put up his hand. "I need to rest for a moment," he told Linnea.

They sat, and Vergil seemed to drift off to sleep momentarily. When he awoke, he said, "If Proserpina's there, I'll introduce you. You'll like her. I have a lot of old friends in the Elysian Fields. You'd like to meet Homer and Ovid, wouldn't you? Being a poetry lover."

It might be exciting to rub clichés with all those famous people. Still, Linnea didn't see how any of her companion's plans would get her closer to making a decision about setting up household in Asphodel.

"Do you think we could have a nibble of those sandwiches now?" Vergil asked. "I worked up an appetite looking at those green shoes." So Linnea pulled the peanut butter out of the brown paper sack they'd brought, and soon they had eaten up all the food that was meant for their day's excursion.

"Maybe we can arrange for a little poetry reading while we're there," Vergil told Linnea. He had a dreamy look in his eye, but his voice was feeble. They moved very slowly toward Puddle Place.

"There's something I don't understand," Linnea said as they walked, Vergil's arm resting on hers. "Why do you choose to stay out here in the world when you could be in paradise?"

Vergil looked up into Linnea's face. "I have to finish my poem before I go," he said. "I can't bear to leave it undone."

"Can't you finish it there?"

Vergil shook his head. "It's a funny thing that happens," he said. "Elysium is so very pleasant—hot tubs, full-time masseuse on staff, fantastic buffet dinners—that people lose their ambition. All my old buddies from there—Ovid, Catullus, Sappho—they haven't produced any new work in millennia."

Linnea wanted to be respectful to the venerable poet, but she couldn't help pointing out, "You've had a long time to work on that manuscript. You died—what?—1,979 years ago?"

"Yes," said Vergil balefully. "As I mentioned, I've had a bit of a writer's block."

"But you're allowed to come and go as a guide."

"Mainly because they like my book."

"Even though technically it's unfinished."

"Yes. My work shored up the Roman Empire, the Caesars, the Gods. It praises the right people, so to speak."

"Do you think I might be able to do something like that? Write something, or..." Linnea doubted her ability to pen a book in a week's time, but she did have a stack of notes on Lucretius and the Empedoclean cosmogony that she might whip into an article, at least. "Not that I could produce something of the caliber of the *Aeneid*," she added, embarrassed.

Vergil patted Linnea on the arm and said, "Do you know, dear? I think we're going to have to make this journey another day. I seem to be quite tuckered out."

Linnea was disappointed but not surprised. Vergil leaned against a telephone pole to rest. When they saw a southbound cab pull up, they shuffled over to it and crawled in beside the unsuspecting customer while the cabbie was putting luggage in the trunk, and Linnea chaperoned the old man back home.

Chapter Ten

A RESHUFFLING

Alice's tattoo idea was out. She needed the money to cover the new college fees. She rounded up all the clothes she could part with and dropped them off at a consignment shop and posted her previous term's textbooks on eBay.

Those things together would bring in maybe a hundred dollars. What else could she sell? Alice gathered up a bunch of notions—"9/11 was an inside job," "Monogamy is inherently oppressive," and "Root vegetables are underappreciated"—and took them back to the notions shop.

"Cash or trade?" the clerk asked. Usually Alice swapped out old notions for newer ones, but of course this time she took the cash.

Tad started moving his stuff into Alice's nook. As soon as they could find one, a new housemate would occupy the stair landing that used to be Tad's. Jillian traipsed past them in the kitchen without saying anything about their living arrangements but with that indefinable air of gloating that

Alice found infuriating.

Tad must have noticed Alice glowering, because he wrapped his arms around her waist and said, "You don't really mind, do you?"

Alice considered. She minded Jillian's sense of entitlement, always getting dibs on the best stuff because she was the pregnant one. Did she mind sharing her space with Tad? She liked having a little corner of the house that was all hers. She had read Virginia Woolf and embraced the teaching that every woman needed five hundred pounds and a room of her own: fiscal and spatial independence. She liked being able to spread her paper-making supplies all over the bed, tape noun declensions on 3x5 cards to the walls, leave the light on all night so she could read Marcuse or sew herself a vest from discarded bubble wrap. All this year, she had noted that though she loved being under the same roof as Tad, she was glad she didn't share a room with him, with his guitars, his bikes, his books, his mess, his man-smells. Now she'd had to deep-six some of her belongings and find alternate places to stash others.

On the other hand, college was supposed to be a time of hippie squalor, of amusing material discomforts and cramped quarters. And lovers were supposed to be together, even free spirits like Alice and Tad. (Though they eschewed the word "dating" as too bourgeois, Tad, who had been taking chemistry the semester they got together, liked to say that he and Alice were "covalent." He'd rub her nose with his sometimes and murmur, "We share electrons.") There was a kind of bohemian romance about this household arrangement they were trying. Alice softened.

"No, I don't really mind," she told Tad, burying her face in his sweatshirt and breathing him in.

Tad kissed the top of her head. "That's good."

"I like having you around," Alice continued. She stood on his feet and let him shuffle back and forth, giving her a ride.

"Good," said Tad. "I like being around." He shuffled from the kitchen sink to the breakfast nook, and they toppled from the doorway onto Alice's futon.

An hour or so later, wrapped around Alice and playing with her hair, Tad said, "Who do you think is hotter? Ryan Gosling or Jake Gyllenhaal?"

Tad and Alice always told each other about their sexual predilections. One of the slogans of their relationship was "No restrictions/no secrets." They would neither imprison one another in monogamy nor be deceptive with each other about their amorous goings-on. So far the no-restrictions part of their agreement was purely theoretical—they were crazy about each other, and neither one had dated anybody else since they'd started going out.

"Oh, Jake Gyllenhaal, definitely," Alice said then.

"That's what I figured," Tad said. "All girls everywhere think he's hot."

"Pretty much, yeah," Alice said.

Tad rubbed her shoulders. "You know who I think's hot?" he said after a minute.

"Who?" said Alice. "Your French professor?"

"Well, her too, sort of," Tad said. "She's kind of old, though."

"Yeah."

"But no. Amy."

Alice had the unexpected sensation of a heavy hand pressing on her heart. "Really?" she said, keeping her voice calm.

"Those legs of hers," Tad said. "I keep imagining them, you know, around my waist."

"I never noticed them."

"Are you kidding? How could you not notice them? They run almost the whole length of her body."

Alice shrugged.

"Well, anyway. I think she's really attractive."

"I guess," said Alice. Then, afraid she sounded defensive, she added, "Yeah. Amy *is* pretty."

Tad pressed on, "She's more than pretty. Those legs. Oh."

Alice felt a certain urgency to steer the conversation away from the subject of Tad's desires, and at the same time to show him how unthreatened she was by them. "True," she said. "Amy's great."

"I'm glad you see it like that," Tad told her.

"Well, of course," Alice said offhandedly. "She's my friend."

Tad pecked her cheek and took off for the library; he had a midterm to study for. Alice sat alone with her thoughts for a long time. It occurred to her that she had never lied to Tad before now.

The housemates composed an ad in search of a fifth roomie, and Alice printed it on sheets of "paper" she'd made from salvaged bits of other wood-pulp products: toilet-paper rolls, magazine inserts, out-of-date phone books. Spending an afternoon fashioning paper out of cast-offs gratified her need to make art and pleased her environmental sensibilities. She was quite satisfied with her homemade paper, mottled and rough-textured, and she set about hand-lettering the ad. The hours she spent bent over her task provided a much-needed respite from her confusions: transition in the household, grief over Dr. Nil's demise, anxiety about expenses.

"I don't understand," Jillian said when she saw Alice at work. "Why don't we just take it over to the library and run off a bunch of copies?"

"Cradle to cradle," Alice told her. "Zero waste. Closing the loop."

"Mm," Jillian said.

Hearing the doubt in Jillian's voice, Alice persisted. "It doesn't make sense," she said, her voice rising, "to throw out usable materials and then make new stuff from virgin resources. Our whole society views the most precious things as disposable."

"Okay," Jillian said.

"People just take their pleasure and then *throw things away*. It's so indicative of the consumption-driven economy that must constantly grow and therefore must constantly exploit."

"Okay," said Jillian.

"You know you can't throw things 'away,' because there's no such place as 'away,'"Alice continued. "'Away' is just a euphemism for *somebody else's habitat*."

Jillian was on her way up the stairs. She said over her shoulder, "Okay. As long as you have the free time."

"Besides," Alice said more quietly, to a now-empty room, "an ad like this will attract the kind of person we want. Not some philistine."

A day or two later, a potential housemate came to see the place. It turned out to be Guppy, Alice's classmate from Western Civ who hadn't combed his hair since the beginning of the school year.

Guppy had had to come in, like everyone, through the living-room window. He laughed as he pulled himself up through the opening and into the common space.

"Hey," he said, and they did a go-around with names and handshakes. Tad, who had the most genial and easygoing nature of the housemates, took charge of the tour. "So," he said, "there's the kitchen. That's a bedroom." He gestured at the hanging area rug that separated Alice and Tad's nook from the cooking space.

"And this," he gestured, "is where we hang out."

The living room at 636 Baudelaire had a mismatched assortment of furniture, most of which the housemates declined to sit on in favor of sprawling on the floor. Where most living rooms would have a coffee table, they had placed an ancient, rusting hospital gurney salvaged from the landfill. They had no TV; instead, a bong sitting on the gurney provided much of the household's entertainment. Guppy nodded in approval.

"I'll show you the upstairs," Tad said, and he bounded up the steps three at a time, Guppy following, the women bringing up the rear. They toured the landing that, if everything worked out, would be Guppy's, and the bathroom that was off-limits to men unless they had to shower or go number two.

"And as soon as the sun comes out," Tad said—meaning in April or May—"we can start using the solar shower." He leaned out the bathroom window and showed Guppy the black plastic bag on the roof of the house that warmed a few gallons of water for outdoor showering on sunny days.

"Dude, that's so tight," said Guppy.

He and Tad grinned together, two clichés in a pod.

The five of them stood in the narrow upstairs hallway. It had been painted fire engine red and sported an orange shag carpet so old, so dirty, so foul that the housemates had never pulled it up for fear of what would be unleashed from the depths of its nap if it were disturbed.

"So, rent's 325 plus utilities," Tad said.

"I'm cool with that," said Guppy.

"Heat, water, electric, garbage and recycling. Works out to about 75 dollars more, per person, per month."

"Yeah. Cool."

"Do you have any questions for us?" Alice asked.

"Well," Guppy said, tilting his head toward the ceiling. "Do you guys have any house rules?"

"We don't believe in house rules," Tad said. "We uphold the ideal of the self-regulating collective."

"Cool," Guppy said.

"Everybody has to do their own dishes," Jillian said. "That's a rule."

"We never find it necessary to enforce it," Tad said quickly. "Everybody pretty much rises to the ideal."

"I don't do other people's dishes," Jillian persisted. "That's *my* rule."

"Okay, I'm cool with that," said Guppy amiably. He placed one hand on the top of his hair-thatch and gave it a wiggle, an idiosyncratic gesture that seemed to signify agreeableness.

"And no cooking fish in the house. It makes me sick," Jillian continued, gesturing at her pregnant belly.

"Oh, hey, I'm, like, totally respectful of your—" Guppy seemed not to know how to finish his sentence. "Are you two, like—?" He looked back and forth between Jillian and Tad, who said "No!" in unison and with equal fervor.

Tad crossed the hall to stand by Alice's side. "Alice and I are together," he said, taking her hand.

Alice felt a surge of warmth at Tad's publicly declared loyalty.

"Oh, yeah. Sorry." Guppy held up a hand. "No offense." He looked at Jillian's belly again. It was smaller than a house but bigger than a breadbox by quite a lot. "Um," he said. "So, will the baby be—living with us, too, when it's, uh, when it comes out? Arrives?"

"I am bearing a child for another couple," Jillian said.

"Oh! That's cool," Guppy said. His boyish face wore an expression of confusion. "I didn't exactly know people did that," he confessed.

Jillian was not forthcoming with details, so after a moment of awkwardness, Tad said, "So I guess you prob'ly have a job, huh?"

Guppy grinned. "Yeah," he told them. "I do drug trials. They pay me to, like, take experimental medicines and stuff."

The three women were stunned into silence, but Tad's face lit up. "Cool!" he cried. "What's the weirdest drug they ever gave you?"

"They gave me this lotion that's supposed to treat hives," Guppy told them. "You rub it on your skin. It made me numb for six days. I couldn't feel anything, man. I couldn't feel my hands; I almost cut my thumb off."

"Dude, that is *crazy*," Tad told him with obvious admiration.

"Aren't you afraid of what the drugs will do to you?" Alice asked.

Guppy shrugged. "I'm still here, aren't I?"

Amy said, "So, do you think you want to live here?"

"Yeah!" Guppy said. "Can I move in this weekend?"

They agreed that he could, and they made a few arrangements. Tad would move the rest of his gear down into Alice's nook this week, and Guppy would scrape together the money for the first month's rent. In his enthusiasm for their new arrangement, Guppy started a round of handshaking. "Roomies!" he said to them affectionately, pumping their hands one by one, and then, draping his arms over the backs of Tad and Alice, he initiated a group hug. He said, "Shall we fire up the bong to seal the deal?"

Chapter Eleven

RIVER OF SORROW

Linnea was prepared to tackle the paperwork involved in asking for a transfer from Hades—the documentation required couldn't be any worse than the MADCAP. But she was pretty sure they'd turn her application down. They weren't going to let her transfer to a paradise she hadn't earned. Unattractive as it seemed, Hades was still Linnea's best backup plan.

Problem was that Vergil, good as his intentions were, was clearly not going to be able to guide her there and back. If she were going to check it out, she'd have to go alone—which meant she had to come up with a sop for Cerberus.

Linnea closed her eyes and tried to get her mythologies straight. At least three ancients had faced down the famous dog. Hercules had bested it in a wrestling match. Orpheus had charmed it with music. Linnea was as unmusical as she was nonathletic—tone-deaf and two-left-footed—so there was no point in trying to imitate the successes of those two Greek legends. But Aeneas had slipped in and out of Hades' gates by

86

plying the hell-hound with honey cakes.

The question remained of what, exactly, a honey cake was, and where she might find one in Bridges. She decided baklava was close enough. The best baked goods in downtown Bridges were served in a crowded, noisy little café downtown called Two Lumps, Please, where Linnea had met with other union organizers on occasion. She headed there.

Linnea slipped into the bakery behind a pair of patrons—invisibility, for once, her friend—and pressed herself into a corner to study the homemade breads and pastries in a display case. The baklava was in the far corner of the case. Linnea waited until the barista was out on the floor and then slipped behind the case and tiptoed to the corner. She'd have to stay there until she was certain no one was looking. She gazed over the crowd in the coffee shop. The place was packed—it was the weekend—and lively with conversation. There were so many people, though, that she saw it was going to be tricky to find a moment when no one's eyes were on the goodies. Patrons kept approaching the case to look them over.

Her lucky break came when a waitress dropped a hot chocolate onto the floor with a crash. Everyone looked her way. Linnea snatched two baklavas from the pastry case and stuffed one into each pocket of her new pants. The warm winter pants she'd woken up in the other day might be unflattering—her fashion sense had not improved, she'd noted, since her demise—but they had good pockets.

When she was alive, Linnea had never stolen anything. She'd not so much as shoplifted a peppermint as a child or, as a professor, filched a pencil from the faculty office supply cabinet. As soon as the sticky treats were safe in her pockets, her face flushed with hot red shame. She looked all around, unable to truly convince herself she couldn't be seen. She wished she had money to leave on the counter.

Now the barista was back, flustered and cross because of all the demands on his energy. Six people were waiting in line. They wanted coffee and pastries and savory pies; they needed extra napkins, sugar, the key to the bathroom; their coffee was lukewarm; they had ordered skim milk and gotten whole; could they please have a water glass. The barista started a fresh batch of espresso and turned to the cash register. Linnea, still squashed into the corner at the end of the pastry case, could see that he hadn't seated the filter in the coffeemaker properly, and that grounds were going to spill into the coffee itself. Once again Linnea waited until all eyes were elsewhere, and then she slipped open the filter drawer of the espresso maker, quickly set the filter aright and scurried out of the coffee shop. She couldn't pay for her baklava, but she could make a barista's day a little easier. It was the best she could do.

The dead formed a line that snaked all the way down the hall and around the corner. Linnea joined them under fluorescent lights, waiting for passage across the famous river.

Many of the patrons of Hades looked unwell, and some sported bloody wounds. They were all dressed in togas, and one or two wore laurel wreaths on their heads. They couldn't be deceased Bridgesians, Linnea thought. She surmised that once she'd passed through the turnstile in the tunnel below the credit union, she wasn't really in Bridges any more.

The fellow at the back of the line was obviously a gladiator. Linnea took her place in line behind him. He stood three feet higher and was half again as broad as she, and he was missing an arm. "Is this the line to the ferry?" she asked.

The gladiator glowered down at her. "No, it's the line to the Circus Maximus."

Linnea was burning with questions, but she was put off by

the gladiator's sarcasm. She glanced at the others ahead of her. No one spoke. Most everyone looked rather miserable. Like Linnea, they were wet, cold, fearful and uncertain. No helpful signs indicated how often ferries ran.

"So, how long have you been waiting?" she asked the gladiator in what she hoped was a deferential tone.

"Two thousand, one hundred sixty-three years," he told her.

Linnea felt her eyebrows jump. "Wonder what the holdup is."

Linnea supposed these conversations had long since been exhausted. She looked up and down the line. Her fellow passengers acted like people who had been waiting in line 2,000 years, without any flicker of hope in them at all, bored into catatonia, feet aching. Couldn't they bang on the window of the ticket booth, assuming there was one?

Then, suddenly, the lined lurched forward and Linnea and the other shades lumbered ahead. They moved down the long hall and around a corner, where a waiting room door had been opened for them. They crowded into the room. It smelled of stale cigarette smoke and urine, and the walls were badly in need of paint. On the other side of the room, another door opened briefly and a few people at the head of the line were allowed to go through. The door closed with a bang.

A few newcomers arrived and took their place behind Linnea. "They could at least do us the courtesy," she muttered, "of telling us what's going on."

The gladiator looked down at Linnea with a mixture of pity and disgust.

"Magazines would be nice, too," she said a little louder. The fluorescent lights above flickered, casting a ghoulish pallor over the already greenish faces of the dead.

"There needs to be some kind of orientation," Linnea

continued. "Or at least a handout. This whole process would be so much more bearable if we knew what to expect."

The door at the far end of the waiting room opened into darkness. Linnea could not see what lay beyond, but whenever a few more passengers were let through, she could hear the slap of the river against the shore. They were close enough to the head of the line now that the next time the door opened Linnea got a glimpse of the man who was opening it. He had a head shaped like a potato and bulging eyes like a pair of boiled eggs. With a shock, Linnea recognized Charon the ferryman.

"Three at a time," Charon said to the crowd. "Two at a time if you're fat."

The line moved forward again, and finally only Linnea and three others were left. When her turn came, Linnea saw that she would cross the Acheron as the sole passenger.

"Have your fares ready. Exact change only," said Charon. He hustled the others through the open door, and Linnea was left alone in the waiting room. She opened the door a crack and peered into the Stygian gloom. A ramp led down to the water's edge. She could make out nothing of the river's banks, nor of the Acheron itself, just the wet-mop smell of the river and the sound of water lapping the shore in the darkness. The air was dank—chilly and humid at the same time—and it clung to her skin.

Linnea had to remind herself that this was not actually Hell. It was only an entryway to the afterlife. Somewhere beyond all this lay not only the reputedly somewhat pleasant Asphodel Meadows, but the palace of Elysium, a paradise.

She waited for what felt like an eternity. Stretching invisibly on either side of the ramp must be the mournful near-side of the river of sorrow, where those who were unloved were dropped off, grown-up orphans, unspooling their infinite days in contemplation of their loneliness. Linnea's stomach knotted again at the prospect—however faint—that she might end up here for all time.

At last she heard the slurp and slap of the returning ferry. Linnea could just make out Charon's stooped figure poling the ferry to the water's edge, and then his pale face, leering at her from the murk. The ferry appeared to be nothing more than a simple wooden raft, lengths of timber lashed together with rope.

Charon's big hands were draped over the top of his pole. She could see the billiard-ball whites of his bulging eyes in the darkness. "The last little duckling," Charon said. "Watch your step!" He cackled then, as though he enjoyed the thought of Linnea slipping. The ramp to the water's edge was slick with moss. Linnea wondered how sturdy the little ferry was, and what would happen to you if you fell off and into the dreary waters. Were there creatures living beneath the river's surface? Did the water have magical powers?

Charon waited on the raft, grinning. Linnea saw that he was missing some teeth. She took cautious steps down the ramp until she was within a foot or two of the raft. Charon did not offer a hand. When she reached him, he simply held out his palm. "Fare," he said.

Crap. Linnea had forgotten about the fare. Traditionally it cost one obolus to cross the Acheron. Linnea, of course, was not in possession of any oboles. She reached two fingers into her pocket and fished out a couple of Canadian quarters she and Dori had found on their office windowsill. She dropped one of the coins in Charon's hairy palm with what she hoped was an air of authority.

Charon studied the quarter. He pulled it up very close to his bulging eye, then pocketed it and said, "Well, come on."

Linnea tried to step out onto the raft without muddying

her shoes or losing her balance. "Need a boost?" Charon said, and with a cackle placed a hand on her behind.

Linnea scooted to the other side of the raft, wanting to ride as far from the ferryman as possible. It was hard for her to walk on the uneven surface. She heard the slurp of Charon's pole in the muck as he shoved off. The ferry rocked, and Linnea lurched.

Charon seemed in no hurry, but took his time dipping his pole in the river and pushing the craft forward. They wobbled across the tenebrous water in near-silence for a while. Linnea could not see the far shore, but she heard the barking of dogs, from the three heads of the famous hell-hound, she supposed.

As though reading her thoughts, Charon said, "Got some goodies in your pockets for Cerberus?"

Linnea was appalled that Charon saw so clearly what she was up to. She said nothing.

"It'll never work," he told her.

"Why not?" Linnea said, her voice small.

Charon giggled. "You're bulging like a walrus," he told her, pointing a long-nailed finger at the pockets of Linnea's pants. "Cerberus won't let you in if he thinks you're angling to get out again. What've you got in there? Sea urchins?"

Linnea didn't know whether honesty was the best strategy with the ferryman. She couldn't imagine that Charon had her best interests at heart. But she couldn't think of anything else to say, so she told him the truth. "Honey cakes," she answered. "I have it on good authority that he likes them."

Charon laughed loudly now, showing a mouth full of black and broken teeth. "Cerberus is a *dawg*," he drawled. "You know what dogs like, don't you?" He leered at Linnea as though she herself were some kind of juicy treat.

It was icky that Charon could see through her plan so readily, and she didn't trust him. Yet, in this instance, she thought he was telling the truth. The ferocious three-headed canine had, of course, a guard dog's personality and a guard dog's carnivorous appetites. "So you're saying he won't accept honey cakes as a sop?"

Charon leered at her—delighted, apparently, by her predicament. "Honey cakes didn't have red meat in them, last time I checked," he said.

"Why didn't you tell me this before I started to cross the river?" said Linnea, grumpy.

Charon grinned. "Do you want to go back, then?"

"Yes."

Charon said, "Suits me. I'll take you back and forth as often as you want." He held out a hairy hand with theatrical exaggeration to make his point and said, "Fare."

Linnea dug in her jacket and gave Charon the other Canadian quarter. He pocketed it and continued to stare at her, draping his hands over his ferry pole. Grinning, he told her, "Charon likes honey cakes."

"Oh, for Pete's sake," Linnea said. She pried a baklava out of one pocket and handed it to him. Only then did he start to pole her back in the direction from which they'd come.

They crossed without speaking. Charon took bites of baklava between strokes, flakes of filo dough flying off and sticking to his face or swirling away toward the dark water. Linnea could hardly wait to escape. As soon as they bumped against the shore, she stepped off the raft and hurried up the mossy ramp as well as she could manage. She didn't want to give the ferryman another chance to put his hands on her ass.

Chapter Twelve

SLaM, 45

The hallway outside Dori's office door had become an ad-hoc memorial to Linnea. Bouquets of flowers, Latin textbooks, hand-written messages and teddy bears were piling up on the floor. Who would leave teddy bears? Dori thought with irritation as she stepped over the offerings to get to her door. As she unlocked her office, she heard a whimper behind her. A student stood in the hall among the mementos. Her eyes met Dori's with a stricken look.

"I brought this to add to the memorial," she told Dori, and she held out a broom handle with no bristles.

Dori paused, waiting for the young woman to make sense.

"Dr. Nil hated the ivy that grows over the windows," the young woman said. "It makes the rooms so dark."

Dori said nothing.

"She said the college never cleared it away. She wanted to pull it down herself, at least from the Latin classroom and her office." A rivulet of blue mascara ran down one of the student's cheeks. "So this one time I said maybe she could use a broom handle. And I remembered I had one"—she drew a breath—"left over from an art project."

Dori was about to suggest that she place the broom handle among the flowers in the hall when the young woman thrust the cylinder of wood into Dori's hands. "Maybe you could still use it," she told Dori. "You could clear out some of the ivy in her honor."

Dori did not think a broom handle would make a particularly good ivy-clearing tool, and there was no place in her office for any extraneous items. But now she couldn't get rid of the thing; the student was so sincere. Heaving a great sigh, Dori leaned the broom handle in the narrow space between her desk and the office door, which she then closed in hopes of getting something done.

The rest of the morning was gobbled up by Dori's trying to sort out Linnea's grade records for the feckless Ned Callow, who seemed unable to manage them by himself. Because of Linnea's murder, Dori had shouldered the Classics department on top of her own duties as Chair of the French and Italian departments. She'd made a valiant effort to find a competent Latin instructor, but none was to be had at such short notice. Ned Callow, however, was always hovering at the edges of campus life, eager for gainful employ. He had been a doctoral student for the past 18 years. He was always "working on his dissertation" and got by on various small instruction-related jobs at which he was famously not very good. Dori hated to do it, but in the end she hired him to finish out Linnea's classes for the semester.

Dori's cell phone sirened. Callow was not the only colleague who wanted something from her. With the Middlebridge faculty in shock and Linnea dead, the union organizing committee feared its efforts were going to stall. Ian Elf from over in the English Department wanted Dori to meet him beneath a freeway overpass that afternoon to talk about union business. Dori wondered if, under the circumstances, she was ill-advised to convene with strange men in out-of-the-way places. Elf was about as big as his name suggested, however, and Dori decided she could hold her own against him if it came to that. Besides, she trusted him implicitly. He taught English. How scary could he be?

Under the freeway, their voices masked by the roar of traffic overhead, Ian Elf shared with Dori what he'd learned at Thursday night's union-organizing meeting. Dori leaned against a concrete pillar, listening. They stood on a steep slope that ran down to the river. Invasive ivy clung to the soil and crept up the overpass, but there was not another human soul to be seen. If Elf wanted to kill Dori and cut out any of her organs, there would be no witnesses here in sight or earshot.

The English prof, though, was squinting earnestly uphill at Dori.

Between thirty and forty Middlebridge faculty members had gathered at the Splash, a pub, the evening of Linnea's murder. Linnea had addressed the group, Elf said.

"I know we've been concerned that part-time faculty aren't on board," she had told the group. It was hard to organize part-timers, who usually taught at three or four different institutions and spent most of their time in their cars or canoes, traveling from campus to campus in order to cobble together the equivalent of a full-time living. "But, I think, *acta est fabula*," she'd said. "The game's up."

Linnea then revealed that she had gotten access to an internal memo penned by Dean Eleanor Fiercey regarding part-time compensation. The Dean of Allocations wanted to swap out a portion of part-timers' salaries for a benefits package. Currently, part-time faculty did not enjoy health insurance or any other benefits from the college. Fiercey proposed one: free overnight parking. Since some part-time faculty made so little income teaching that they could not afford housing and instead lived in their vehicles, the free parking, Fiercey said, would be a "supportive gesture."

Ian Elf went on to explain to Dori that Fiercey also planned to provide part-time faculty with a "wellness hotline," given their lack of health insurance. The hotline would include recommendations that faculty get adequate exercise and sleep and advice on how to get the most out of food stamps. Fiercey had not yet unveiled the plan, Linnea had told them, but it looked as though the board was going to approve it and it would be quietly put into effect before the school year ended. When part-timers found out about it, Linnea felt certain they would want collective bargaining rights. "Linnea was proposing that we go to the media with the information, and then hold a faculty-wide vote on whether to unionize shortly afterward," Elf said.

As he laid out the details of Dean Fiercey's plan, Elf began to wring his hands. Linnea had had documented proof of Fiercey's designs. No one knew where that proof was now. Her colleagues were still reeling from Linnea's death, but they were also worried that Fiercey would get her plan approved before the faculty had time to regroup. "We want to go ahead with Linnea's proposal," he told Dori. "But it would be easier if we had her records. Do you by any chance have access to them?"

Dori thought of Linnea's flowered notebook, the one where Linnea kept all her union notes. There was plenty of Linnea's stuff in their office, and Dori had been to Linnea's house many times and had a copy of her house key. A semi roared overhead, giving Dori a moment to think. What if Ian

Elf were a mole from management?

"I might," she told the diminutive composition instructor, who looked innocent enough with his floppy hair and earnest face. "I can look," she half-shouted as another truck approached overhead. She'd have to give some thought to what to do if she found the papers. She'd better present them to the whole organizing committee, and not just pass them to Elf, guileless though he appeared.

Elf thanked her with a handshake. Before they picked their separate ways across the shrubby slope, he looked her in the eye and said, "Dori, be careful."

It had been weeks since Bridges had had an island of dry weather, so when the clouds parted briefly that afternoon after class, Dori decided to take her bicycle for a spin. Fencing was rigorous exercise, but for endurance, Dori liked to take long, hilly bike rides. Anyway, exercise was a good way to work through emotional trouble. Dori oiled her chain and pumped up her tires, pulled rain gear on over her sweats just in case, and carried her Fuji Absolute down two flights of stairs.

"Oh, my, aren't you virtuous?" Chesterfield, one of her downstairs neighbors, said to her. "Frannie and I only bicycle in the sunny months."

Dori lifted the bike frame down off her shoulder and smiled. She liked Chesterfield and Frannie Pheasant, an older couple who often invited her downstairs for biscuits, the kind that came in a cylindrical cardboard package and could be popped straight from the packaging into the toaster oven.

"It's not virtue, really," Dori told him. "I'm just trying to stay in shape."

"Well, that's a form of virtue," Chesterfield said, patting his stomach, which was something like a beach ball. "One I gave up some decades ago."

Dori mounted her bike, buckled her helmet under her chin and took off pedaling. She'd have to stick to the hills, foregoing the riverside bike path she enjoyed in the less waterlogged months. She rode three or four blocks through a commercial district, past coffee shops and second-hand clothing stores, bakeries and magazine vendors, around the corner from the French soup place called Soupçon and a combination auto shop/massage parlor called Lube Jobs. The district was anchored by an alterations shop that Dori sometimes patronized. They would alter most anything in there, not always with felicitous results. A man in Dori's acquaintance had reportedly wished for more sex in his marriage, only to have his wife start parading boyfriends to their marital bed. Dori had heard of a woman who'd told the shop she wanted to lose 40 pounds, and who soon afterward was involved in an unfortunate alligator incident. With fairytale-like predictability, the good citizens of Bridges continued to request alterations, certain they could outwit the system if their wishes were cleverly worded enough. Dori herself had gone there only for the simplest of changes: pants that needed hemmed or waistbands taken in.

Dori turned away from the mini-malls and into a residential district and began to pedal faster. The wind sang in her ears and made them sting with cold. A hard workout focused her attention. If she slowed, her thoughts fluttered back to Linnea's murder. So she stood on her pedals and pumped, driving up her heart rate and her breath, pushing to outrun her troubled thoughts.

This was the night Dori had rescheduled to have dinner with the man from the dating website. Dori knew she wouldn't make much of a date right now, but she didn't want to back out of their second get-together after standing him up for the first. Also, she needed the distraction. "Go have some fun," Jaspar had told her in the library that morning. "You look like you need it."

Pablo was soft-spoken and gentle, with a bald dome and round glasses. He worked as a medical transcriptionist in the county forensic lab and in his spare time played the lute. Over dinner he told her about a group he was in that aimed to preserve Renaissance music and play it on period instruments.

Dori was having a hard time concentrating on his words, though. In spite of the pleasant ambiance of the restaurant, dreadful images of Linnea's murder kept popping into her head—Linnea alone in the women's room, a man with a knife, a struggle, a horrible end. The fear and pain Linnea must have felt in the moments leading up to and at her death were almost beyond comprehension. Dori wouldn't wish them on anyone, but to have them happen to someone she was close to left her practically paralyzed. Then there was the matter of Linnea's brief appearance in her condo on Saturday night. She wondered if Linnea's ghost had been a manifestation of post-traumatic stress, or perhaps of perimenopause.

Dori stared at the menu.

"I recommend the shrimp," Pablo was saying. "They cook it in coconut and ginger and coriander and something delicious I can't identify. Do you like seafood?"

Dori strained, trying to remember what seafood was. She couldn't conjure her opinion of shrimp, but she wanted to appear good-natured, so she said, "Yes."

A waiter appeared. "Are you ready to order?"

"I am," Pablo said. "Dori?" He smiled at her, so warm and encouraging that Dori, struggling to stay attend to dinner, wanted to cry. "I'll have what you recommended," she said.

To Dori's relief Pablo ordered two of whatever it was. Pablo was an able conversationalist, and if Dori had had any focus, she would have been impressed at his easy manner and ability to ask good questions. He wasn't thrown by her answers, which she knew were disjointed and incomplete. Pablo managed to find out what she did for work, what she did for fun, what cities she'd lived in. Dori should have been asking good questions as well, but she kept losing her train of thought, and images of Linnea in the women's room kept jumping into her view.

Finally, near the end of dinner, Pablo said to her, "You seem distracted. Are you all right?"

Dori shook her head, her blond curls bobbing. "I'm sorry," she said. "I shouldn't have come tonight." She crumpled her dinner napkin. "A colleague of mine was murdered on campus last week."

"I wondered if I should ask you about that when you said you worked at Middlebridge," Pablo said, empathy in his face. "But it didn't seem like great first-date material."

"So you knew about it. I guess it's been all over the news."

Pablo ducked his head. "And in my line of work... My employer is the county forensic lab," he said. He didn't elaborate, and Dori didn't want to hear more. "Was it someone you knew?"

"She was my best friend. We shared an office at the college for seven years." Dori was numb, staring at the tablecloth as she spoke.

"God, I'm sorry."

"I've been pretty poor company tonight," Dori explained. "I just can't get it off my mind."

"Of course not, my God," Pablo said. "It's only been— what?—five days? You must still be in a state of shock. I'm honored you decided to keep our date, given the circumstances."

"I shouldn't have dragged you through this, though," Dori said. "I wasn't thinking clearly."

Pablo gazed at Dori with kind eyes. "Is there anything I can do for you?" he asked.

Dori bit her lip. She didn't have any idea if she was romantically interested in Pablo, but sex could be therapeutically distracting, and she thought the comfort of human warmth would do her good. "Would you come home with me tonight?" she said.

In the middle of the night Dori sat straight up in bed. She clutched her hair for a minute, thinking, and then drew the sheets around her.

"Hey," said Pablo softly, stirring. "Everything okay?"

"You work in the county forensic lab," Dori said.

Pablo's eyebrows drew together. "Yeah?"

"I think there may be something else you can do for me," Dori told him.

Chapter Thirteen

IN THE DARK

Linnea hesitated to tell Vergil what she'd done with her afternoon. She didn't want to hurt his feelings. "I went back," she said, trying to be as gentle as she could.

It was evening. A last sliver of yellow-gray light was seeping through the curtains at the lone window in Vergil's apartment, and it fell on the old man's face, which crumpled with disappointment.

"I'm sorry," Linnea said.

"No, no, *I'm* sorry."

"I just thought—we had the day-pass, you know, and I might as well…"

"I let you down," Vergil said. "I was deceiving myself. I simply can't do what I used to do any more."

Linnea gave Vergil's hand a squeeze. "Was I gone a long time?" she asked. "A man in line told me he'd been waiting over two thousand years."

"Poppycock," said Vergil. "It only *feels* like two thousand years. You were only away a couple hours."

Time probably did funny things when you were dead, Linnea thought. Or maybe the gladiator had just been messing with her. Linnea told Vergil about her encounter with Charon and what the horrible ferryman had said about honey cakes and Cerberus.

"I'm afraid he's right," Vergil told her. "Cerberus has wised up over the years. He's very suspicious of anyone trying to pull an Aeneas."

Linnea's throat tightened. If Vergil couldn't help her, and she couldn't bribe the three-headed guard dog, she might really be in trouble.

They sat in the dwindling gray light without speaking. Then Vergil said, "It's hard to let go. One has one's pride, you know."

"Let go?"

"Of all the things I used to do. The adventure. The excursions. I'm a world traveler—I've even been to death and back—and now it's all I can do to get to the grocery store." Vergil looked smaller than ever, shrunken and papery, his eyes oversized in his tiny face. "I should have crossed over for good a long time ago," he continued. "But I can't bear to leave my book undone."

Linnea didn't know what to say, so she sat in the gloaming with her friend in silence.

As Linnea saw it, she should now turn her attention to two other matters. The first was practicing the art of appearing and disappearing at will, what Vergil called *wefting*. She didn't think she'd be able to weft on demand into Dori's apartment again if she needed to, so she'd have to work on that skill. The second matter was the continued investigation of the afterlives available to her. She needed to hedge her bets against the possibility that Dori should fail her, and she remained unenthused about Asphodel. In spite of Vergil's admonitions, Linnea decided she should give her old body a try. She'd spend a little time in her corpse, she thought, and then, if she couldn't stand it, she would reconsider her options. At the moment, eternal boredom seemed preferable to eternal damnation.

Linnea showed up at the county forensic lab during business hours the following morning. She didn't dare open the door, since the front desk clerk had a clear view of the entrance, and Linnea didn't want the clerk to see a door opening and shutting of its own accord. He'll think he's seen a ghost, she said to herself with a smirk. So she simply stationed herself at the door. Eventually someone would arrive or leave, and she could time her entrance to coincide.

Linnea was used to waiting—she seemed to do a great deal of it at Middlebridge. The week before her murder, for example, she had spent the better part of an hour just trying to pick up some registration documents. The college was already two weeks into its spring semester, but some students hadn't gotten around to signing up for classes, so Linnea had walked over to the Student Data-Intake and Entrance-Status Processing Building (historically called Registration) to pick up a stack of late-registration slips. She thought it would be a quick errand, since the registration building sat close to Verizon Wireless Hall. She only had to tromp past the Center for Supplemental Instruction and Assistance Procurement (formerly called the tutoring center) and the Department for Digital and Print-Based Information-Access Tools (once known as the library) and hang a left at the copper beech.

But there had been an enormous line at the registration window and only one clerk at work. Linnea remembered it clearly, because she had waited for 45 minutes, and with nothing else to do, she'd studied a display of student ceramic work from the fall semester. In a glass case sat bowls and cups, teapots and plates. Linnea liked them very much, even the warped and asymmetrical pieces that represented the early efforts of beginning ceramics students. They were ash-glazed, she learned by reading a helpful placard, which gave even the most deformed of them a gorgeous stippled pattern.

When Linnea ran out of pottery to admire, she had turned her eye to the registration clerk. He was a handsome fellow, with sleek hair pulled into a ponytail. In spite of his workload he remained calm and friendly, handing over papers and looking up data with a prize-winning smile, all good white teeth and dimples.

Just before Linnea approached the registration counter, someone behind her had said, "Wait." It was Eleanor Fiercey, looking buxom and authoritative. Linnea didn't know her personally, but the dean's reputation preceded her, and Linnea felt her heart quake a little. Dean Fiercey stepped past Linnea and leaned in close to the handsome clerk. "May I see those? I hear there is some irregularity in them." She frowned at the papers, and then barked, "No, these aren't they. May I see a prerequisite-override form?"

The clerk had looked around uncertainly.

"I believe they're behind you. In a box on the floor, there." Dean Fiercey studied the clerk as he moved toward the box of forms. Linnea saw the dean's eyes slide over the young man's tush as he bent to pick up a stack of papers. When the clerk returned with the yellow form, the dean said brusquely, "Yes, here it is," and rapped the paper with her knuckle. "That will do." Her face was severe, but as she turned to leave, her eyes slithered down over the clerk's body again with a kind of oily greed.

Linnea and the clerk had exchanged a look, as if to say to each other, "Weird."

Replaying this scene in her head now, Linnea almost missed an opportunity to slip into the forensic lab. An amiable-looking fellow with a bald pate and round glasses was headed through the doors with a clipboard in his hand. Linnea just had time to dash in behind him.

After a few minutes of stealthy investigation, Linnea located the refrigeration unit, a long, cool room of stainless steel drawers, each one holding a lifeless form waiting for autopsy or burial. Linnea found the drawer where her own shell was kept and tried to prepare herself for the emotion of seeing herself dead. Her body might be partly decomposed, she told herself, or the violence done to it might come as a shock. Linnea drew a brave breath. She pulled the drawer open, yanked back the sheet and took a good look.

It was strange, but not necessarily frightening, to see her likeness lying there. She had already gotten used to the hole in her chest and the awkward ribs that poked out here and there through her torn flesh. No nasty surprises awaited her. The body that reposed on the roll-out shelf was identical to the form she currently inhabited. Linnea's spirit, if that's what it was, had suffered the same insults and injuries as her carnal version.

Linnea hopped onto the table beside her body and lay, face-up, atop it. After some wiggling to get her fingers and toes exactly lined up with those of her corpse, she melded quite nicely into it. Linnea lay still for a time, staring at the ceiling. Then she sat up briefly and drew the sheet over herself, pulling it smooth, to the best of her ability, from underneath. This isn't so bad, she thought. A sense of comfort and calm settled over her. The room was wonderfully quiet.

This was a place where she could think. Perhaps it would be a place where she could lie in quiet contemplation forever—though it would be nice if she had something to read.

Linnea wondered what had happened to her at the end. She raked over all her recent memories but could come up with nothing that might have led to her murder. *Cui bono?* Who would benefit? Who might have had a motive to do her in? She wondered what her survivors were thinking. Dori, when Linnea had popped into her kitchen, had honestly not seemed glad to see her. Was Linnea mourned by anyone?

The door to the refrigerator unit opened. Linnea realized with a start that she was still lying out in the open. She had never shut her drawer—nor could she have, while she herself was occupying it. Linnea shut her eyes and tried to hold very, very still.

She heard shoes on the polished floor and then a man's voice: "Shit!"

"Oh," said another. "What's going on?"

"Did you leave this drawer open?" The voice was angry, and his angry footsteps crossed the room to where Linnea lay.

"No! Why would I?" said the second man.

"You must have," barked the first. "You were the last one in here."

"I didn't touch that drawer. I'm not even assigned to that case."

The angry man pulled back Linnea's sheet and inspected her. She held her breath. He seemed to lean over her for a long time.

Linnea's body might be lifeless, but her ghost—or whatever it was—seemed to have the same needs as a living organism. Linnea didn't know how long she could sustain this game of freeze-tag without drawing breath. A sensation of panic began to rise in her chest. Fingers prodded her wound, then held her jaw and turned her head back and forth. She tried to snake a tiny bit of air in through her nostrils without moving her ribcage. That tactic would delay, but not for long, the need to pull in a full breath.

"Huh," the man's voice said. She could feel his eyes on her, and wondered if he perceived that this dead body was not like the others. Her form lay perfectly still, but her mind grew increasingly hyperactive. She could not hold out. She would have to abandon pretense and take the consequences.

Linnea was on the verge of taking in a breath when she felt the sheet fall over her again.

"I don't see any evidence of tampering," said the forensics lab worker, his voice a little calmer now. "Still, I'd like to know what the hell somebody was up to." Linnea felt herself going on a little ride: the man must be sliding the drawer back into place. It shut with a click, and Linnea was left alone in the dark with her thoughts.

Chapter Fourteen

WAKING UP

At night Alice had taken to falling headlong into bed without a word to any of her housemates, not even Tad. She would sleep with her head on his shoulder but she wouldn't speak to him, not about Dr. Nil, not about anything. Tad said he wasn't sleeping well either, and she accepted that as perfectly natural. Never mind that Tad had never met Dr. Nil. Alice imagined the whole campus felt bereft of her favorite professor and must be grieving. To Alice it made sense that all Middlebridge students would be stricken with sleep troubles—that they, like she, must be lying awake wondering who could have done in Dr. Nil and whether they were morally obligated to try to track down the murderer themselves. So she didn't really notice when Tad stopped coming to bed at the same time as she did, and she didn't really notice a few days later when he stopping sleeping in her bed altogether.

It was Guppy, the new housemate, who finally shook Alice out of her somnambulant state. He said to her, "You're kind of a zombie. You know that?"

This, coming from the mouth of a guy who'd boasted that he'd once spent five weeks in a state of catatonia induced by an experimental cold medicine he'd been paid to take.

"I'm having a hard semester," Alice told him.

"Yeah, I heard your teacher died," Guppy said.

"Somebody murdered her."

"That's so rude," Guppy said.

Alice was sometimes amused by Guppy's happy-go-lucky understatements, but today it felt like he was rubbing sandpaper on her eyeball. She was so offended that she awoke from her daylight sleepwalking.

She started noticing then what a sack of moldy potatoes had replaced Dr. Nil in Latin 102. Days were slipping by, and the students were still working on the short chapter they'd been studying at the time of Dr. Nil's murder. Mr. Callow had a way of using up almost all their class time doing things like opening his briefcase and lining up the dry-erase markers in the trays at the white board.

For Alice this was more than a waste of time—it had implications for her pursuit of a Classics degree. She was already in a hurry, because she hadn't started Latin until her sophomore year. She had intended to take an accelerated second-year course over the summer so she could jump into third-year as a junior and be back on track. Now she doubted she would be prepared for her summer class. If she couldn't take the accelerated course, she'd be delaying her graduation by a full year. That was 16,746 more dollars, or 540 additional nights of stripping. In short, her life had been deeply, deeply interrupted by the presence of Mr. Callow at the head of her Latin class.

"I have to find a different Latin teacher," she said to Mick and Brian. But they all knew it was too late.

"You can take a different teacher next term," Mick told her.

"I won't be ready!" Alice wailed.

"Come on, Alice," Brian told her. "You're the smartest student in the class. You'll catch up."

Brian was right. Alice set her jaw. She could and would catch up. She'd do the work on her own, go to tutoring, sit in on another section of the class. She'd do on-line exercises, get handouts from another instructor. *Aut viam inveniam,* Alice thought.

It was Wednesday, costume night at the club. Alice had amassed a considerable collection of get-ups: firefighter, welder, librarian, EMT, house painter, corrections officer. Some of her costumes were pornography clichés—her 60s-style nurse's and flight attendant's uniforms, for example—and others were more clever. She liked to mix it up.

Alice kept all this gear in a plastic milk crate which (topped with an empty pizza box) had doubled as a night-table next to her futon all year. But now that Tad was living in her bedroom, Alice didn't have space for the box. Instead, she'd found a handy hiding-place for it on campus. Right upstairs from Latin class was a faculty lounge with a large closet that was apparently unused by anyone who worked at the college. Alice slipped in early one morning before the professors started showing up for their coffee and stashed her box there. She was always in the building on Wednesdays anyway because of Latin class, so it would be easy to zip upstairs and pick out a costume for the night's dance routines.

More alert than at any time since the tragedy, Alice started wondering where Tad had gotten to. She wandered through the house looking for him. He wasn't in the kitchen. He wasn't playing darts in the living room. She checked the back yard; no sign of him under the basketball hoop, where he could sometimes be found, even in the dark and in the rain.

"Tad?" she called down the basement stairs.

"I think he's up there," Guppy said, gesturing at the ceiling with his thumb. Alice tripped up the shaggy orange stairwell and climbed over the stuff piled in Guppy's alcove. From the top of the stairs, she could see the room at the end of the hall belonging to Amy. The door was wide open and there were two sets of legs on Amy's bed, Tad's outstretched ones and Amy's, wrapped around his waist as she lay on top of him like some extremely long-legged, long-bodied frog. Alice strode up to the doorway and cleared her throat.

Tad peered around at her from behind Amy's head. Amy, who had her back to Alice, turned her head to the side so she could see Alice in her peripheral vision.

"Hey, Alice," Tad said.

Alice said nothing.

"You don't mind, right?" Tad said.

Alice considered. Her heart had lurched when she saw them there together, but, she reflected, she had no right to mind. She and Tad had always agreed they didn't own each other. No restrictions/no secrets. Amy rolled off Tad and stretched out against the back wall. "Yeah, you're okay with it, aren't you, Alice?" she said. Her words were casual, but her voice sounded unconvinced, Alice thought.

"Yeah, I'm okay with it," Alice said, her voice light. She shrugged and turned away.

"You wanna join us?" Tad called after her.

"Nah, that's all right," she said over her shoulder and went back downstairs.

When Alice got to work that night, the Larries seemed

unusually present. They always sat front and center, their hands wrapped around their respective bourbon glasses and their posture bad, two big toads on bar stools. It wasn't possible for them to get any closer to the dance floor than they already were, but they were louder than usual—maybe they'd started drinking before they got to Cootchie-Coo—and lewder than she had ever heard them.

Patrons could pretty much make any crude comments they wanted. It was part of what they paid for when they plunked down their covers. Alice was usually able to keep herself behind an invisible shield of self-respect and self-determination. Tonight, though, the Larries were getting to her.

She remembered an evening from early on in her time at Cootchie-Coo. Once she'd gotten used to the drill, it had occurred to her that she could be creative with her routines. Dance, was, after all, a form of self-expression and an art, whether it was performed clothed or naked. She'd gone out on the floor that night and done something all new, pushing herself to the outer limits of her physical abilities and her imagination. She finished the routine knowing she'd danced well. Really, really well.

She got almost no tips.

Shell-shocked, she'd returned to the dressing room and said to Ember, who shared her vanity table, "What just happened?"

Ember was an older performer who'd been dancing a long time. She shook her head at Alice. "Look, if you want to do that, you have to go to Portland or Seattle," she told Alice.

"I thought they'd find it interesting," Alice said. "I thought I'd getter *better* tips."

"Look, honey," Ember said. "You don't go out there trying to earn anything. *They* have to earn *your* goodwill. Got it?"

"Nuh-uh."

"Make them prove to you that it's worth your while to make an effort."

"Oh. I see," Alice said. Ember's point was an important early lesson for her.

"Anyway," Ember said then. "Look at them." She jutted her chin past the stage curtains in the direction of the clientele. "Do they look like connoisseurs of the arts to you?"

Alice thought of that night now, watching the Larries ogle her coworkers. Bridges had just a handful of skin clubs. If you were Asian, you could get a job at an uptown club called China Dolls, where the staging was uniform, suggestive of subservience, the dancers sylph-like and blank. If you were pretty and black, like Ember, or pretty and plus-sized, like their co-worker Tigress, or not mainstream-pretty but skinny and young and white, like Alice, then you had Cootchie-Coo and two or three other venues like it. If you were over forty, unconventionally proportioned, or supporting an addiction that was getting the better of you, you danced at the clubs among the used-car lots on 105th Street. Those were the choices.

At the time, Alice felt that her own goal—her B.A.— would be compensation enough for whatever she had to do to earn it. Tonight, watching the men at the front of the club trying to wheedle and intimidate their way to sexual favors, she felt less certain.

"Do you have any eyeliner?" someone asked Alice. She poked around in her drawer and produced the item but didn't have the heart to carry on a conversation. She had twenty minutes to study, but she couldn't concentrate.

Tonight it was Alice's turn at the Larry Pole. Sometimes the dancers took the stage together, each to one of the three poles on the floor. Out of fairness they rotated poles, because only one of the three was mounted in a desirable spot on the floor. It was nearest to tipping patrons, and therefore that dancer was likely to collect more tips than the dancer at the back of the room. The third pole was right in front of the Larries, and no one wanted to dance near the Larries.

Alice had just finished a number when the Larry on the left said, "I'd like to take a piece of that home." The Larry on the right said, "Huh-uh, not if I get to it first." Then the first Larry grinned and said, "Grab a leg and make a wish."

Alice turned and walked off the stage and out of the room without collecting tips from anybody. She found Renee taking inventory in the back room. "Can you do something about them?" she asked her manager.

Renee shrugged. "Don't worry about them—they're harmless." She wrote a figure on her clipboard and moved on to the next shelf.

"They're threatening me."

"As long as they don't touch you," Renee said, "they're within their rights." Her mouth was a grim line of non-budging.

"They *have* touched me," Alice protested. Some months earlier, before Alice knew not to get too close to the tip rail near the Larries, one of them had shoved a crooked finger right between her legs. Renee knew all about it.

Renee stopped what she was doing and turned to face Alice. "You're a bright girl," she said with no praise in her voice. "There's a long line of other girls out there willing to uncover their booties to cover tuition. Do you understand what I'm saying to you?"

Alice said nothing, but turned and went back to her dressing room. She closed the door hard behind her and took up her Latin text.

Chapter Fifteen

COLDHEARTED

In the morning, Dori followed Pablo to work. She didn't dare tell him, of course, about Linnea's request. She kept wondering if her friend's strange appearance in her kitchen had been a hallucination. The dishtowel she'd used to mop up her spilled coffee still lay soggy in the laundry basket. She'd checked several times.

Dori had told Pablo that she wanted to view Linnea's body for closure. Pablo had balked. "She—really isn't fit for viewing—after what happened," he told her, wincing. "I'm sorry."

"Can I at least come in and see her body covered in a sheet?" she'd asked. "I'm struggling to believe she's dead. I think it would help me put the issue to rest." She hated to lie to Pablo. He seemed like such a nice guy.

Pablo looked distressed. "It would be in violation of the strictest rules," he said. "Especially in an ongoing investigation. Only a few people are authorized to have anything to do with the body. I'm sorry, Dori."

In a desperate last-minute effort, Dori said, "What about the heart? Could I—say good-bye to it?"

Pablo searched Dori's face for a few seconds and then told her, "I could show you the box it's in."

Maybe that would do the trick, Dori thought. And if Linnea weren't satisfied, at least Dori would know where the heart was, and she could try again another time.

As they entered the county forensics building, Dori looked around surreptitiously. Pablo led her past a sea of cubicles—it was early, and his co-workers hadn't yet begun to arrive—to the refrigerator unit at the rear of the building. There must be a back door, Dori thought. They wouldn't wheel bodies through the front offices, would they? They passed through a stainless steel door and into a cold room lined with a bank of drawers that Dori supposed must house the bodies. Off to one side was a smaller room where she guessed autopsies took place; Dori could see through its open door a cabinet of supplies and operating-room lights. On a third wall of the room was a pair of swinging doors that seemed to lead to another corridor, and another exit, a steel door to the outside. There's my back entrance, Dori thought.

Pablo went to a freezer case at the back of the room and retrieved from it a metal box labeled with Linnea's name and date of death. "I can't take it out of the box," Pablo said, "but you can have a little time with it."

Dori placed her hands on the box. Now what? Dori wondered if this moment would satisfy Linnea's request, but she doubted it. What had Linnea meant by being "reunited" with her heart, anyway? Was Dori supposed to take the heart from its box and stuff it back in Linnea's chest cavity? And why was reunification necessary in the first place? *Le Coeur a ses raisons que la Raison ne connaît pas*, she thought. The

Heart has its reasons that Reason doesn't know.

Pablo's cell phone rang. "Excuse me," he said. "I have to take this." He turned away from Dori.

Dori set the box down, then pushed open the heavy steel door. It led to a concrete stairwell. Dori slid to the ground in the open doorway. Pablo looked her way, and she gestured as though to say she was all right. She slipped her hand in the pocket of her Stylin' Jacket, found and fished out a Canadian quarter, and leaned it up against the doorjamb behind her back so that the door might remain propped open just the tiniest crack when she shut it.

Pablo ended his phone call and came and squatted before Dori.

"You okay?" he asked.

"I got lightheaded. I thought I should get a breath of air," she said.

"You're pale. Do you want a glass of water?"

"I'll be okay," she said. "I really appreciate this, Pablo." She let him pull her to standing and then, with care, she eased the door closed, hoping Pablo wouldn't notice it wasn't shut tight. He returned the box to the freezer case. Then he took Dori's hand and said, "Um, this little visit needs to stay between me and you." Pablo was visibly uncomfortable, and Dori knew he had broken a rule, probably a big rule, for her.

"Of course," Dori said. "I'd better get to campus. I have a class in less than an hour. Thanks for everything. I mean it."

"Don't mention it," Pablo said. He gave her a hug and asked, "Can I call you?"

Dori's mind floated over the previous night. Pablo had been an attentive lover, but Dori could hardly remember their dinner together. Under ordinary circumstances, she probably wouldn't go out with him again. But these weren't ordinary circumstances. Dori couldn't distance herself from Pablo—

she might need him again to gain access to Linnea's heart. She stood on tiptoes and kissed him. "Yes," she told him. "You can call me."

An engine murmured outside the building and a yellow light beside the swinging doors began to flash. Dori could hear the banging of doors and the squeak of a metal gurney on the concrete driveway out back. From the corridor beyond the swinging doors, someone shouted "Incoming!"

"Scoot," Pablo said. "Fast. Now. They're delivering a body."

Dori hustled past the room with the operating lights, through the stainless steel door to the office area, past the empty cubicles and out the front of the building before her mind could catch up to her legs. Once outside she smoothed her skirt and did her best to smooth her face. She followed the sidewalk around to the back of the morgue and peeked at the ambulance idling there before returning to her canoe to paddle to Middlebridge.

Dori was acutely aware of the possibility that the murderer still lurked nearby, and that, being single, she lived and often made her daily rounds in solitude. A murder had taken place, not just on her campus, but in the very women's room where Dori herself peed half a dozen times a day. Yet fear was something she could contain by following the prescriptions of Campus Security: don't walk to the water taxi stop alone; avoid unpeopled areas; leave campus before dark; report suspicious behavior. Fear she had dealt with.

Grief was something else. Grief came with no sensible prescriptions. Besides, Dori hadn't had the leisure to address it. Since the beginning of the week, she'd been all business— running two departments, shepherding Ned Callow through the Latin curriculum, reading student applications for the

Millicent Vena Cava Scholarship in the humanities, teaching. And thinking about how to get the heart into Linnea's hands. Or chest, or whatever.

Shortly after she got to campus following her sojourn at the forensic lab, she was summoned to Dean Budgie's office.

"I'm sorry to have to ask this of you," the dean said to her as soon as she arrived—dispensing with greetings and niceties—"but since you've agreed to shoulder the Classics department I must ensure that you include the completion of the Mid-Year Assessment of the Department's Continuous Academic Progress among your responsibilities." Dean Budgie tugged on the cuffs of his dress shirt. He was in his yellow suit again. "I must impress upon you in the strongest possible terms the importance of this document. The accreditation team is to visit us in May. Our re-accreditation may rest on our having the appropriate self-assessments in place."

Dori must not have disguised her feelings very well, because Budgie held up a hand as though to swear off protests. "I understand the tardiness of this particular document is not your fault. French and Italian's Mid-Year Assessment came to me with time to spare, and I thank you for it. Still," Budgie cleared his throat, "that of Classics needs to be on my desk at the earliest possible opportunity."

"I see," Dori said.

"I do appreciate your efforts," Dean Budgie told her, unsmiling, as he held his office door open for her to leave. If she didn't already think of him as a sort of large bird, Dori might have described him to herself as a cold fish.

When she returned to her office, Dori sat at her desk with her head in her hands, exhausted. She heard a tapping at her window and swiveled in her chair. The familiar crow was there, eyeing her with its shiny eye, a long, flat silver object in its beak.

"What do you want?" she said crossly.

"Grak," said the crow. The object fell from its beak to the sill, and as Dori approached the window, the black bird flapped away. Dori slid the window open. It was drizzling. No students were out and about. The only other person Dori saw was a handsome registration clerk walking past the window in the Data-Intake building across the way. Hank was his name. Dori picked up and examined the object the bird had dropped. It appeared to be the detachable blade of a saw. "Huh," Dori said to herself, dropping it into a pocket of her Stylin' Jacket.

After leaving work that night, Dori returned to the part of the city where Pablo worked. The morgue and its neighbors stood on high ground, so she tied her canoe at the bottom of a hill and approached the building—glancing around to see that she was alone—on foot. Slipping around to the back of the building, she descended the three or four steps into the concrete stairwell and checked the emergency exit door. It was shut fast. Her quarter trick had failed.

"Now what?" she muttered. She couldn't approach Pablo for another favor. She hoped he hadn't been the one to discover the quarter, or if he had been, that he didn't suspect her of anything.

She poked around in her jacket pockets to see if anything there might be of use. The saw blade; a ball of tinfoil; a marble. Nothing she could use to pick a lock. How else did one get into a locked building? Scale a wall? Tunnel a hole beneath? She walked the perimeter of the building, examining it, and stopped before the front entrance. While she stood there doubting herself, a woman in a lab coat came to the door from inside. "May I help you?" she said.

For all Dori knew it was the County Medical Examiner herself. "Oh—I was hoping to find Pablo," she said.

"We're closed. He's not here."

"Well—can I leave him a note?"

Dori scribbled a friendly, "Just stopped by to say hi—D." She folded the scrap of paper and handed it to the woman with a guilty pang. When Pablo got the note and learned she'd popped by his workplace just hours after having left it, Dori knew he would imagine she was getting very interested in him. She hurried back to her boat in a clammy sweat.

Before heading home, she canoed over to Linnea's house. She let herself in and spent an hour looking for the documents Ian Elf had asked about. It was spooky and disheartening to be in her dead friend's home, and Dori didn't feel good about rifling through Linnea's things, even for a worthy cause. She didn't turn up anything of use.

Before bed, Dori settled onto the nubby loveseat in her living room to go through Linnea's Latin class papers for Ned Callow. She opened a manila folder and pulled out the top sheet. When her eyes fell on her friend's familiar handwriting, they filled with tears. It seemed impossible that Linnea was really gone. Linnea, her dearest friend at Middlebridge, with whom she had shared so much of what it was to teach there. How would she be able to manage without her? Their shared little office, always cramped and cluttered, now seemed horribly empty. The thought of working there alone in perpetuity was excruciating. But the thought of someone else taking over Linnea's desk—replacing her—was unbearable. Linnea was irreplaceable. Then Dori's mind bent toward the unthinkable, the moments of the murder itself. In helpless horror, she lay down and sobbed.

Some part of her separated and observed the strangeness of grief, witnessing her own small form huddled on the loveseat, noticing the feel of the yellow nubbins under her face, the foreign sounds that rose from her unbidden, while the rest of her gave itself over to feeling and lay curled and keening like a wild animal.

Chapter Sixteen

HEAVEN

Luckily, Linnea was not claustrophobic, nor did she really have issues with the dark. That was a good thing, because it was extremely dark, and extremely close, in the long safe-deposit box in the forensic lab where her body was stowed. She could just hear the sound of the door to the refrigerator unit opening and shutting from time to time, footsteps, indistinct voices. Mostly she lay in long stretches of silence.

Varieties of darkness were part of life in Bridges, with its short winter days and constant cloud cover. Even Linnea's classroom had been dark, despite its ample windows. The founding fathers of Middlebridge had planted English ivy on the grounds, hoping to evoke the great university campuses of the east coast and of Britain. But in the Pacific Northwest, English ivy was an invasive species. Over the decades it had grown up over the walls of the classroom buildings, lending them at first an air of dignity and then, as the years passed, of decrepitude. Ivy had reached the full height of the buildings and had crept over their peaked roofs, encasing them in its dense leaves, so that these days the campus appeared to be filled in less by architectural structures than by vast dark pods. Indoors, a muffled green light seeped through the windows. Studying in Linnea's classroom was like learning Latin inside a submarine.

You no longer have a classroom, Linnea reminded herself. You're here to wrestle with the future, not the past.

Another problem leaped into Linnea's mind. What if she and her body were to be cremated? She had assumed that her body would be buried, and she could rest inside it forever if she cared to. What would become of her if her housing went up in smoke? Linnea strained to think. Had she left any documents specifying her last wishes in this regard? In the absence of instruction from the deceased, what was the default means of disposal?

On the other hand, as Linnea lay on her sliding drawer in the pitch dark she realized there was an important aspect of being a corpse that she'd overlooked: it was cold as stainless steel. The longer she dwelt there, the more uneasy she became. Her toes grew numb, then her fingers and ears. Inch by inch, over the course of the day and night, Linnea began to feel miserable.

The damp cold was a part of life in this climate that Linnea had barely tolerated. For nine months of the year here, the rain was of Biblical proportions. When she had first moved to Bridges, she'd been charmed by the thought of taking a water taxi to school in the morning, and the small boats that replaced city buses in the rainy season did, in their way, evoke Venetian gondolas and vaporettos. But the delight of riding to campus in a downpour daily for many months, and of walking around all day in damp pants and wet socks, had quickly worn off. Instead of acclimating, Linnea had found each winter here a little harder than the last.

Linnea remembered now how eagerly she'd been anticipating her weekend trip out of the wet, gray city. The conference of the National Association of Classical Studies was to be this weekend in Arizona. Linnea often found the papers given there to be on the dusty side, but she didn't care—she'd been looking forward to the sunshine, as well as to the conference's delightful extracurricular events. Someone would no doubt bring a slide show of Sicily or Corfu, and on Saturday night they'd serve a multi-course Italian dinner, complete with Tuscan wine. One year some clever person had brought a scale model of ancient Rome fashioned entirely of gelato. Linnea had lingered there a long while, in love with the Coconut Temple of Castor and Pollux, the Mocha Rostra, the Pistachio Pantheon.

Discomfort in her extremities jolted Linnea out of her daydream. She wasn't going to the Classical Studies Conference; she was dead, and in storage at the county morgue. And if she had imagined briefly that she would be eternally content under six feet of cold, wet Bridges clay, she awoke now to the truth. She would never be able to bear it. She hadn't been able to tolerate even 24 hours of refrigeration. Her body as a permanent casing was an option she had just crossed off her list.

And now she was trapped. She couldn't open the steel drawer from the inside; there wasn't even room for her to sit up. "Hey!" she shouted, banging the wall with her fist, and then hoping no one had heard her noise. Panic began to rise in her throat.

Then she remembered she could try *wefting.*

With effort, she willed herself out of her corpse and through the stainless steel drawer. In her clumsy novice's attempt to move herself with her intention, she landed on the polished floor of the refrigeration unit in a heap.

Linnea picked herself up and strode out of the building. She didn't even wait for one of the living to open the front door, but left through the back exit of the body bank, kicking a quarter out of the way as she pulled open a big steel door and stepped into a stairwell. She wouldn't return to her body unless it was to be cremated. Dubious an option as that was, she believed she would choose to come back for cremation. Anything to get warm again.

Acutely aware of the hatch marks of her days on Earth—there were four now, leaving just nine for her to resolve her fate—Linnea left the county morgue and headed once again for the entrance to Hades. All that time in the dark had given her time to think. If her recollection of the first chapters of Dante was correct, the far side of the Acheron marked the entrance not only to the underworld of the ancient Romans, but to the dwelling places of other sorts of believers. She was pretty certain she could get to the Christian portion of that underworld without having to get past Cerberus, and she knew how to deal with Charon now.

Linnea stopped by the bakery on her way, this time pushing the baklava into a side pouch of her big briefcase. At the mouth of Hades she descended and entered the fluorescent-lit tunnel. The ferry service waiting room held no line. Maybe Tuesday was a slow day. When Charon arrived, she handed him a coin. He said nothing to her about what might be in her pockets, and he made no demands.

Linnea was not as nervous on this second trip across the sorrowful river, and she found herself burgling glances at the ferryman. He seemed to be paying no attention to her, but the third or fourth time she let her eyes scamper over him, he said, "Isn't nice to stare," and made a face at her.

Linnea was embarrassed. It was hard not to peek at

Charon; his face was so fascinating in its grotesqueness.

"It's the eyes, isn't it?" Charon said. His eyes were a pair of ping pong balls, white and round and protruding.

Linnea said nothing.

"Exophthalmoses," Charon told her, "Due to hyperthyroidism. Now you know."

Linnea could feel herself blushing and was glad for the dim light. "And you thought I was just ugly," Charon said, widening his eyes even more and thrusting his head in her direction.

Linnea didn't know what to say, and they made the rest of the crossing in silence.

When the bottom of the raft scraped the sludge at the far side of the river, Linnea hopped off and asked, "Which way to the Christian realm?"

"Going to take Jesus as our personal savior, are we?" said Charon. "Might be a tad late for that."

"There's a honey cake in it for you," Linnea told him. "And another when I return, if your information proves accurate."

"Let's see it," Charon croaked. Linnea pulled one of the two squares of baklava, wrapped in a paper towel, from her briefcase. Charon swiped at it with a hairy hand, but Linnea, anticipating his tricks, jerked her hand away in time.

Charon stared, licked his lips. "That way," he said. He waved upstream. "Through the trees, always going uphill. Look for an arch." Charon held out his hand for the baklava, which Linnea gave him. He stuffed the whole thing in his mouth, shedding flakes as he began to chew. He continued to stare at her, chewing, as she backed away. Linnea turned and began to walk swiftly toward the trees. She glanced back, remembering to note some landmark by which she could find the ferry launch again. Charon was just visible in the shadows. "Mind the She-Wolf!" he called after her with a little cackle.

A poorly maintained trail paralleled the river for a few yards and then turned and led uphill among dark trees. The air was chill and clammy. Linnea wondered how many miles of hiking she was in for. She supposed the Darkling Wood was a very large and very wild place.

Linnea had to slow to step over fallen logs. Her bag was heavy and the strap bit into her shoulder. Cold drops of water fell on her from the branches above, sometimes rolling down the back of her neck. From the shadows beyond the trees she heard moans and groans and sounds not human. She shuddered and picked her way through the mud as quickly as she could.

Eventually Linnea encountered the arch with its famous inscription, just as she remembered it from *The Inferno*, and sighed with relief that she'd gotten this far without encountering any wolves or lions. Linnea passed under the arch and set out to navigate what she supposed was the first circle of Hell. The trees opened into a clearing, at the far side of which was a drop-off. The overhang afforded a prospect of, if memory served, the Valley of the Abyss of Woe.

Linnea tiptoed to the edge. From this vantage point she could see that here, as everywhere, the urban growth boundary had been expanded, and development had swallowed up nearly all of what in Dante's time had probably been a mighty forest. Linnea looked out over a maze of cul-de-sacs and cheaply built three- and four-thousand square-foot homes, Dodge Rams in their driveways, lawns edged and fertilized, covering the whole valley and marching up the slopes. The valley had become a suburb. Coming from the other side of the clearing was the sound of speeding cars. It appeared that what was left of the Darkling Wood was now little more than a windbreak between a housing development and a freeway.

Linnea wasn't sure where to go from here, but she surmised that all those cars must be on their way to somewhere. She stepped through the underbrush in the direction of the auto noise and walked out onto the shoulder of the road. Several cars passed her. She was curious about the drivers, but kept to the weeds along the side, well off the asphalt. In the distance she could see what she took to be the Christian afterlife proper. It resembled an airport.

Linnea stuck out her thumb, but motorist after motorist passed her by, sometimes with a disapproving stare. Normally Linnea didn't mind getting around on foot, but the traffic noise and pollution here were unpleasant and not conducive to pedestrian safety. At last a white Lincoln Continental pulled over and idled. Linnea trotted up to it and pulled open the door. The driver, a man in a suit and tie, had the head of a bull. "Thanks," Linnea said as she slid onto the passenger side of the red vinyl seat.

The bull-headed man said, "Headed to Heaven, huh? I've heard it's 70 degrees there year-round."

"Nice," said Linnea, feeling she shouldn't reveal too much about her errand. "And you?"

"Oh, no, they wouldn't have me," the driver said. "I'm just dropping off a package."

"I see. Where do you live?"

"Tartarus."

"I've heard of that," Linnea said, and then, wishing to be diplomatic, she asked, "Do you like it pretty well?"

"Tartarus? Oh, yes. Everybody has a good time in Tartarus, steeping in human excrement, having the soles of their feet burnt, marching in a circle while being whipped by minor demons."

"Oh!" said Linnea.

"Being immersed in a lake of boiling pitch or frozen slush or steaming blood. Getting chopped into confetti with a steak knife."

"Oh, yes, I see," said Linnea, hoping to put his litany to an end.

"Sometimes it rains fire," said the bull-headed motorist. "Sometimes pigs eat your entrails."

"I'm getting the picture."

"Hard labor, bad smells, unbelievably bad music. *Basso loco.*"

"Crazy bass player?" Linnea asked.

"No. A 'low place.' Where Satan chews your nose."

"How does a person end up *there*?"

"Oh, all the usual ways. Gluttony, sloth, rage. You know."

"Mmm."

"Fraud. That's a big one."

"Fraud?"

"Oh, yes. Especially those who willfully deceive the authorities by lying about their status, hiding, trying to sneak into the wrong afterlife." The bull seemed to lift a furry and knowing eyebrow in Linnea's direction. "They always get caught."

"Do they?"

"Are you familiar with Malebranche and Malacoda?"

"I don't think so."

"Otherwise known as Evil Claws and Evil Tail. They work as a team, going after cases of fraud."

They must be the goon squad Vergil had told her about, Linnea thought.

"You can imagine," the bull-headed man said, turning his vast bovine head toward Linnea so he could look right into her eyes, "you can imagine what they do to a person when they catch him. Or her. And when they're done, they send people to the ninth circle, even people who normally would end up floating around on the first or second circle, or even over in Asphodel." He paused to let Linnea take this in. "It's because of the mandatory minimum sentencing laws."

They had come to the passenger drop-off lane, and Linnea said, "Anywhere here is fine." She thanked the driver and he nodded, the ring in his nose swinging back and forth.

"Take care now," he said, and he pulled away, leaving Linnea staring after him, wondering what he knew about her, and whether he was telling her the truth.

Linnea entered the main terminal. The Christian afterlife was as bustling as any major hub for air traffic. It was packed with people of every nationality, some passing the time with a copy of *USA Today*, others standing in line with their shoes hooked over their fingers.

She walked down the wide passage, passing sports bars and magazine vendors, until she found a monitor showing departure times and gates. Domestic or International? Roman Catholic, Protestant, Greek or Eastern Orthodox? Mainline, Evangelical, or Fundamentalist? Oh, dear, thought Linnea. She continued to scan the screen. Lutheran, Methodist, Presbyterian? Reformed? United? Coptic or Gnostic? Jehovah's Witness, Seventh-Day Adventist, Charismatic, LDS? Independent, Old or Non-Chalcedonian Catholic? Anglican, Quaker, Restorationist, Christadelphian, Baptist or Anabaptist, Alexandrine or Antiochene, Non-Trinitarian, non-denominational, ecumenical? Open or closed communion? Pro- or anti-gay ordination?

Feeling less and less prepared to buy a ticket, Linnea peered down the wide hall. At one end she saw escalators, one going up, one going down.

She approached a ticket counter, hardly knowing what to ask, and said to the clerk, "How do I get a ticket to Heaven?"

The clerk, dressed in blue with a three-cornered hat, gave Linnea an aspartame smile. "Come now, Ms.... " she said.

"Ms. Nil."

"Ms. Nil. You are a product of Western Civilization. I'm sure you know the answer to that question already."

Linnea swallowed. "'That whosoever believeth in me...'?" she ventured.

"That's right," sang the airline representative, her joyless smile growing wider. "No believee, no boardee passee." She raised an index finger and waggled it back and forth.

Linnea had suspected as much. She was sure there was a way to get around the rules, but she didn't know what it would be. "Thank you anyway."

Linnea thought she'd poke around the airport a little for good measure. She didn't relish the walk back along the freeway and through the Darkling Wood to the river.

As she walked away from the counter, a porter approached her from behind and said, "Take your bag, Miss?"

Linnea was startled and for an instant foolishly pleased— she hadn't been addressed as "Miss" in a long time, having fallen to the ranks of "Ma'am" sometime in her 30s. In the time that it took her to compute the man's question, he had lifted her bag—the oversized leather briefcase that held Linnea's last remaining worldly goods—and flung it onto an enormous cart loaded with suitcases.

"But, wait—I don't have a—" Linnea started to say, but the porter had already turned his back on her to help other passengers, and two other burly men were wheeling the cart away. She ran a few steps after them and then slowed to a stop. What was in that bag that she needed, really? Linnea tried to remember. She knew it held a tall stack of Latin 102 quizzes and other assorted homework assignments still waiting to be graded. She had notes in there from a Faculty Office Insulation Inspection Committee meeting, a Passive Voice Mission Statement Committee meeting, a File Alphabetization Committee meeting, and a Photocopy Collation and Stapling Committee meeting. She knew the bag didn't hold her house keys—they'd been lost in the hubbub of her murder—and that her ID was in her pocket. She had carried no personal letters, keepsakes, mementos, tokens of affection, pretty little stones, meaningful jewelry or other accessories, love notes, favorite quill pens, small objects of art or original poetry, photographs, or even an address book in her briefcase.

"Hunh," Linnea said aloud, beginning to wonder why she'd held onto that bag so long and so tightly.

"What happened?" said someone standing next to her. She turned to look. The individual at her side—man or woman, she couldn't really tell which—had the face of an angel.

"He took my baggage," Linnea said, indicating the porter, who was trundling away far down the wide passage with a suitcase in each hand.

"That's his job," said the person who looked as if he, or she, had just stepped out of a painting by Raphael.

"But I'm not going to be able to get it back," Linnea said.

"That's the idea. He's relieved you of your burden."

"He has?" Linnea stared after the porter, who at that moment started helping a man with a backpack, lifting the weight from his shoulders. "Hunh," she repeated. "I didn't even tip him."

"It doesn't matter," said the person of cherub-like beauty. "'His yoke is easy and his burden is light.'"

Linnea squinted down the passage at the slightly overweight, Middle Eastern-looking fellow with male pattern baldness who had taken her briefcase away. Her mouth dropped open and she turned to confirm her suspicions with her companion, but angel-face was gone. So Linnea bought herself a latte and lingered in the hall to study a line of pardoned sinners waiting to pass through security. She noticed that they, like air passengers everywhere, still had to take all the metal out of their pockets, send their carry-on items through the X-Ray, walk through a scanner and sometimes be subjected to a more thorough search. She also noticed that the security personnel were inspecting boarding passes with great care, studying them with magnifying glasses and examining them with special lights. Linnea didn't know how to square the rigidity of these personnel with the apparent generosity, unlooked-for and unthanked, of the baggage porter. But she thought her chances of slipping past security without a valid boarding pass were very skinny, so she stepped out onto the causeway to look for a cab, stopping to marvel, from time to time, how much lighter she felt without her bag.

Chapter Seventeen

BREAKING AND ENTERING

Antoine had his root canal on Tuesday and, according to Jaspar, was feeling very low. "In spite of the fact that he's living on mashed potatoes and ice cream," Jaspar had clucked. "So much for the Atkins. Three months to lose 30 pounds, and he's going to gain it all back in a week."

Before school Wednesday morning, Dori ran over to Bovine Divine and got Antoine a large vanilla milkshake to deliver to her friend, who was propped up on the chaise longue watching Claudette Colbert and Clark Gable in *It Happened One Night.*

"You are a gem," Antoine told Dori. He pushed the stop button on the remote and patted a chair next to him for her.

"I hear you're not feeling so hot," Dori said.

Antoine proceeded to tell Dori with obvious relish all about his dental surgery.

"And I'm just frazzled from playing nursemaid," Jaspar said with theatrical exaggeration. "Thank God you're here, Dori, to provide some respite care."

"Does your mouth hurt?" Dori asked.

"Mm-hmmm." Antoine looked over his paper cup at her with baby harp seal eyes.

"Oh, you'd say anything for a Percocet," Jaspar teased. He triangulated their seating arrangement by pulling a bar stool in from the kitchen, hopping up on it, quick and lithe like a rabbit.

"Come. Distract me from my pain, Dori," Antoine said. "Tell me some happy news. What's going on with you? Any interesting men on the horizon?"

"Well, there might be one," Dori said, hesitating.

Jaspar leaned in, his boyish hair flopping over his forehead. "Really? Do tell."

"Is he hot?" Antoine wanted to know.

Dori smiled. "Warm," she said.

"And? Well? Who is he, what is he like? Is he good enough for you?"

Dori described Pablo briefly, his background, his interests.

"And when do we get to meet him?" Jaspar said, leaning forward and hooking his sock feet under the crossbar of the stool.

"I'm not sure I'm ready to trot him out yet," said Dori. "We just had our first date."

"Just don't let it go on too long without letting us vet him first."

"Promise," Dori said.

They went on in this vein for some time, until Jaspar sobered and asked, "Have you heard the update on Linnea's case?"

Dori shook her head.

"It was on the news this morning." Jaspar and Antoine exchanged a look, as if in doubt about whether to let Dori in on it.

"The killer—well, obviously—sawed through Linnea's ribcage with some kind of power tool. The heart was removed carefully, probably with proper surgical instruments or something very like them."

Dori's eyes widened.

Antoine said, "And they discovered the heart had been injected with potassium chloride."

"But why?"

"To preserve it. The killer must have had plans for the heart. They're saying it couldn't have been his original intention to dump it in the sink and leave it there."

Jaspar said, "I'm sorry you have to hear this, Dori." He pulled his knees up to his chest and wrapped his arms around his calves. "It's too horrible."

Dori looked from one friend to the other. "I'd rather hear it from you two than from the evening news," she said.

They sat in aggrieved silence until Antoine said suddenly, "Oh, no. My milkshake has gone to soup."

Dori had a class to teach and papers to grade and six students to see during her office hours. She had a meeting with Ned Callow to show him how to calculate weighted averages. The Vena Cava Scholarship Committee was still waiting on Dori's recommendations for promising students in the Romance languages, and she hadn't finished reading the applications yet. Dean Budgie had asked to see her again— Dori knew he was going to press her for the Classics department MADCAP. She needed to make another effort to find Linnea's union organizing notes for Ian Elf. And then a siren wailed from inside Dori's jacket pocket.

It was Pablo. He'd gotten her note. "I have the day off and I wonder if you might be able to slip away for a few hours," he said.

"A day off," Dori said, stalling. "That's pleasant."

"Well, they're fumigating my office building," he told her. "We have bugs. So we had to evacuate."

"That's not very convenient," said Dori. "I suppose people continue to die even though the morgue's closed."

"They do." Dori could hear the smile in Pablo's voice. "Anybody who is thoughtless enough to die today will be diverted to a nearby funeral home. So, could I steal you away from work for a little while?"

Dori sighed. "I wish you could," she told him. "I don't dare. I just have so much going on this week."

"I understand," said Pablo. "This is very short notice. Well, how about some evening soon?"

They made plans to see a Fellini film the following night. As soon as Dori had pressed "end," she left school and went straight to Pablo's workplace. She walked once around the building just to be sure she was alone. The fumigators had not yet arrived.

Dori studied the area some more. A second-floor window on the west side was open. Well, she'd have left her window open if they were spraying her office with toxins, too. At the northwest corner of the building grew a cherry tree that Dori ascertained was pretty good for climbing. She pulled off her rain boots and stashed them in some foliage. Grabbing onto a low limb of the tree, she hoisted herself up, finding footholds among the gnarls as she could and smiling at her own bravado. While she was up among the branches, two men came splashing down the sidewalk. Dori held still. There was no leaf cover. Bridges' trees wouldn't leaf out for weeks yet. But if the men noticed her, she was sufficiently small that they might mistake her for a child. Dori could hope, anyway.

They passed without looking up. She waited until they had gone down the hill and were wading across the street;

then she ascended two more limbs to reach the second-story window ledge.

"Not bad, Amore," she said to herself. She began to scoot toward the open window.

Dori wasn't afraid of heights, but a second-story ledge was a second-story ledge. Don't look down, she told herself. When she was beyond the cover provided by the tree, she stopped to scan, and the temptation to drop her eyes overcame her. It was the wrong thing to do. Dori blanched and leaned her head against the sand-colored brick of the building, willing herself stable. "*Merde,*" she muttered. She was halfway to the window—as far from safety in one direction as in the other—so she figured she might as well keep going. She inched, hugging the brick, until she reached it. She stopped and listened to make sure no one was in the room, and then lowered herself, one leg and then the other, inside.

Though Dori knew the building was empty, she moved with stealth and high anxiety. She padded downstairs to the refrigeration unit she'd visited with Pablo the previous morning. The bodies were stashed in drawers in a bank along the wall like great big post office boxes. Her plan was to find Linnea's body, then fetch the heart from its box in the freezer and tuck it back inside her friend. She hoped that would do the job.

Dori started at one end of the bank of drawers and began reading labels. Did the bodies repose in alphabetical order? Or were they shelved by date of death? Realizing she didn't have her reading glasses, Dori squinted at one label, then another. It appeared the occupants of the drawers were identified only by number.

She stalled around for a minute, but no brilliant alternatives presented themselves to her. She eased open the first drawer and held her breath as she peeled the sheet from the form lying there. It was an elderly man, stiff and yellow as wax, mouth wide open. Dori squeezed her eyes shut and dropped the sheet.

In checking the next body she was careful just to peek under the sheet's bottom corner. When she saw that the bloodless foot was a man's, she covered it again and moved on. Dori tried very hard not to think about what it would be like when she finally found Linnea, and how she might react to the sight of the violence done to her. It was bad enough laying eyes on dead strangers.

She had to stand on a chair to open the top drawers, but Dori went up and down the rows and checked every body. It took nearly forty minutes to inspect them all. Some were aged, some were young; some were ravaged by disease; some were bruised and bloodied; some were in the throes of an overdose. All were cold as porcelain and pale as fish and hard as mannequins—and not one of them was Linnea Nil.

Chapter Eighteen

CATO

Linnea was not troubled by she-wolves on her way back toward the Valley of the Abyss of Woe. She saw no Lions of Ambition, nor any Leopards of Malice. Those wild beasts, she reflected, must represent vices that weren't her particular hang-ups. Lust? Nope, it had been a long time since she'd had an opportunity to give in to lust. Gluttony? Linnea looked down and cast a disapproving eye on the tummy bulge that distended the waistband of her pants and on the zipper handle that would not lie flat, but stuck out like a stubborn little tongue. The extra pounds that had come with lunching at Greasy Horrors did not, however, precipitate the appearance of wild animals. What are my vices? Linnea wondered. Her principal vice, she decided, was giving herself over to joylessness: a pessimism, a dullness of spirit. She seemed to remember that some of the sufferers in Dante's Hell were said to be guilty of Sullenness, but how that ranked among the various sins, and whether a wild beast was associated allegorically with it, Linnea didn't know. Her thoughts wandered off into trying, not altogether successfully, to name the seven deadly sins, and to discerning what sort of beast would be a good representative of sullenness. Badgers were said to be ill-tempered. And zebras. Zebras were undomesticatable; they bit. Linnea felt that she was not a biter, but more of a moper. Which animals moped? Basset hounds? She doubted that any basset hounds had made their way into medieval verse.

Linnea was sufficiently tangled in these thoughts that she did not notice the way growing darker. Now she realized that she could not see the path before her, and that her shoes were picking up clods of wet soil. The way was no longer paved and smooth.

"Crap," she said aloud. She'd missed the turn to the valley, with its housing development and trails that led back to the Acheron. Instead she'd ended up deeper in the Darkling Wood. She couldn't see well in the dim light and didn't recognize any rock or turn in the path.

Linnea turned to go back the way she'd come. In the gloaming ahead of her were two yellow eyes. There it was: some Wild Beast of Sullenness, come to punish her for her ungrateful ways in life. Now she would be ravaged, and she would spend eternity nursing pus-oozing, burning wounds. The thing with the yellow eyes growled. Linnea held very still. What would be a proper defense against it? If she could summon some anti-sullenness, some opposite of pouting, some counter-listless feeling, she might be able to fend off its attack. Linnea racked her brains, trying to conjure the things that energized and inspired her. She could only come up with an image of the gelato scale model of the Coliseum from last year's Classical Studies conference. She did flash on the real thing—her trip of ten years before to Rome and the days she'd spent wandering around its ruins—but the image only filled her with vague longing and a sense of defeat. The Beast leaped and in an instant was upon her, knocking her over backward onto the earth and standing on her with its full weight on its paws, pinning her and growling. Linnea could hardly breathe. She could not see the Beast—its body blocked out what little light was left in the Darkling Wood—but she felt its hot foul breath on her face. Perhaps this was not even a creature of allegory, but one of the dreaded members of the goon squad, coming to take her to the part of Hell that the taurine motorist had described to her in such dreadful detail. Linnea braced herself to be ripped limb from limb.

"Ranger!" called a man's voice a short distance away. "Come on, boy."

The big animal turned its head. Far above her in the dimness, Linnea could make out the tops of trees.

"Bad boy! Come!" The man's voice took on a tone of command, and the beast leaped from Linnea—she let out a cry as it pushed off with its massive feet—and trotted back to its owner. She sat up on her elbows. A short distance away, a man was bent over a great black shape. He was affixing a leash to its collar.

"Are you all right?" he called to Linnea. A minute later he was at her side, offering his hand to pull her to her feet. A graybeard in a white turtleneck sweater, he said, "I'm sorry about Ranger. This is an off-leash area. I didn't expect to run into anybody."

"I think I'm lost," Linnea told him, brushing the dirt off her fleece. "I need to get to the overlook near the valley."

"Oh, that's not far," the man told her. "I can take you." He gave a little tug on the leash, and his pet fell into an easy trot at his side. "I'm Cato, by the way." He extended a hand, and Linnea shook it.

"Cato the Younger?"

"Yup."

"No shit," Linnea said softly.

"Where're you headed?"

As they walked back the way Linnea had come, she explained briefly what her errand was.

"So, you're still in your grace period then," Cato surmised. "Newly dead."

"Dead and heartless," Linnea told him.

"We have something in common then," said Cato, amiably lifting one corner of his turtleneck to reveal a terrible gash in his belly. Cato's abs were not a pretty sight. Linnea knew what had happened to him; he had sliced himself open with a knife and pulled out his own intestines as a gesture of political protest against Julius Caesar. Linnea had always thought of Cato as a bit of a drama queen, but now that she'd met him, she thought better of him.

"Well, I'm flattered," she said, "but my wound isn't self-inflicted. I was attacked."

"I'm just the man you want to see, then," Cato told her with some enthusiasm. "I'm in charge of assigning an afterlife to those who died a violent death."

"Really?" Linnea said, perking up.

Cato described life in the Inferno. "I'd want to get you into one of the outer circles, of course. They don't smell too great, and there can be a problem of stinging insects, but that's about the worst of it."

To Linnea it didn't sound like much of an offer.

"We're working really hard to make improvements." Cato waxed expansive then, describing Hell's hard-won cost-of-living increases, grievance procedures and paid overtime. Linnea recognized a kindred spirit, and told Cato about her efforts to unionize the Middlebridge faculty.

"You could join our efforts if you like," Cato said. "We

could use someone with your skills."

Linnea hesitated. She wasn't ready to give up on Dori and Redemption yet. "Do you mind if I pass?"

Cato looked disappointed.

"So, I have to ask," Linnea said. "You were born during the era of the Roman Republic. What are you doing in the Darkling Wood? Isn't this a Christian afterlife?"

"That's an interesting question." The side-path they'd been on met up with the main path then, and Linnea thought she recognized it. "I started out down in the Asphodel Meadows. You know them?"

"I do, as a matter of fact. I might end up living there."

"Don't go if you suffer seasonal allergies. The blooming asphodel is a killer."

"Oh. Good to know."

"You know, Asphodel was where I expected to land originally. Then I was given what they called a promotion. They told me that Hades corresponded to the Catholic Inferno, but that because I had led a righteous life, though a 'pagan' one, I was allowed to come to Purgatory and spend eternity here guarding the gates. But you know? I wasn't any more righteous in life than thousands of others who are moldering away down in Hades or in the Christian equivalent."

"Well, I don't know about that," Linnea said, gesturing at Cato's belly. "You sell yourself short, Cato."

"Whatever the case may be," Cato said modestly, "I realized that they wanted to keep us apart. There's strength in numbers. If we band together, they won't be able to oppress us. Thousands of my compatriots are stuck in Hell for the crime of being born too early. And there are others here in Purgatory who are doing time for crimes they didn't commit. So we formed a union. I'm president of Local 4409."

The wood opened out into a parking lot. "Hang on, I need to chain Ranger here," Cato said. He busied himself at the edge of the wood securing the creature to a tree.

"What kind of bargaining power do you have?" Linnea asked.

"Well, there are an awful lot of us," Cato said. "We could pretty much overrun Heaven if we chose to. The thing is, we don't want a bastion of privilege for ourselves. What we want is decent living conditions right here. We want an equitable distribution of light, beauty, happiness—all those things they've monopolized in Heaven."

"I see," said Linnea with approval. "And what about the non-righteous?"

"We take the position that punishment is a crude and antiquated way of addressing wrongdoing. We advocate counseling, rehab, and community service."

"That's an impressive agenda," Linnea said. She recognized ahead the suburban landscape she had seen earlier in the day.

"Step by step," Cato said. "Our contract is up for renegotiation next month, so we'll see how it goes."

Linnea knew how to get back to the Acheron from here. She shook Cato's hand and thanked him for his assistance. "Cato? Can you explain something to me?" she asked. A question had been nagging at her throughout their conversation. "It seems as though the Christian God and the Roman Gods are in cahoots. All that shuffling people around between afterlives—it seems like a divide-and-conquer tactic."

Cato put one finger on the tip of his nose and pointed the other at Linnea. "You're absolutely right!" he cried. "Publicly they disparage each other, but behind closed doors, they're always cutting deals to keep themselves in power." Cato gave

Linnea an admiring look. "We really could use you," he added wistfully. Linnea, though, was not eager to try to wrest power from gods and goddesses. She had seen enough of that sort of behavior from the Middlebridge College administrators.

Chapter Nineteen

TO AND FRO

So Linnea was still waiting for her heart.

Or was she? Dori found herself in doubt about her own mental state. In the stark light of overhead fluorescents and with Linnea's death starting to retreat behind her on the calendar, Dori once again began to question her dead friend's appearance. A more reasonable explanation was that she had imagined Linnea's visit to her kitchen. Could post-traumatic stress disorder give a person hallucinations? What about hormone imbalance—could it make you see things? Maybe Linnea's ghost was only a figment of her estrogen.

Jaspar might know. Librarians knew everything, didn't they? When she faced him on the fencing strip that afternoon, she thought about how she might bring it up. She could come right out with it and tell him what she'd experienced in her kitchen the previous weekend. Or just bring up the appearance of a ghost as a theoretical proposition.

Dori's worry distorted her practice. Thrust, parry, thrust, parry. *Tic tac tic tac.*

"You're struggling," Jaspar said, removing his helmet and tucking it under his arm. "Having trouble concentrating?"

Dori nodded.

"It's not surprising," Jaspar said.

It's not, Dori thought, but you don't know the half of it.

Jaspar patted Dori's back. "Have you thought about getting some grief counseling?" he asked. "I hear Tim Fimbria is pretty good."

Jaspar reminded Dori that the psychiatrist was working extra hours for Middlebridgers who wanted to talk about Linnea. Fimbria was an expert; Dori reasoned he'd be able to tell her if hallucinations might come with the territory of shock and grief, or of perimenopausal madness. A diagnosis could put her mind at ease. It would be a relief to know she was merely a little crazy.

Later, Ned Callow paid Dori a visit. He appeared at her open office door, hands clasped in supplication.

"Come on in," she told him, wondering what he would be asking her to do that he should be able to do for himself. Callow, a tall, stooping bean pod of a man, took a step inside but did not unclasp his hands. His shoulders were up around his earlobes. Dori said, "I'm glad you stopped by, Ned. I've been meaning to call you."

Something like hope lit Callow's long face, but was extinguished as soon as Dori continued, "Several of your students have been attending class without being registered. You've got to get those late-registration slips signed and turned in."

"I don't know, uh, where to go to do that," Callow said.

Dori pointed out her window at the registration building. Hank, the clerk with the sleek ponytail, was standing at his own window over in Data Intake, looking out. "Talk to him,"

Dori told Callow.

Hank saw Dori pointing at him and gave a dimpled smile and a wave.

"Now, what can I help you with?"

Ned Callow fetched his briefcase from the hall, lifted it onto Linnea's old desk and set to fiddling with it. He seemed too tall for the room. Dori wondered if he had ever played basketball, but the thought of him in athletic shorts was absurd. She imagined he had spent his whole adult life indoors. He seemed to have spent the last twenty years just traipsing from one classroom to another, briefcase in hand, with no particular purpose. Callow bent over a sheaf of papers. He tapped them together and laid them attentively in the bottom of his briefcase, moving like someone who wanted to put something off, and he closed and locked it again.

"The reason I came?" He turned to Dori and cupped one palm over the other. "I wondered? Now that Linnea Nil is out of the picture?"

Out of the picture? Dori sat up straight.

"If this post might be made a permanent one."

"What?" Dori said.

"If I could, if I could, have her job. Her position. Since it's available," he added meekly.

Dori was having a hard time processing Callow's words. "You want to know," she ventured, "if, since Dr. Nil has been so conveniently murdered, you could slip into her place, circumventing the usual processes for applying for a faculty position, and overlooking the fact that you haven't got the qualifications? Is that what you want to know?"

"Oh." Callow had his answer. He flipped his cupped hands so that the hand that had been on bottom was now on top. "I felt it would behoove me to ask. Perseverance is a virtue, isn't it?" He gave Dori a wan little smile and reached behind him for his briefcase. For an instant, Dori imagined him swinging it around and bashing her in the head with it. But he only took it in both hands and said, "I'll be seeing you."

Dori closed the door behind him and sat down hard, thinking. Ned Callow had often been a nuisance to the language departments, but she had not really considered him a threat. He wouldn't have killed Linnea to create a job opening for himself, would he? The whole idea of his ever taking her place was ridiculous. Did he himself realize that? No, she decided. But could he have committed murder? No. He was simply too incompetent. Unethical, perhaps, and short on social skills, but probably not murderous.

Could he be involved in the murder indirectly? The irresponsible and perpetually broke Callow had few loyalties except to himself—certainly none to the college and to the well-being of the people here. Was it possible, for example, that he could have taken a bribe to spy and report on Linnea's organizing activities? Dori began to imagine a network of Middlebridge's worst sorts conspiring to prevent collective bargaining at any cost. Callow was probably too dim to understand that unionization would be in his own best interests. Dori's thoughts whirred. These thoughts had gone around and around in her mind so many times that she couldn't tell any more if she was being insightful or paranoid.

Who else could she talk to about this? Jaspar and Antoine? Kristin? Pablo? Tim Fimbria? More than anyone else, the person who used to help Dori think clearly on issues like these was Linnea. Ned Callow's outrageous inappropriateness was the kind of behavior Dori and Linnea used to laugh about together. *Les tonneaux vides*, Dori would have said to Linnea, *font le plus de bruit.* It's the empty barrels that make the most noise.

It was time to heed Dean Budgie's summons. Dori was certain he was going to press her about administrative matters, but he didn't mention any. Instead, he told her that Linnea's next of kin, a brother who lived on the east coast, had declined to collect Linnea's belongings. Budgie knew because he himself had called the brother to offer his condolences on Linnea's death. "Legally, Linnea's things belong to the state now, and they'll be auctioned," the dean told Dori. "But I assume you knew her well, and if there were anything of sentimental value to you…" Dean Budgie spread his hands, palms up.

Dori had never had anything but the most businesslike exchanges with the dean. She was startled now by his gesture of human kindness. The more she thought about it, the less she liked the idea that state bureaucrats would be going through the material remains of Linnea's life and hocking them to strangers. She bristled at the distant brother who couldn't even be bothered to fly out and take care of the task himself.

She thanked Dean Budgie, and he bowed his head slightly before ushering her out the door.

Dori had just left Budgie's office when her cell phone howled from her pocket. It was Kristin. She and her husband and daughter would be driving down from Seattle Saturday to see Dori in the fencing tournament. Would Dori be willing to keep eleven-year-old Elsa for the remainder of the weekend?

"You bet!" said Dori. She and Elsa were great buddies. She started to brainstorm things she and Elsa might do together, but Kristin was in a hurry and said simply, "I trust your judgment," before ringing off. If the weather were at all decent, Dori thought, she and Elsa could go bike riding. Maybe there'd be a suitable movie, too, or Elsa might like to go to FEAR and fool around with fencing foils or shoot some hoops. Elsa was about the only person Dori could play basketball with, since she herself only stood as high as a pre-teen. Dori smiled. It would be the first time in days she could simply enjoy herself.

A pale Pacific Northwest sun had been shining, however feebly, and the waters in Bridges were low enough for driving now, if not dried up altogether. Dori was relieved. She usually welcomed the workout provided by paddling, but she had a lot of to-ing and fro-ing to do and was glad to be able to carry it out in motorized fashion. When she finished grading papers, Dori got some cardboard boxes and drove to Linnea's house, where she spent the rest of the afternoon going through everything that looked as though Linnea had ever cared about it. Dori took a few mementos for herself and other colleagues at Middlebridge. She packed the rest away with care, taking down the artwork, folding the scarves, arraying the necklaces and earrings, wrapping the pretty little flower vases in paper, organizing the book and CD collections. She emptied drawers and medicine cabinets of all the private junk you wouldn't want a stranger pawing through. She emptied the refrigerator, too, and cleaned the kitchen. It wasn't her job—someone else would do it, and probably be paid to do it—but she felt called to it. In traditional cultures, she reflected, friends and family sometimes washed and prepared a body for burial, and that was part of how they came to terms with a death. In Linnea's case, such rites were not possible, but Dori felt that by thoughtfully, lovingly packing Linnea's things, she could achieve something of the same closure for herself, and honor her friend in the process.

Toward the end of the day she returned to campus for a session with the school psychiatrist. Dr. Tim Fimbria had a deep, soothing voice and that most excellent therapeutic tool, a sense of humor. Dori hadn't been in Merck Hall since it had been made over, but she thought she recognized Fimbria's office as a former women's restroom. "Didn't this used to be a ladies' lounge?" she asked him, looking around. "I remember it being pink and flowery—excessively sweet."

"Yeah, I remember when they were remodeling." Fimbria chuckled. "You could get diabetes just walking in here."

The doctor eased Dori into a discussion of her feelings, nodding, tipping his head from time to time to elicit more details as she spoke of her grief.

"Your reactions are all normal," Fimbria told her. "Linnea's murder came as a shock to the whole community, but you were especially close to her. It's very difficult."

Dori blew her nose.

"And," the doctor pointed out, "you're under a terrific amount of stress beyond the stress of grief, shouldering Linnea's workload like you have."

"Oh. Yes. Right," Dori said. She'd simply been doing what needed to be done. It hadn't occurred to her that the extra work might complicate the grieving process.

"Are you letting yourself have time off?" Fimbria asked.

"It doesn't seem to really help to have time off," she told him. "I'm almost better off working too hard. At least then I'm not obsessing about Linnea." She looked around at the houseplants and handsome oil paintings in Fimbria's office, looking but not really seeing. "I keep finding myself trying to think like a private eye. Combing through every detail of the case. Looking at it from every angle. I just can't stop thinking about it. Who could have done this to her?" Dori laid out several theories—a student, an instructor, an administrator. "Do you think it's possible?" she asked.

Tim Fimbria said, "Anything is possible. But I'm concerned about you taking this on. You already have a job to do at Middlebridge—two jobs, in a sense; yours and Linnea's. You're not really in a position to crack a murder case."

Dori shook her head. "And I'm not qualified in any way. But I just can't seem to get the wheels to stop turning." She spilled out other thoughts, about the deans, about the union. "I know none of this is particularly rational," she concluded. "Maybe it helps to just get it out of my system."

"If it helps, I'm all for it. Now, are you having trouble sleeping?"

"Yes."

"And concentrating?"

"Uh-huh."

"Yes," said Dr. Fimbria. "That's not surprising."

"It's not just that," Dori said. "There's something else." She took a deep breath and then plunged into an account of Linnea's post-mortem visit to her condo. She described the vividness of Linnea's appearance, though she omitted the part of the story that involved creeping around the morgue trying to get her hands on the heart. It unnerved Dori to realize how seriously she'd taken the illusion, if that's what it was, and she wasn't quite ready to come clean, even to a shrink. When she finished, she looked up from the plush carpet of Fimbria's floor and into his attentive face.

"Do you think the hallucination can be explained away by stress?" Dori asked, feeling wretched.

Obviously Fimbria wasn't going to tell her Linnea was real, but he might say that hallucinations were far beyond normal—grounds, perhaps, for serious psychiatric treatment.

Tim Fimbria was listening with a thoughtful but not a worried look on his face. "I think it was a dream," he said. "Survivors frequently have quite vivid dreams of loved ones who have died, dreams that seem convincing, even if their content isn't rational."

"But I wasn't lying down. I mean, I didn't wake up from it. I was in my kitchen."

"You may have dozed off without realizing it. Or your memories of the past days might have gotten distorted and confused," Fimbria continued. "That happens. I wouldn't worry about it."

He stood and went to his desk. "I'm going to write you a prescription for sleeping pills," he said. "I don't imagine you'll need to take them for more than a few weeks. They'll reduce the intensity of your dream life and allow you to get some rest so you can get through the semester. And of course," he added, "if they keep happening, or even if they don't, you're welcome to come back and see me any time."

Dori blew out a long breath of relief. The Boston ferns and spider plants in Fimbria's office seemed more real. They were grounding—green, living things that seemed to offer the possibility of health and serenity. "Okay," she said at last. "I feel better. Thank you so much."

"Don't mention it. Come back and see me any time. Any time at all."

Dori blew her nose again and wiped her eyes.

Fimbria handed her a tissue. "And be sure to replenish those fluids."

Chapter Twenty

I SPY

Linnea felt badly for Vergil and the problem of his unfinished poem, so when she went to fill him in on the results of her research, she took him a little something that she thought might make him feel better.

When he lifted the lid off the box, Vergil's mouth formed a perfect *o*. "You shouldn't have!" he gasped, clearly very glad she had. "Oh, my dear."

Vergil lifted one of the green velvet ankle boots from the shoebox and stroked it. His eyes were shining. "It's been so very long," he told her in a near whisper. "I haven't let myself buy any shoes in such a long time. And look at these. Just look at them!" He held it up. "They are magnificent! Oh!" He clasped the boot to his bosom. "My dearest dear. Is this what you've been up to? When you should be out trying to get into Paradise? Now, where shall I display them?" Vergil stood and placed the shoes atop a thick volume of poetry on his bookcase. "What do you think?" He beamed.

Linnea had to admit they looked rather splendid there.

Vergil hobbled to the kitchenette. "Do you remember when I told you," he said, "that my rule is I have to give up one pair of shoes to make room for another?"

"I think so."

"Would these fit you?" Vergil lifted a pair of shoes from his cabinet and held them out for her to see. They were red pumps with wickedly sharp heels and a curlicue of red sequins wrapping round them.

Linnea would never wear such things. She couldn't even walk in heels, and she had no clothes whatsoever that would go with red sequins. But Linnea didn't want to hurt Vergil's feelings or burden him with stuff he had no space for.

"Yes," she told him. "That's lovely, Vergil. Thank you." She put them in the empty shoebox and stashed them by the door before he could ask her to model them.

Linnea didn't want to dog-ear her welcome at Vergil's, so after filling him in on her adventures across the water she took her leave and walked to the Middlebridge campus. She thought she might practice wefting there, since Vergil had advised her to start developing wefting skills by willing herself in and out of familiar locations. The campus lawn was thick with crows. Linnea disliked them—horrible, defiant birds. A glossy crow, big as a house cat, had been in the habit of visiting her office every afternoon, staring at her and at Dori in silence. Dori would sometimes remove her Stylin' Jacket and wave it with vigor at the window glass. The crow would fix its shiny black eye on her, as though to show her it was not afraid, and flap away only at its leisure.

Linnea approached Verizon Wireless Hall, her old home, and Pepsi Hall next door. She could glimpse the registration building behind, and the old ivy-encased library and the school cafeteria, Greasy Horrors. She stood off to one side of the quad, out of the way of students crossing the wet grass, and closed her eyes, trying to envision the second floor of Verizon Wireless. A crow uttered a hoarse caw and Linnea felt a blow to her head. Her eyes flew open. She had wefted up into a copper beech and bonked her head on an overhanging limb.

Linnea placed her palm on the hurt spot, wincing. The thought that her fate might soon depend on her skill at wefting made her anxious. She scanned the campus, which looked different from her vantage point high in the tree. She started counting crows in the grass until the number was so large that it horrified her and she made herself stop. Her eyes traveled to the Student Data-Intake and Entrance-Status Processing Building. A long box hedge, seven feet high, ran the length of the building. Part of the hedge was rustling in an unnatural way. Linnea squinted. From the ground, no one would be able to spot a human being back there, but from here Linnea could see down into the space between the dense curtain of shrubbery and the brick. There was a man's head, ducking and then popping back up again. A minute later, a figure appeared at the end of the hedgerow and slipped into the registration building. What could he have been up to? Did he slip back there to take a leak? Did he want to smoke without having to make the trek to the nearest smoking shelter? Linnea thought he looked familiar—handsome and young, with a sleek ponytail—but she couldn't place him.

A few minutes later Linnea spotted Dori. The smartly dressed department chair left Verizon Wireless Hall and strode toward the west end of campus. I should just go talk to her, Linnea thought, and see if she's tried to get the heart. She knew Dori had not enjoyed her last visitation. How could she encourage Dori, and impress upon her the urgency of her task, without frightening her? She hoped she'd given Dori enough information to go on. Linnea hadn't had the know-how, or the stamina, to hang around explaining herself. Had she told Dori she was on a deadline? She couldn't remember. Dori had pressed her for details about her murder, and Linnea of course didn't know anything. She hoped her office mate wasn't getting distracted by trying to solve the crime. That wouldn't help.

Linnea got out of the copper beech with some difficulty and trotted after her friend, dodging the occasional student. Dori was headed for Merck Hall, which housed the School of Pharmacy and where the school counselors worked. Though small, Dori was swift, and Linnea was having trouble catching up. In through the double doors she went. Linnea scrambled after her. Dori moved down a hall and into a suite, and Linnea just had time to slip in behind her before the door swung closed.

"I have an appointment with Dr. Fimbria," Dori was telling a receptionist.

Crap, thought Linnea. There would be no revealing herself to Dori here. She'd have to wait until Dori was finished with her appointment. Linnea took a seat in the waiting room and tried to remember who Fimbria was. Ah, yes—the school psychiatrist. Dori had never mentioned him to Linnea before, though they always shared that sort of personal information. Linnea was sure Dori hadn't been seeing a therapist before. A cold custard of unease settled in her stomach. Had she impressed upon Dori that the business with her heart was a secret?

I should listen in just a little, Linnea thought, and at the same moment she was appalled at herself. She sat gripping the arms of the waiting-room chair, trying to decide what to do. Look, Nil, she finally said to herself. Dori wouldn't put her right to privacy over your right to a decent eternity. Anyway, if you were still alive, Dori would probably go right back to the office after this and tell you everything that happened here.

Linnea tiptoed across the carpet to Fimbria's door and pressed her ear against it. Of course she could hear nothing.

She couldn't bring herself to try to weft right into Fimbria's office. A little overhearing she could justify, but she hated the idea of blatantly spying from the back of the room, assuming she could even get herself in there. After another moment of dithering, she closed her eyes and managed to weft just her head through Fimbria's office door. There was Dori, wiping the corners of her eyes, and Fimbria leaning toward her in his chair with a sympathetic face.

"Do you think the hallucination can be explained away by stress?" Dori was saying.

Just as I suspected, Linnea thought. She listened, increasingly disconcerted, until her neck and shoulders grew uncomfortable from standing half-in and half-out the door. With effort she pulled her head back through the steel. She would have to catch up with Dori later and have a word with her.

Chapter Twenty-One

HEARTSTRINGS

Dori tossed her purse into the back seat, started up the Prius and began to cruise down E. Gorey Street. Her fifty minutes with Tim Fimbria had put her mind at ease. She thought she'd stop by the pharmacy to pick up her prescription for sleeping pills, then go home, have a nice hot bath, and mellow out for a while. Without the task of procuring Linnea's heart, the remainder of spring semester was starting to look more manageable.

Dori was idling at an intersection and looking at the traffic to her left when Linnea said to her, "We need to talk."

Dori jumped in her seat.

"Sorry. Didn't mean to startle you."

"What the hell is going on?" Dori barked.

Linnea was sitting in the passenger seat, buckling her seat belt. "I'm getting anxious about my heart." In a tone of utmost reasonableness she added, "Once I'm reassembled, I can go about my business."

"For God's sake," Dori said.

"Your light's green."

Dori pulled ahead.

"Why do you come and go like this?" Dori said. "It freaks me out."

"Sorry. I don't have the hang of it yet," Linnea said. "But I need you to know I'm not a hallucination, Dori. I'm not your imagination or a manifestation of grief. I'm real, and I'm asking you for a sincere and urgently important favor."

Dori glanced in the rear view mirror and could see a miserable look on her own face. "But *why*?"

"I'd rather not say."

Dori was silent. She was waiting for her own heart to stop kettle-drumming.

"But I'm running out of time," Linnea continued. "I really need you to try your hardest to get the heart. Right away. This week."

Dori really, really hoped she was dreaming. "What will happen if I can't—if I can't pull it off?"

"I don't want to alarm you."

"It's too late for that," said Dori almost bitterly.

"Well. They want to send me to a Roman afterlife."

"'They' who?"

"The bureaucrats from the beyond. Upper Management. They're telling me the ancient Romans are the only ones who will let me in."

"And so the heart... would protect you from that somehow?"

"I'm not at liberty to reveal more," Linnea said. A difficult silence settled between them. "Anyway, I wanted you to have these," Linnea continued with forced brightness. She had a pair of red shoes hooked over her fingers, and she extended them toward Dori.

Dori glanced over at the shoes. "Why?"

Linnea said, "Truthfully, I'm re-gifting them. A friend gave them to me. But I want you to have them. They're such fun shoes—they're really you."

Dori glanced again. The shoes were bright red and sequined, with pointy toes and sharp, pointy little heels.

"Do you think they'll fit? What size do you wear?"

Dori stared at her dead friend, dazed. "Um, five," she said, thinking with some relief, well, this is clearly a dream. "They *are* fun," she admitted. She slowed and turned a corner onto E. Gorey. "Linnea, can you please explain a few things to me?" She felt that Linnea was being deliberately obtuse.

"Look," Linnea said. "Do you trust me?"

Dori didn't trust her perception of Linnea's ghost. And she didn't trust her friend's strange request. But she thought about their seven years of friendship—the times they'd cried on one another's shoulders, the advice they'd exchanged, the encouragement they'd given each other in their endeavors, their inside jokes, the way they'd covered for each other before the deans. She said, "You've never given me a reason not to."

"Thank you," said Linnea. She lifted one hand, waving her fingers in the merry way she always used to when she was finally quitting work for the day. Then she wavered out of view, leaving the Fun Shoes on the passenger seat.

Chapter Twenty-Two

THE DHARMA HALL

After wefting out of Dori's Prius, Linnea made a bumpy landing on a park bench. She hoped that this second visit hadn't made matters worse. She needed to motivate Dori, but it was possible she was immobilizing her with fear instead. When Dori had pressed her for details, Linnea hadn't known what to do. Intuition told her she didn't dare be explicit about the nature of redemption. That seemed like cheating, and it might void the redemptive task.

Linnea sat watching the afternoon drip and run down the rain gutter and studying the map of the underworld in her mind. It stood to reason that if two unrelated afterlives could be reached from the same portal near the credit union, others might be down there as well. But where? Linnea did not want to face another crossing with Charon if she could help it. It seemed to her there was another cranny she had yet to poke around in. She tried to picture the entrance to the underworld and the grimy hall outside the ferry dock's waiting room. She remembered that the passageway went around a bend beyond a vending machine.

Linnea hurried out of the city park and back downtown to the parking strip near the credit union. She descended and walked past the waiting room and the vending machine.

In a room at the end of the hall was a single long table with fold-out legs, and seated there was a young man wearing a hoodie, jeans and Converse high-tops, perusing a catalog. Beside him, with a laptop, sat a donkey.

"Hello," the donkey said in a pleasant voice. "Come on in."

Linnea ventured into the room and pulled up a chair.

The donkey smiled, revealing two rows of very large, yellowed teeth. "Do you have your paperwork?" she asked Linnea.

Linnea shook her head.

"That's all right," the donkey said. "We can probably proceed without it. Do you remember what you've taken?"

"Taken?"

"What lives you've taken."

Linnea gasped. "I've never taken anyone's life!" she exclaimed.

The donkey gave a gentle whinny of a laugh. "What lives you've *lived*."

"Oh," Linnea said. The young man cast her a look of faint derision, and she squirmed. "Just this one. This one that I've just finished."

"Oh! You *are* a beginner," the donkey told her. "Well, now. This should be straightforward, since you don't have many options." The donkey pushed a catalog across the table with one hoof and said, "Turn to page four. You can choose from 'List A' or 'List C.' You'll find detailed descriptions of each entry in the catalog."

Linnea read through the list. "I don't understand this," she said.

"Those are your choices. You can go back as one of those."

"Go back? To being alive, you mean?"

The long hairs of the donkey's eyebrows drew close enough together to touch. "Did you not attend an orientation before your first life?"

Linnea was accustomed to being in the donkey's position, the one who advised, at Middlebridge. She was finding it very uncomfortable to be in the seat

of a confused and naïve newcomer. "I don't know," she said. "If I did, the details aren't clear in my mind."

The donkey paused, thinking. She raised and lowered her long ears. "Well, normally, I'd send you packing," she told Linnea. "But we're not very busy today. So I'll try to give you some guidance." She turned to the young man. "How are you faring, Zach?"

Zach's curly locks fell down over his eyes. He pushed them out of the way with one hand. "I'm just trying to make up my mind," he said.

"All right, then." To Linnea she said, "Technically, since you've only lived one life, you're supposed to be limited to these choices for your next." She tapped 'List A.' It read, "Sociopath, Murderer, Rapist, Warmonger."

"But," the adviser continued, "since you killed no one in your first life, you may proceed to one of these." 'List C' read: "Lout, Thief, Chronic Liar, Narcissist, Rake." The donkey told Linnea, "If you bring in your paperwork, you can sign right up for whichever one you choose. If you can't lay your hands on your papers, then you'll have to take a placement test first."

"These are my only choices?" Linnea said.

"That's how it works, dear. You're only just getting

started."

Zach turned to Linnea. "I don't meet very many of the pre-reqs myself," he told her.

"Which lives are you considering?" Linnea asked.

The young man flipped open to a page in the thick catalog and showed it to Linnea. "It's pretty much down to these six."

Linnea glanced at the list. It consisted of options like "Fun-Loving Dropout," "Clever Packrat," "Uptight Do-Gooder" and "Artistic Insomniac."

Linnea flipped through the whole section of "human" entries, which ended with "Organic Farmers, Mothers, Yoga Teachers, Saints." Successive sections of the volume were devoted to mammals, reptiles and amphibians, invertebrates, plants of all kinds and single-celled organisms, in that order.

"Why do the animals come after the people?" she asked.

"Well, obviously," Zach said, shaking a lock of hair out of his eyes, "the more complex a life form you are, the farther you can wander from the truth."

"Really?" said Linnea. "I was under the impression it was the other way around."

The donkey said, "Your expanded capacity for mental activity distracts you and gives you all kinds of things to do with your reality besides be awake to it."

"If you're a planarian, you pretty much can't avoid being at one with your true nature," Zach added. "You don't have a choice. Once you get to planarian, enlightenment is pretty much a slam dunk."

"I see," said Linnea. "Where are donkeys in the lineup?" Then she flushed, thinking she'd asked too personal a question.

The donkey gave Linnea an indulgent smile. "Domesticated animals are essentially extensions of humans," she told Linnea. "I'm only a slightly higher life form than the two of you." She turned back to Zach. "Well, which one are you leaning toward?"

He shrugged. "I think maybe the woman with the no-nonsense personality. It'd be refreshing to be someone who doesn't take any crap."

Linnea leaned over and read the catalog description. It was kind of chummy, this process of picking out next lives together. "It says that she doesn't know how to cry," Linnea said. "That she carries her sorrows in her body and might develop a lung disorder if she doesn't learn to work it out."

Linnea looked from Zach to the donkey.

"That's the human condition," said the donkey.

"It sounds hard," Linnea said.

"You have to be willing to get your heart broken over and over again," said Zach. "Because if you're not willing, well, you have to become an inorganic compound. Or a stone, or a sandy beach, something like that. But then there's not much opportunity for promotion."

Linnea said, "What if you don't have a heart to get broken?"

"Oh," the donkey said with sympathy, patting Linnea's hand with her hoof. "Well, they'll issue you a new one."

Zach set about filling out his registration form. Linnea wanted to sign up for something, too, but she didn't know which incarnation to pick. She wished she could consult with Vergil.

"All right," said Linnea. "I guess I need to take that placement test."

"Tuesdays and Fridays at 1 p.m.," the donkey told her. "Be here 15 minutes early to check in, and bring your mantra. You'll have to have it notarized."

Linnea gulped. "I don't have a mantra," she said.

The donkey lowered one long ear slowly toward Linnea, then the other. She said, "Are you not... any kind of Buddhist?"

Linnea shook her head regretfully.

"Well," the donkey said, raising her ears again. "I think the only thing you'd be allowed to do is start at the very beginning."

Together they flipped open to the first page of the catalog. On it were lists of people whose descriptions were so remorseless and hateful Linnea could not even finish reading them. "Oh," she said. "No, I don't want to do that."

"I couldn't in good conscience recommend it."

Zach said, "You should have become a Buddhist in your last life. Then you could start incarnating from where you are now."

Linnea's shoulders slumped. "Is there anything you can do for me?"

The donkey flicked her long tail, studying Linnea. "I can think of one thing that might come in handy, no matter where you end up. Let me see." She opened a website on her laptop. "Here's a good one," she said after a moment. She printed it, folded it and slid it into a plastic sleeve and passed it to Linnea. "It's a mantra. I'll just make a note in your file that it's been issued to you, since you might be back at some point."

"Oh! Thank you," Linnea said. She pushed her chair away from the table. She and Zach wished one another luck and she wiggled her fingers goodbye, relieved to be done with this puzzling step in her process.

Linnea waited until she was in the hall again to read her mantra. It said, "Always come back to the breath." Linnea slipped it into her pocket. She had only a vague idea of what the mantra meant.

Chapter Twenty-Three

WATERY DISCHARGE

Dori's concentration was still shaky from Linnea's second visit. It was not improved by the continuous drumbeat, fast and intense like the heartbeat of a hummingbird, that was coming up through the floor and rattling the windowpanes in her office Thursday morning.

Punk rockers in the basement had been making the humanities building tremble all year. Dori had wanted to put a stop to it early in fall term, but Linnea had pleaded for clemency. The band members were her students, they were good kids, and there wasn't anyplace else on campus for them to practice. Dori had been gritting her teeth against their noise two or three times a week all year. Lately she hadn't heard guitars, thankfully, but the relentless banging of drums still made it hard for her to concentrate on her work. After 15 or 20 minutes of vexation, she laid her pen on her desk and walked down the two flights of stairs to the student lounge in the basement of Verizon Wireless Hall. The sharp heels of her new shoes tapped in counterpoint to the furious drumming.

Dori had decided to wear the Fun Shoes in Linnea's honor until the heart issue was resolved. The shoes were concrete reminders that Linnea was no hallucination, and Dori seemed to need that constant reassurance as she moved forward with her plans to suspend her disbelief, deceive Pablo and break the law.

She rounded the corner at the foot of the stairs. The student lounge was a desultory place with a concrete floor and peeling sea green paint. The building's old boiler sat in one corner and a few folding chairs had been pushed to the periphery to make room for the band. The space was otherwise unfurnished. Two electric guitarists and a bassist were playing with the drummer, but their instruments were not plugged in, and they sounded like autoharps. Dori recognized one of the guitarists, a lanky, likable B-minus student named Tad, from her French 202 class.

Just as she opened her mouth to make her request, the drummer burst into a frenzy of percussion. To Dori it sounded like the soundtrack to a nightmare. The bass player, an abundantly tattooed young woman, closed her eyes in blissful concentration. She looked familiar, but Dori couldn't place her. It was probably only a few minutes, but for Dori the sound of instruments being beaten to death did not come to an end soon enough.

"Hey, Dr. A," Tad said with a grin. "You here for our autographs?"

"Actually I'm here to ask you to keep it down." Part of Dori was sorry to shatter their brief illusion of her as a groupie and establish herself as the curmudgeon she was.

"Oh." The band members looked at each other. "We thought it was okay to practice down here."

"This is an office building," Dori said. "People are upstairs trying to get work done."

"We're a lot quieter than we used to be," the lead guitarist said cheerfully. "We were really loud 'til we fried the electrical system with our amp." He gestured at an electrical outlet in the wall behind Dori. Someone had taped a stern "Do Not Use" sign across it.

"Yeah, we don't amp up any more," the tattooed bassist added.

"It's the drums," Dori told them.

"Oh." The other band members all looked at the drummer. "You're gonna have to chill, Mick."

Mick said, "I can chill."

Dori's annoyance began to dissipate. These 20-year-olds were so guileless in their various loud forms of self-expression, she couldn't help liking them a little bit.

"Guys, this is my French professor," Tad said. "Dr. Amore,"—he held out one arm with a flourish—"my girlfriend and bass guitarist *par excellence,* Alice. On drums, the inimitable Mick. And our lead guitarist, Brian."

Dori raised a hand in greeting.

"You're Dr. Nil's office mate," Alice said.

Dori recognized her then as the anguished young woman who had foisted a broom handle on her a few days earlier. That length of hardwood still leaned pointlessly against the wall next to her office door.

The young woman had an air of wistful urgency about her. "Okay, guys, let's take 15," she told the others. She set her guitar in its stand. "Three of the four of us were in Dr. Nil's Latin class," she told Dori.

"Actually we met in her class," Brian added. "That's how our band got started."

"Oh! You're Watery Discharge," Dori said. She smiled for the first time since she'd come downstairs. The students were visibly pleased that she had heard of them. "Linnea was fond of you."

Alice said, "We're still in shock."

"Me, too."

"Do you know if they've found anything new?" Alice asked.

Dori shook her head. Of course there was the news that Linnea still walked the earth in search of her missing heart, but that wasn't information she was prepared to share. Dori sensed the students expected something of her, but she didn't know what it was. Sometimes in grief, she supposed, people just needed to talk to someone else who'd known the deceased, someone else who understood how the living were left suddenly forlorn.

Mick returned. Alice and the boys plopped down on the floor, Mick tapping his own knees with his drumsticks. Mick was probably one of those young men who never stopped drumming. He probably drummed in his sleep.

"How is Mr. Callow working out?" Dori asked them.

The students looked at each other. "Mr. Callow is a catheter bag," Alice volunteered.

"Oh, dear," said Dori.

"I don't even think he knows Latin," added Brian.

It made Dori feel ill to know what she'd done, saddling these students with that sorry excuse for an instructor. Hiring Callow had been an act of desperation.

"I became a Classics major because of Dr. Nil," Alice told Dori. "And now I'm not sure I'm going to be ready for next year. Mr. Callow has kind of screwed up my whole plan of study."

"You'll be able to catch up," Dori told her. "You seem very capable."

Alice stared at the floor. "I just can't stop thinking about it. Her being killed."

Dori knew the feeling. She pulled up a folding chair. The other band members drew in a little closer, too.

"We were down here the night she died," Alice spouted.

That was something Dori hadn't expected to hear.

"It was freaky," Alice said. "We were practicing. It was late. And she was upstairs. We didn't know. We didn't know what'd happened until the next day."

Dori was startled. "You told the police?"

"Oh, of course," Alice said. She was sitting cross-legged on the floor beside Dori. "We all got interviewed, like, three times. It feels so weird that we were down here while she was…"

Dori made a sympathetic murmur.

"We feel awful."

"There wasn't anything you could have done to stop it. You didn't know."

Alice said, "But she was so good to us, and it's like we betrayed her." She tugged on a thread in her sweater, making the fabric pucker. "I feel like we should have done something."

Dori said, "If you had gone upstairs, you might have put yourselves in danger. We don't know if there was more than one assailant, or if he was armed. We just don't know."

Alice said, "Then we should be doing something now. To help with the investigation. Or something."

Dori couldn't help smiling at the young woman's earnestness. "That doesn't seem very feasible," she said gently.

"We got into trouble as it was," Brian said.

"What do you mean?"

"We started an electrical fire with our amps," the guitarist explained.

Dori raised an eyebrow. "You're the ones who tripped the

fire alarm that night?"

"That was us," the bass player said. "All three of us were plugged in and we blew the circuit."

"So the fire department came," Dori said, trying to recollect the details, "and they're saying that's when the assailant took off."

"That was crazy," Mick said with some enjoyment. "Firefighters running around all over the place."

Chickens with their clichés cut off, Dori thought. "You know," she told the students, "It might actually be a good thing you started the fire. Because if the murderer hadn't left in a hurry, he might have left less evidence behind. At least this way the police have something to work with."

This seemed to make the students feel better. Mick got to his feet. "Anyhow, I'll be quieter," he told Dori. "I'm the only one left who makes any sound."

"Yeah," Tad chimed in. "Watery Discharge is not allowed electrical access any more."

Chapter Twenty-Four

A FAVOR

Amy and Alice were walking to campus together when Amy said, "I want to ask you a favor."

Alice did not particularly feel she owed Amy any favors. Tad had been as cheerful with Alice as ever and had kissed her goodbye that morning, but he had spent several consecutive nights in Amy's bed. The women did not discuss this arrangement, here or anywhere. They talked every day, sometimes at length, about anything but Tad. Still, it was important to Alice that she bore Amy no ill will. "What favor?" she said.

"Do you think you could get me a job at Cootchie-Coo?"

Amy, who had begun the school year scandalized by skin dancing, had spent the school year quizzing Alice about her livelihood. Amy's awed curiosity had grown chummier as the months went by.

Alice studied her housemate and considered her—on the one hand, her high splits and her glossy blonde hair; on the other, her modest clothing, un-made-up skin, and wide blue eyes. Amy had come to the west coast from Missouri. She had just turned 18, had probably slept with one guy before Tad, and spoke of stripping as though it were a life of unsurpassed glamor.

"Let me think about it," Alice told her.

"Because, I was thinking? You could kind of show me the ropes, and it would be fun! And—"

"Let me think about it."

They approached the campus in silence. "I'm gonna stop here," Alice said to her housemate when they stepped on the lawn.

Smoking on campus was restricted to clear plastic structures, similar to bus shelters, called *fumettes*. They were so full of smoke that only the feet of the smokers could be seen thrusting from the bottom of a thick, swirling cloud. Alice wasn't much of a smoker—she needed good lungs for her line of work—but in this moment she wanted to establish an authoritative cool and felt a cigarette would be the best way to do it.

"Can I bum one?" she said to a smudge of human form lost in the toxic whorl inside the fumette. Someone handed out a lit cigarette. Making sure Amy was still watching—her housemate was stalling around, wondering if they were parting ways or not—Alice took a drag, narrowing her eyes and standing a rebellious foot or two outside the designated smoking area.

"Um, I guess I'm gonna go," Amy said.

"Okay," said Alice. "See ya."

She took one more drag after Amy had turned away and then thrust the cigarette back into the cloud bank and headed her own direction.

Alice had a paper to write for Art History. She had settled, as a topic, on paintings by Degas and Forain of ballerinas, as she felt a certain kinship with the dancers. She'd been surprised to learn that in 19th-century Paris, ballet didn't pay the bills, so dancers sometimes supplemented their incomes by going home with patrons.

Alice spent an hour in the library researching and poring over reproductions. In some paintings, the dancers appeared with their benefactors, top-hatted society gents who met them at the door after a performance. Alice recognized in the dancers both the alluring poses they struck and the resistance in their faces. She recognized in the benefactors the same look of predation that she saw on some of the faces of patrons at Cootchie-Coo.

She sat cross-legged on the library floor and began drafting her paper. *Dance,* she wrote, *being a supremely difficult art to master, should have paid well enough to provide for the dancers, but it didn't. Ballet was to the society patrons nothing more than foreplay.* The book on the floor before her lay open to a Forain painting in which a man in coat and top hat gripped the chin of a dancer in his hand. *The wink-wink system of allowing wealthy patrons backstage access after the show,* she continued, *commodified the women.*

Alice was indignant on behalf of these 19th-century Parisiennes. She wondered how much autonomy they might have had. Alice had muddled and muddled about this issue in her own life. Some of the patrons at Cootchie-Coo pressed the dancer—requesting, cajoling, demanding, begging, threatening, attempting to bribe, attempting to take by trickery—for services the club did not sell. They wanted to touch, to pinch, to stroke; they wanted lap dances, hand jobs, private peep shows, and they wanted to meet their favorite dancers at the back door after hours. Alice studied a sketch of a ballet dancer with her back to her patron, flinching slightly at his touch on her bare shoulder. Here was a worker being pressed to go beyond what she wanted to offer.

Alice stretched her legs out and bent over them, resting her head on her knees. In her own life, she didn't want to be judged, and she also didn't want to be pitied. "My patrons are looking for a service like any other, and I have a service to offer like any other," she had told her housemates. "As long as the playing field is even, it's a business transaction, pure and simple." Alice gazed at the painting again. The extent to which women were victimized by sex work depended on their work environments, she thought. She wrote in her notebook, *The playing field for Paris ballet dancers and their patrons was not even.* She scribbled out the metaphor, searching for something less clichéd, and then reinserted it. If she wrote too well, professors sometimes thought she'd plagiarized.

But victimization also depended to some extent, Alice mused, on the dancer herself. She thought about what it took—the timing, the acting, the sense of space, the hard stare or the clipped words she brought out when necessary—to give patrons what she was willing to offer, right up to the limit, and no more. Alice knew she could hold her own at the club. But maybe not all the dancers there could.

She narrowed her eyes and made a decision about Amy.

Chapter Twenty-Five

STAYING IN

That night Pablo picked Dori up at her place for their date. He told Dori when she climbed in the car that he'd forgotten his wallet and needed to swing by his house before they headed to the movie theater. Dori said she didn't mind.

They traveled a few blocks down side streets.

"This is it." Pablo pulled his Volvo into the driveway of a rowhouse. "I'll just be a sec. Do you mind waiting here?"

Dori stayed in the car and marveled at how there was not a speck of lint on the floor or even in any of the little crevices that were such crud magnets in cars. She looked over the neat lawn and clipped azaleas of Pablo's property. She played with her hangnails. She slipped in and out of her red sequined Fun Shoes.

When more minutes had gone by than it should have taken Pablo to fetch his wallet, Dori decided to go to the door and see what was up. As she climbed the front steps she could hear the roar of an electrical appliance from the other side of the door. She leaned over the rail at the doorstep to peek into the front window.

Pablo's living room was tidy, much tidier than her own. She saw framed prints on the walls and a wide bookcase full of books. Pablo's profile appeared at the window. He was pushing a vacuum cleaner back and forth. He looked up and saw Dori, ducked out of view and appeared at the front door.

"I'm sorry to make you wait," he said. "There was a spill, and I just wanted to take care of it really quickly." He pulled the door open all the way. "Come on in."

Dori stepped inside. The floor was spotless—the carpet looked as though it had never been stepped on, actually, and Dori could see that the kind of spill that might go unnoticed for days in her own living space would spoil the pristine state of Pablo's.

"This looks like a no-shoes-in-the-house house," Dori said.

"Thank you for your sensitivity to that."

Pablo knelt to wind the vacuum cleaner cord around its handles. Dori slipped off her Fun Shoes.

"And thanks for being so patient," Pablo told her from the hall closet. "I know it's a little strange that I stopped to vacuum. I just didn't want to come home to a mess."

"No worries."

On the far wall hung several lutes. "Those are beautiful instruments," Dori said.

"They are, aren't they?" Pablo said. "They have sweet voices, but they're pretty just to look at, too."

"So, those are the Renaissance instruments you play?"

"Yes."

"Nice." Dori pulled out her cell phone and checked the time. "Doesn't our movie start at 7?"

"Oh," said Pablo. "Oh. I thought it was 7:30."

They both looked over at the freshly vacuumed spot on

the rug. The theater wasn't far, but it was just far enough. Pablo's vacuuming had kept them from Federico Fellini.

A certain awkwardness fell between them now that they had no movie to go to. Pablo was probably worried that Dori was annoyed at him. She wasn't, but she found herself at loose ends. Pablo was all right, but she wasn't invested enough in him to want to spend the whole evening just making conversation. On the other hand, she could use the extra time to try to learn where Linnea's body was, if she could find a way to bring it up.

At least he was a gracious host, bringing Dori a glass of Chardonnay and growing expansive when she asked him to tell her more about the lutes.

Dori padded in her stocking feet to the wall to look at the instruments more closely, and from there to the titles on Pablo's bookcase and the framed photos that shared space with them.

"That's Mom," Pablo told Dori. "She's 87."

"Does she live in Bridges?"

Pablo shook his head. "San Diego," he said. "I try to get down there to see her every couple months or so."

"And who's this?" Dori indicated a photo of a chocolate Labrador.

"That's Gordon. He died last year at the age of fourteen."

"Aw," said Dori.

"He was a very good dog. A dear friend."

Dori settled onto the couch with her wine. She thought she might as well plunge into the subject most on her mind. "I packed up all Linnea's things," she told Pablo. "Couldn't stand the idea of strangers doing it." She picked a thread off her pants. "So, is Linnea...? Are they...?" She wasn't sure how to ask. "Are they done with her?"

Pablo looked surprised. "The Medical Examiner and company? They are, as a matter of fact," he said.

"And what happens now?" asked Dori, squirming for fear her line of questioning would arouse suspicion. "Is she going to be cremated or buried?"

Pablo shook his head. "I wouldn't know," he said. "That's up to the family."

Dori frowned, thinking of Linnea's neglectful brother. "So she must be at some funeral home."

"Yes."

"But you don't know which one."

Pablo shook his head, and Dori thought she'd better change the subject. "Nice color scheme," she said. The living room walls were painted in warm, earthy colors Dori didn't know the names of. Ochre, maybe? And burgundy, and, oh, olive or something. She definitely liked Pablo's style. Still, some element was missing in the whole package that was Pablo. Dori couldn't quite find a foothold in their interactions. She was relieved at the end of the evening when her conversational responsibilities came to an end and her date took her by the hand and led her off to bed.

Chapter Twenty-Six

THE AUDITION

"So, what do you think she's gonna ask me?" Amy said. She and Alice crossed 6th and headed south. The streets were dry enough now to bike on, but Amy had asked that they walk to the club so that Alice could prepare her on the way. "Is she gonna make me audition?"

Alice remembered her own initial conversation with Cootchie-Coo's manager, Renee. "Yes," she told Amy. "But mostly she's going to want to know that you'll show up for work when you're scheduled."

"Oh, my God," Amy said. "It's going to be so weird, to, like, dance for her."

"You'll be fine," Alice said.

"Do you think I'll have to perform tonight?"

"Maybe," Alice told her. They had had this conversation several times already.

"Oh, my God," Amy said. "Your clothes are going to look so stupid on me." They had brought along an extra set of Alice's things in case Amy needed them. Amy hadn't wanted to shell out money for clothes unless she knew she'd be getting the job. But she was much taller than Alice, and the outfit wouldn't fit her well.

"You won't be in them for very long," Alice told her.

They continued toward the club in silence. When it came into view, Amy clutched Alice's arm. "Oh, my God, oh, my God," she said. "I don't know if I can do this."

"Everybody's nervous at first," Alice said. "You'll catch on fast. Anything you want to know, just ask me."

Amy looked like she'd just swallowed a cracker whole.

Alice punched in the security code and they entered the back of the club. In the dark hall, Amy reached into her shoulder bag for her résumé. "If she calls my references," she asked Alice, "she's not going to tell them I'm applying to be a stripper, is she?"

"She's probably very professional," Alice said.

"Oh, my God," Amy repeated. "Do I have to do this?"

Alice turned and searched her housemate's face and thought about what she might say. She could tell her, no, you don't have to do this. You have free will. She could say, this is one kind of opportunity, and you can go after it if you want to, but if you decide it's not the right thing for you, that's okay too.

Alice looked into Amy's wide blue eyes and told her, "Look, I went to the trouble to set this up for you. And we're already here."

"Okay," Amy said. "Okay." She chewed her lip for a few moments. Then she said, "I'm ready."

They found the club manager at her computer in her office, bifocals on, typing figures into Excel.

Alice tapped on the open door. "Renee?" she said. "This is the friend I was telling you about."

Amy stepped forward and offered her hand. "Hi." Amy

and Alice had talked again and again about the job, and Amy had rehearsed all kinds of things she might say to Renee.

Renee slid her bifocals down her nose to look at the young blonde. She took in Amy's long legs in a single glance and said, "Fine. You can start right now. Alice, show her the dressing room." She turned back to her computer.

In the hall the two women stared at each other.

"Oh, my God," said Amy. "Oh, my God, oh, my God, oh, my God."

Chapter Twenty-Seven

BASSO LOCO

Bridges got a first tease of spring each February when its sweet-smelling *daphne odora* bushes bloomed extravagantly, releasing their intoxicating scent all over the city. Those days were declared blossom days—Bridges had blossom days the way other municipalities had snow days—and no one went to work, because it was not possible to go outdoors without getting drunk. Driving was banned. Some citizens sealed up their doors and windows with duct tape and hunkered inside. Others rushed outside and spent the day in a state of debauchery. Most just got a pleasant buzz and enjoyed a little vacation.

The business community hated the daphnes, because blossom days interfered with productivity. They had tried to have the bushes removed, which provoked an enormous public outcry, with angry demonstrations at City Hall and grandmothers chaining themselves to the bigger shrubs. One time, business leaders persuaded the city to cover the blooming bushes with elasticized plastic bags like giant shower caps. It didn't work. Polyethylene covers were no match for the daphnes' heady scent.

And now the flowers were in bloom. Most years, Dori looked forward to three or four days of forced vacation during the otherwise wet and gloomy late winter. But this year's blossoming was poorly timed. She was aware to the point of nausea of her urgent errand, and now she was trapped indoors.

She could only use the time to catch up on other tasks. A student of Linnea's had come to see her the day before about a bureaucratic problem that popped up often: the student had received a letter stating that she hadn't paid tuition for her Latin class, even though, she said, she absolutely had paid. "Mr. Callow didn't know what to do about it," she'd said, "but he thought you would."

Dori had tried not to sigh aloud at the mention of Ned Callow. She'd asked the young woman with the tuition problem if she had talked to Registration.

The young woman had said yes. She had the eyes of a doe and the unblemished skin of someone who has not been in the world very long. "Their computer was down," she'd told Dori. "Monday is the deadline to pay or I'll be automatically withdrawn from the class. And if I drop below twelve credits,"—the student's doe eyes had filled with tears—"I'll lose my financial aid."

Dori had agreed to help. Bureaucratic bungling at Middlebridge could set off a chain reaction that could take months to undo, sometimes with dire consequences for students. The problem was that many areas of the vast lair that was the college's computer system were off-limits to her. "Give me a day to work on it," she had told the student, who was wiping tears off her alabaster cheeks with the back of her hand.

Dori peered out her condo window. Below her she could

see many daphnes in bloom on her street, their pale pink flowers quite small and innocuous in appearance given their impact on the local economy. Dori had an idea for the Latin student. She picked up her phone and called Jaspar at home.

Unlike faculty, librarians had access to student financial information, because they needed to record students' library fines and stop grades, transcripts and degrees from being released to students if fines weren't paid up.

"Jas? It's Dori."

"Well, hello, Dori dear. This is Antoine," Jaspar's boyfriend said to her. "How are you holding up? We've been thinking about you."

"I'm managing. I just have so much to do."

"Well, don't over-do, darling." Antoine sounded merrier than the conversation merited. "You just step outside and take a deep breath. It's good for what ails you." Antoine had obviously been outside already this morning.

"Let me talk to Jaspar a sec," Dori said.

"I'll see if I can rouse him," Antoine said. "He's in something of a state of bliss."

Perhaps because of the extremities of natural phenomena they experienced here—blossom days, omnipresent crows, streets that became canals in the winter—the residents of Bridges tended to embrace nature's rhythms. It seemed Dori was alone in her exasperation over lost time. Jaspar greeted her, and Dori explained the situation with Linnea's student. "Can you take a look at her registration records for me?"

Jaspar, unsteady on his feet from the sound of it, went to his computer and in a few moments said, "Got it." He scrolled down. "Her account is marked 'unpaid,' and of course I can't change that. Even if I knew for a fact that she *had* paid. The only people who have the password work in Registration. Hhmm." Jaspar clicked around in silence for another moment. "You know what's strange? A lot of students are paying in cash these days. It's not a good idea, because then there's no paper trail. And besides, tuition is up to almost $8,400 a semester. Who carries that kind of cash?"

"Mmm," Dori said, distracted. She was thinking that if Financial Aid weren't able to stop the doe-eyed student's automatic withdrawal from Latin, the poor thing might be fasting for a month before her checks were reinstated.

"Here we go." Jaspar's voice interrupted Dori's gloomy speculation. "I'll set the 'last day of class' as July 31. That'll buy her some time." The computer would automatically withdraw a non-paying student when a class was one-fifth complete. Jaspar had tricked the computer into thinking the class was longer than it really was, giving the young woman a couple more weeks to sort her situation out.

"Jaspar, you're the best."

"Don't mention it. Now go outside and play."

Pablo called to say hi. Dori had left his house not six hours earlier, and his attentions felt like cling wrap on her skin. After wriggling away from him, Dori called her sister. Krizzle was Dori's mentor on all questions connubial. She was four years younger than Dori but had always been socially savvier. She'd coached Dori through all Dori's college dating when Kristin herself was still in high school. "I'm having trouble deciding whether I like him or not," she said. "I mean, I like him, but I don't know if I *like* him like him."

"Tell me about him."

"He's my age. Attractive enough, in a safe, bald kind of way. Soft-spoken. Sweet. Seems responsible, solvent, well-adjusted. Works in a lab. Makes music in his free time."

"So far, so good," said Kristin. "I guess the chemistry just isn't there."

Dori could hear water running in the background, and she knew that her sister, ever efficient, was probably cleaning the kitchen in her headset while they talked. Dori herself was lying on the floor with her feet up on the loveseat.

"Oh, the chemistry's all right," Dori said. "I don't mind diddling him. I just don't know if I want to date him."

"What's wrong with him?"

"He's just a little... tame. I like 'em a little edgier, I guess."

Kristin sighed the sigh of faint exasperation she seemed to so often use on Dori. "You've got it backwards," she said. "The edgy ones are for diddling. The tame ones are for dating."

"Maybe 'tame' isn't the right word. Maybe 'geeky.'"

"Tells-you-more-than-you-want-to-know-about-his-hard-drive-specs geeky, or takes-all-jokes-at-face-value geeky?" Dori heard clanking and knew Kristin was loading the dishwasher. "Or does he just have better personal hygiene than you?"

"Maybe 'geeky' isn't the right word," said Dori, feeling she was getting nowhere. "Maybe... 'boring.'"

Kristin shut the dishwasher door with a bang. "Well, then, don't date him. That was easy."

"I like the sex," Dori said. "I'm not ready to be done with him just yet."

"Then tell him you're just in it for the sex," Kristin said, openly impatient now. "Come on, Dori, this isn't a hard assignment."

Dori couldn't tell her sister the truth—that she feared Pablo *liked* her liked her, and that he might not accept a no-clichés-attached arrangement, but that Dori needed to hang onto him long enough to snag Linnea's heart.

To use him, in other words. Dori hadn't planned it that way. It wasn't by design that her personals-ad bonk-buddy was employed by the Medical Examiner. And it wasn't her fault if he was getting emotionally involved.

"I guess you're right," she told Kristin, her voice flat. "Thanks. Hey, can I say hi to Elsa?" Dori wanted to run some ideas past Elsa about their upcoming day together.

"Yeah. Sure. Talk to you later." Dori could hear the sounds of Kristin's feet padding through the house. She handed the headset to her daughter.

"Hey, favorite niece," Dori said.

"Hey, favorite aunt. Have you ever noticed? If you shut one eye and then the other, you don't see exactly the same thing? Everything moves over, like, an inch."

"I know this," Dori said, a smile in her voice for the first time that day.

"I went back and forth between eyes for about ten minutes today," Elsa continued. "It was pretty fun."

"Sounds like an afternoon well spent."

"It beats pre-algebra. That's what everybody else was doing."

"Pity the fools," Dori told her.

Dori stretched out on the yellow loveseat, rubbing her temples and willing herself to relax. She was uncomfortable, and got up after an hour without being able to tell whether she had fallen asleep. Her mind kept running over the same ideas, rubbing them raw. Was the murderer a student? Dori still hadn't been able to conjure up the name of Linnea's most anxious pupil, the young man who had been flunking out of two of her classes. What about the members of the punk band? Dori had liked them, so it wasn't until hours after she'd met them that she started to wonder if they could be the killers. They had had the means—with four of them, it would have been easy to overpower Linnea and later carry her body to the Art department—and they had had the opportunity. Dori came up empty-handed, though, when searching for a motive. Unless they were, say, part of a Satanic cult—she should have paid more attention to their song lyrics, she thought—she couldn't fathom why the four young people would do such a deed. They had seemed to genuinely adore their teacher. Anyway, if Alice was telling the truth, the police had already pursued that line of reasoning.

What about Ned Callow, then? What was the likelihood that Callow had butchered Linnea to try to create some job security for himself? Did he imagine that homicide was a workable job-search strategy? Dori had doubts about whether Callow was competent to plan and carry out a complicated scheme like murder.

Was the murderer from Upper Management? This was the most likely scenario, she thought. She mulled over what Ian Elf had told her and the others about the recent board meeting. She thought of Elf going undercover, and of how much care he'd taken to communicate with her in secret. The hairs at the back of her neck stood up. The most likely explanation for Linnea's murder, Dori reasoned, was that her organizing efforts had been found out. Fiercey, or someone in league with her, must have discovered what Linnea knew and was determined to keep her quiet.

Dori tried to run down the list of deans. In addition to Fiercey, the Dean of Allocations, and Budgie, the Dean of Documentation, Middlebridge had several others—a Dean of Deliberation she'd worked with a couple times; a Dean of Implementation she saw now and again; and a Dean of Obfuscation, whom she'd never met. But only faculty would have attended the union organizers' meeting at the Splash.

Could there be some instructor who had infiltrated Linnea's group? What faculty member would do such a thing? Then there was the unresolved business with the items left on Dori's windowsill. Who had access to Dori's office? It had to be someone from Middlebridge. Why would that person leave curiosities for her to find? Was it a practical joke, or something more sinister? The hamster in Dori's mind kept running in its exercise wheel, going nowhere.

This blossom day posed an additional problem that was troubling Dori—it could interfere with the following day's fencing tournament. Meteorologists were predicting a giant windstorm that would blow the city clean of the inebriating scent (in effect moving the problem to communities west of Bridges). But Dori wasn't going to take any chances. She pulled a balaclava over her head and double-wrapped her face in a long knit scarf and set out on foot to buy a gas mask. An outdoor-supply store in her neighborhood stocked them, she knew, for this and other emergencies.

Dori had just come home and was carrying the gas mask under her arm, hurrying toward her front steps, when Pablo arrived. Without saying anything about it, Pablo took the mask out of her arms, then drew him to her and said "Hi" into her hair.

"To what do I owe the pleasure?" Dori said, trying not to stiffen. This was altogether too much Pablo. His inhibitions must have been lowered by the *daphne odora*.

"I want you to run away with me."

"What?" Dori was alarmed.

"Just for the weekend. Are you free?"

They began to climb the stairs to Dori's condo.

"I have a fencing tournament tomorrow."

"No kidding!"

"Keeps me on my toes."

"Can I come cheer you on?"

In spite of her resistance to Pablo, Dori felt a little wave of affection lap over her. She'd often been a teeny bit envious during tournaments, where so many competitors had supporters on the sidelines. Antoine was always there for Jaspar, a stockpile of Jaspar's favorite treats in a cooler at his side. "All right," Dori said, surprising herself.

"And maybe we can make a little getaway that night."

"Actually I have my niece then. She and her family are coming down for the tourney and then Elsa's staying for the rest of the weekend." Dori was relieved to be able to say so. A weekend away together was the next step in dating, a gesture of enthusiasm for the relationship that Dori didn't feel, and she was glad she had a ready excuse to decline.

"Well," Pablo said, "Monday is Presidents' Day. Do you get the day off? There's a red-eye special that goes to San Diego on Sunday nights. It's a good deal. And San Diego is such a treat for Pacific Northwesterners in February. Reliably awesome weather."

Dori opened her door. "Here, I'll take that," she said, relieving Pablo of the gas mask. They stepped inside, and Dori set about prying apart the mask's plastic clamshell packaging and trying to come up with a reason why she couldn't leave town with Pablo a few days hence. When she glanced up, she saw he was gazing about him with a look of something like horror. "Sorry about the mess," Dori said. "I would've tidied up if, you know, I'd known you were coming over."

"It's okay," Pablo said, his voice feeble. "It's not very messy. Just—it could use vacuuming."

Dori flushed. He was probably right, even though she herself wouldn't vacuum for another week. To distract his attention from the way she lived, she burst out, "I do have

Monday off. I think going away together is an excellent idea."

After Pablo left, she called Kristin yet again. "I need an objective assessment," she told her sister. "Is it creepy and stalkerish that he came over to my house unannounced?"

"Mmm," said Kristin. She was driving; Dori could hear traffic in the background. "How many times have you gone out now?"

"Twice."

"Has he been to your house before?"

"Yeah. He spent the night here once."

"And you're getting along just fine?"

"Yeah," Dori said in a lukewarm voice.

"You don't sound convinced. Have you had conflict?"

"No! Of course not."

"Have you told him you're not interested in dating?"

"No, huh-uh."

"Hang on."

Dori could hear the rumble of Kristin's engine. She was probably squeezing into a tight parking spot.

"Okay, I'm back. Weren't you going to have that conversation with him?"

"Oh, I don't know."

"It doesn't sound to me like he's stepped over any lines," Kristin told her. "It sounds to me like he's more interested in you than you are in him, and he doesn't realize it."

Dori could see that Kristin was right. She told herself she should be grateful for Pablo's interest, since it could only help her get to Linnea's heart. What she would do with him when the deed was done, she'd figure out later.

"Do you have problems of any substance you'd like to discuss?" Kristin asked.

Dori said good-bye and set thoughts of Pablo aside. She had a tournament to prepare for.

Chapter Twenty-Eight

BROKENHEARTED

One place Linnea wanted to visit now was her own home. To save energy, she took a bus rather than wefting to her old neighborhood. It hadn't rained much in recent days, and the streets were passable. Linnea was glad, because it was easier to slip unnoticed onto a bus than into a water taxi, where her invisible weight affected the ballast of the boat. She walked the three blocks from the bus stop, wistful about her old haunts.

Linnea's spirits sank when she saw the house. The curtains were drawn and it stood empty and, it seemed to her, forlorn. In the absence of a will, Linnea supposed, the house would be sold and the proceeds held in probate until the state could decide what to do with it. Why didn't I ever write a will? Linnea thought. So many human endeavors, from dating to cultivating friendships, from going back to Italy to finding pants that really fit, from scraping the moss off her roof to putting her affairs in order, had escaped her grasp during her lifetime. What did I do instead? Linnea thought. 43 years seemed like ample time to have put her last wishes on paper. Mostly, Linnea knew, she had worked. She had kept the Classics department running, she had taught, she had served on committees, and her personal life had suffered a lot of deferred maintenance. Now some of those mossy inner matters were coming to light and might even affect the outcome of her eternity. Linnea frowned, remembering Esme, who had been concerned only with Linnea's soul. There was probably no record in Esme's database of Linnea's stellar student evaluations, excellent annual performance reviews and robust MADCAPs.

Linnea approached her front stoop with something akin to fear. The house was dark. She shut her eyes and concentrated. With terrific effort to shut out images of Esme, of her office, of deans and of spreadsheets, Linnea willed herself into her living room. She opened her eyes and found herself sprawled on the front lawn. It was a good thing no one could see her.

Linnea brushed off her pants and tried again. This time she opened her eyes to the sight of her living room wall. It was bare. The painting that should have been hanging there had been taken down. Her furniture was draped in sheets. Stacked six high on either side of the fireplace stood cardboard boxes full of her belongings. She walked through the empty house. Every plate, every appliance, every book and photo album, every hairbrush and pillow and article of clothing had been packed up—by strangers, no doubt—to be sold or given away, and the proceeds to disappear into the pockets of probate lawyers. Linnea slid down to the floor and sat among the boxes in silence. She had never seen such a lonesome sight. The trappings of her life had become Goodwill donations, all physical evidence of her existence reduced to cardboard containers. She'd been dead just a few days, but no time had been wasted in clearing her away. No one had stood up and said, "These things have value to the college, to the community, to loved ones." No—her effects had been instantly drained of meaning, indistinguishable, anonymous, dissipated, unmourned, forgotten.

Chapter Twenty-Nine

TAD

In the stairwell of the student union building, Alice heard familiar voices. They rose from two stories below and piqued her curiosity.

"*You've* subjected yourself to all kinds of physical trials, and *you're* still okay."

"Dude, no, my situation is totally different. I'm, under, like, constant medical supervision."

"I don't know…"

"I think you need to come clean, man. You gotta tell somebody and get help."

When Alice came within view of Dexter Beet and Guppy, they stopped talking. "Oh, hi," she said. "I didn't know you two knew each other." She hadn't seen Dexter in a while—he'd disappeared from Latin class. That wasn't surprising, given the way he'd quailed in the presence of *nē* clauses.

"Yeah, we failed statistics together last term," Guppy said cheerfully.

"I gotta go." Dexter did not look at Alice, but gave Guppy

a little nod and hurried down the stairs.

"What was that about?" Alice asked after Dexter's footsteps had faded.

Guppy moved his hair-thatch back and forth a few times. "I feel like I should tell you," he said. "But he asked me not to tell anybody. I don't know."

"Okay."

"Yeah. I don't know. I feel like you should know, but then, on the other hand—I don't know. "

Not wishing to be held hostage to Guppy's indecision, Alice said, "All right. Well, I'll see you back at the house," and went on her way.

Alice was in a state she thought of as medium-miserable. She was still picking herself up by the scruff of her neck to get herself to work and class. Yet her thoughts ran around the same track over and over again: how would she make it through college? How could she dance 540 more nights—or longer? Would the Latin she was teaching herself be good enough to see her through the summer class? Thoughts of Latin plunged her into a cold sea of sorrow. How could Dr. Nil have been murdered? Alice was adjusting to the idea that Dr. Nil was dead. But the violence and the mystery of the death continued to gnaw at her.

It seemed like a good idea while she was dialing, but once Alice had Dr. Amore on the phone, she felt foolish.

"Have you learned anything?" she asked after stammering out who she was and why she was calling, "about the investigation?"

"No," said the professor. She sounded puzzled.

Alice took a dim view of police, who were sometimes unhelpful to, and sometimes aggressive with, sex workers. She was imagining Dr. Nil becoming a cold case due to official indifference, and she couldn't bear it. But she hadn't really thought through what she might say to Dr. Nil's colleague.

"Do *you* know something?" Dr. Amore said. "Something you think would help solve the case?"

"No," Alice said in a sad little slip of a voice. "I wish I did. I want to *do* something." Didn't police sometimes rely on the vigilance of common citizens? Weren't cases sometimes solved by amateur sleuths? Alice wasn't sure if amateur sleuthing and citizen arrests only happened in fiction. Dr. Amore seemed like the kind of person who would know things like that. Alice had been hoping Dr. Amore would give her encouragement and direction. But the phone call was becoming more awkward by the minute.

"I want to help with the investigation," she said finally. "To help figure things out."

"I don't know what to tell you," Dr. Amore said. "I don't really see that there's any way for you to do that, Alice."

"I guess not," Alice said. "I just want to do something for Dr. Nil, you know?"

"I do know."

Alice went back to her flashcards, but they didn't have her attention. Some little detail of her day was tugging at her, but she couldn't quite think what it was.

She was lying on her futon surrounded by grammar books and 3 x 5 cards. Tad knocked on the wall outside the kitchen nook. Without leaving her bed, Alice used her foot to push back the area rug that divided her space from the kitchen.

"Hi," said Tad, his eyes big and brown and sad. "Can I come in?"

"Sure."

They hadn't seen each other in a few days except at

mealtimes. Alice had been working a lot of hours, and she knew Tad was spending those hours with Amy. Whatever.

Tad flopped down on her bed. She was startled by how much of her bed he consumed. Tad was thin and lanky but nevertheless, with his rubbery Gumbyness and big hands and feet, he seemed to take up a lot of space.

"I'm not happy," Tad announced.

Alice waited to hear what he meant.

"I'm having a lot of orgasms," Tad continued, "but I'm not happy."

"What's up?" Under Alice's breastbone, hope like a helium balloon began to rise. She knew she shouldn't feel that way—she and Tad and Amy were all free, independent beings—but Alice understood with sudden, painful clarity that, in secret, she wanted to be the favorite.

"I miss you," Tad told her. "I miss *us*."

"Oh," Alice said. She made her voice very calm. "All right."

"Amy's great and everything," Tad said. "I don't mean her any disrespect. But she's not you."

Alice didn't mean any disrespect to Amy, either, but her heart leaped. She might not have Amy's inseams, but she had other qualities, evidently, that mattered to Tad.

"I want us to spend more time together again," Tad said, "like in the old days."

The "old days" were only about a week behind them, but time made strange accordion movements, Alice had noticed, in periods of emotional intensity.

"Okay," Alice said. "That's fine with me."

"Can I sleep here tonight?"

"Yeah, sure. Of course," Alice said.

Relief washed over Tad's face. "Whew," he said, making a gesture of wiping sweat from his brow.

"What?" Alice said.

"Oh, I was worried that you might not, I don't know, really be into sharing me."

"We've always agreed it would be okay."

"Yeah."

He crawled up to the head of the bed and settled in beside Alice, draping his long floppy arm around her shoulder. He was wearing a moth-eaten orange sweater, the one Alice loved best.

"How are you?" Tad asked her.

"Not so good."

"What's up?"

"Dr. Nil," Alice said.

"Oh. Yeah. Of course," Tad told her.

Under the gaze of Tad's warm brown eyes, Alice's internal coil of misery began to loosen. "I just can't get used to the idea that someone murdered her. While we were in the building!" she told him. "It's like it happened before my very eyes. I feel like we should have known what was happening and done something to stop it."

"Hey," said Tad, and he pulled her close to him. She felt the old familiar drape of his long arm on her shoulder, and smelled his old familiar smell, a safe haven. She buried her face in his neck and began to sob.

Tad stroked her back and let her cry. "You aren't responsible for what happened," he told her softly. "You couldn't have known."

What he said was true, but Alice kept crying. Tad ran his big Gumby hand over her hair. While Watery Discharge was down in the basement messing around with chord sequences, someone's life was being snuffed out three floors above. The thought made Alice nauseous with a sense of failed responsibility. It wasn't rational, she could see that, but it swamped her nevertheless.

In Tad's absence these past few days, Alice had half forgotten the comfort a boyfriend could be. Now, while his arms were around her, she thought she might be able to begin uncoiling her wound-up sadness. She pressed her nose under his warm chin, breathing in the Tadness of him.

"So," Tad said in the same gentle voice, still stroking Alice's hair. "I was thinking?" It was the voice Tad used when he had a little scheme, a voice with a twinkle in its eye. He was probably going to propose they leave town for the weekend, go to the beach or up to Seattle, so Alice could have a change of scenery and the two of them could have time alone together. Alice lifted her face to his. Tad stroked under her chin with one long finger. "I was thinking I could make a circuit. One night with you, the next night with Amy, back to you, like that. Would you be cool with that?"

Chapter Thirty

THE TOURNAMENT

A fierce wind scoured the town of the smell of daphnes in the night. Dori was relieved—the gas mask was one less piece of gear she'd have to think about in preparation for the tournament.

Under the enormous ceiling and pale filtered light of an airplane hangar, aluminum fencing strips had been laid out one after another in rows. The hangar was the only space in Bridges big enough to accommodate a multi-club tourney, and it was lent out to the region's fencing schools and university teams every year for their annual competition. Lining the walls were tables of vendors' wares—gear, snacks, epée key rings, saber tree ornaments, teddy bears in lamé.

Dori checked in and reviewed the schedule posted on a bulletin board at the door. She would bout several times. If she were victorious in the semi-finals, she would face Aldous Adipose at 4 p.m.

In a makeshift locker room, she changed into her gear. She inspected each item of clothing—pants, plastron for protection, socks, glove, lamé—before slipping it on. Dori was glad she'd arrived early. A tournament was a noisy affair—the air vibrated with loudspeaker announcements, the ringing of blades, the shouts of spectators, and the high whine of the scoring apparatuses at every touché—and she needed time to adjust to the ambient noise before her first match.

She walked up and down the aisles between rows of strips, making sure she knew the locations of all her bouts. Low green curtains separated spectators from competitors on their strips. At any given moment five or six matches were taking place, and everywhere she turned, fencers were getting ready. The space was strewn with long equipment bags. Green and red lights flashed on scoreboards. Dori paused to watch one match, a Class A men's epée competition between two fellows she knew slightly, when someone knocked hard into her shoulder, throwing her off balance.

"Oh, I'm *so* sorry," said Aldous Adipose to her with a tiny smirk, clearly not sorry in any way. "*Pardonnez-moi.*"

He moved along without any further words to her. He'd obviously bumped into her on purpose, hoping to rattle her before they faced off later in the day.

Dori found a corner where she could shake away his energy. She pulled her body cord out of her equipment bag and made sure it was untangled, then took all her gear to an inspection table for an official weapons check. Fencing competition was electrified: competitors' blades were attached to a box with a retractable cord like a leash, which allowed each touché to be registered electrically even if a ref didn't see it.

"Aunt Dori!" Elsa's cheerful voice sailed over the ruckus of the crowd. Dori went to greet her family members and advised them to go ahead to the strip so they could get good seats. Dori's first bout would be with another Class B woman of about her own age.

"What's Class B?" Elsa asked.

"Not the best, but pretty good."

Dori and her opponent were two of 15 competitors in their pool. After they'd fenced everyone in the pool, they would be ranked according to the number of bouts they'd won. Then they'd move to the next level of competition, in which they'd face off with others similarly ranked in their respective pools. A bout was just three minutes, or five points, whichever came first. Still, at tournament-level intensity, it could be a tiring day.

Dori scanned the space for Pablo once or twice, though she wasn't expecting him until later. Then she put him out of her mind. Stretching and warming up, she began to get into the Zone, a dreamy yet alert state in which she could shield herself from the stimuli of the competition space and focus on her game. The *tac, tac* of the blades and the occasional ringing of metal on metal became a kind of mantra, as did the slap of cords hitting the aluminum strips behind the fencers.

Dori won her first two matches handily and lost the third. Elsa, who was attending her first tournament, looked crestfallen. Dori winked her way, then remembered that her expression could not be read behind her mask. She removed the mask and held it under one arm. "It's all right," she told Elsa. "I'll get lots more chances."

They broke for lunch, Dori eating a sensible sandwich of lean turkey and whole-grain bread, Kristin and her family choosing hot dogs from one of the food booths. Jaspar, also a Class B fencer, joined them. He was in a different pool but might face Dori later in the day.

"I've got a little pain in here," Jaspar said, rubbing one calf. "I hope I didn't pull something. How are you feeling?"

"I'm all right," said Dori. She felt well, peppy, but she

was afraid to jinx herself by saying so aloud.

As the afternoon wore on, Dori's pep only grew. She bested Ollie Watson, an opponent with a much more aggressive style than hers. Men tended to do a lot more jumping around than women, a lot more thrusting, bouncing, thumping, stabbing, charging, lunging, posturing before the crowd and wordless hollering (they could be disqualified for shouting intelligible words, though Adipose sometimes insulted Dori mid-bout in French, confident no one else could understand). Like Muhammad Ali facing George Foreman, Dori waited for Ollie to tire himself out with all his commotion, then deftly scored on him five times in the last thirty seconds of the bout. The spectators enthused noisily. Dori and Ollie shook hands, saluted the referee and the crowd, and removed their masks.

"Good game," Ollie said. "Very well bouted, Dori. I'm taking notes." Ollie might be a thumper and a charger, but he did not posture. His praise was sincere. Dori appreciated him.

As the afternoon wore on, Dori worked her way through all the scheduled bouts. She finished that portion of the competition with a standing of third in her pool. Now it was on to repêchage—the fencing equivalent of sudden death, in which one opponent would be eliminated in a single round. Dori's opponent, who was ranked third in his own pool, was Aldous Adipose.

Dori felt fit, energized, by the morning's work. She bent her blade over her head. (All around the airplane hangar, fencers were in a constant state of lifting their blades over their heads and bending them back into shape. Though they did it for good reason—blades could lose their "temper" in use, getting bent out of optimum curvature when a fencer scored on an opponent—all this bending looked like a nervous habit or act of superstition, like gamblers blowing on their dice.)

Dori scanned the crowd. She couldn't help wondering if Pablo were going to show up. He'd said he'd be there in the afternoon, but there was no sign of him. Dori felt a peculiar mixture of relief and disappointment.

She went to her strip and hopped from one foot to the other, a warm-up that was really a pretext for siphoning off nervous energy. Jaspar was there, having already lost his last bout of the day. He sat in the audience with Dori's family and several of their other fencing buddies. Everyone hoped to see her defeat Adipose, save for a small but noisy group of Adipose's own fans.

Just before the judge called her name, Dori caught sight of Pablo. He was hurrying down the center aisle toward her *piste,* and when he saw her, he waved. He took a seat in the front row next to Antoine just as the referee called out, "Amore, Adipose."

The opponents approached one another on the strip. With their sabers they saluted the referee, then the crowd, and then shook hands. The non-dominant handshake of fencing tradition (one must offer the ungloved hand) took getting used to, limp as it was compared to a business greeting. But the handshake of Aldous Adipose always seemed especially lackluster. Perhaps he wanted to start getting under her skin from their very first contact on the strip. Dori didn't care. She felt strong, zippy, able to rise above the petty insults of her old rival.

The referee said, "Ready, fence!"

Tic tac tic tac clash, *tic tac.* Too much arm, not enough wrist. Dori was excited. She could feel herself being a little too wild, using strength in place of technique, wasting energy. Exercise control, Dori. Retreat. Loosen your grip. She met a cut, moved in to score, and missed as Adipose slipped away like silk. Damn him! He might be obnoxious, but there was no denying he moved like a cat, graceful and silent, quick and cunning. One minute into the bout and neither had scored.

Cut, parry, cut, parry, feint, thrust, don't lean, Dori; riposte, retreat, bend your knees, loosen your grip, cut, parry, cut, advance. She met another cut with excessive force in spite of lecturing herself; she scolded herself, took a breath, almost scored on Adipose with an elegant thrust (but almost chicken doesn't make soup, she thought), then almost got scored on because her timing was off (don't think about your mistakes, Dori thought; just concentrate). Moved in for an obvious cut but gave Adipose too much time to see her coming. Two minutes into the bout.

Then she saw what looked like the tiniest flagging of Adipose's energy—a momentary pause during which his usual erect bearing seemed to slump just a little. I'm wearing him out, Dori thought. I should strike while the cliché is hot. Adipose moved into *en garde* position, giving Dori a moment to coil for the spring. The very instant Adipose lunged, Dori, full of adrenaline, met his blade with hers, but jerked her arm and sent her rival's saber clean out of his hand. It flew off to the side of the strip and clanged against one of the rods holding the knee-high curtain between the strip and the spectators. Dori was disqualified. The bout, which had stood at 0-0, was awarded to Adipose. It was over.

Adipose moved in to Dori to salute her, as was customary. As they shook hands, he said with mock sympathy, "*Quel dommage*, Dori. *Quel dommage.*"

Dori's jaw tightened, not at Adipose but at her own performance. She'd told herself over and over to maintain control—she'd made this very same mistake in the gymnasium with Jaspar just days before.

A cloud settled over Dori's supporters. No one could

accuse Adipose of playing dirty. Dori had simply screwed up.

If she'd been unambivalently fond of Pablo, Dori would have been humiliated to have him present now. As it was, she was merely embarrassed. He'd made the effort to attend her tournament, and she'd been a dud. Dori wished she'd never told Pablo she was a fencer.

Jaspar said, "Damn! Damn damn damn! Rotten luck, Dori."

"Not rotten luck. Rotten fencing on my part."

"It happens to all of us sometimes."

"Maybe."

"You're better than that guy," Elsa said darkly. "I don't care about the other bouts you lost. But *this* one…"

This one hurt—Dori felt the same way.

"He's so horrid," Elsa continued. "And he has that horrid little mustache."

It was true. But Dori didn't want to model poor sportsmanship, so she said, "We have to be gracious, whether we win or lose."

"I know." Elsa yanked her hat over her blonde hair.

"We have to be gracious in our words and our deeds," Dori said in a low voice, "but we can *think* all the ungracious thoughts we want."

Elsa's eyes widened. "We can?" she said. Dori figured it wasn't a message eleven-year-old girls heard very often. Girls were supposed to be nice right to the marrow.

"We can," Dori said solemnly, and they grinned at one another.

"We all wanted to see you put Adipose in his place," said Antoine.

"Thanks," said Dori, unhooking her electronic belt. "There's always next year."

Pablo stood from his folding chair and joined the gloomy

circle that had gathered round Dori, and she was faced with the moment of introducing him. She didn't want anyone making too much of Pablo's presence. She began a round of introductions. Her sister's eyebrow lifted and Dori knew Kristin was remembering their last conversation about Pablo.

"And these are my friends Jaspar and Antoine..."

"Yes, we've met already!" said Antoine, a little too merrily. Dori took his meaning. He and Jaspar knew exactly who Pablo was.

Dori unzipped her equipment bag and placed her helmet inside. She pulled her jacket on over her lamé.

"Before you leave, Dori," Jaspar said, slipping his arm under hers and steering her out of the circle. Antoine joined them, taking Dori's other arm, leaning into her with his great Pooh bear shape.

"We've checked out Pablo," he said to her, *sotto voce*.

"And we think he's the cat's meow," said Jaspar.

"The bee's knees," Antoine added.

"Like falling with your bum into butter," said Jaspar.

"What?"

"Okay, too many metaphors and similes. Here's some straight talk: we *liiiiiike* him." Jaspar sang the last bit.

"We like him a lot. Well done, Dori," said Antoine.

"Thanks, guys," said Dori, flustered. She craned her head around, self-conscious about the possibility that Pablo was taking notice of their little football huddle and knowing they were talking about him.

"Now don't screw it up," said Jaspar.

"*Jas*," Antoine clucked. "Dori won't screw it up. We have complete faith in her."

"Yes, we do." Jaspar loosed his arm and picked up Dori's equipment bag for her.

"Okay," said Dori. "Thanks? I think."

Chapter Thirty-One

QUICQUID POSSIS PERDERE

On Tuesday nights all the housemates had dinner together. Tad and Guppy often engaged in what they called "recreational dumpster diving," and Thursday was the day they went around to grocery stores that had chucked whatever had passed its sell-by date. They usually found some sad but edible vegetables, and meat that would be okay if they used it that day. The bakeries put out bread that was fine if you toasted it. In the summer and fall months you could glean nuts and fruits from trees around town, too, though pickings were slim in February and March when everything was just germinating. But Tad was resourceful and had done some guerrilla gardening, sowing salad greens in empty lots. So he and Guppy came home with a good assortment of stuff that the five of them could compel into dinner with a little imagination and some barbecue sauce. Tonight he also brought home a couple six-packs of beer.

"What's the occasion?" asked Amy.

"I'm feeling flush," Tad said. "I made a deposit today."

Tad occasionally donated to the cryobank—what he and Alice called the Jism Center—a sperm depository that paid $50 a pop. He set the beer at the center of the table. Guppy laid out table settings; Amy brought out a hot casserole dish. They took their places at the table. Amy pushed the casserole to Jillian to dig in, and the others passed her the bread and the salad. By mutual agreement, Jillian got first crack at anything that was in short supply, since she was eight months pregnant.

Guppy told the others, "So, I landed a gig in a Phase I drug trial."

"What's that mean?" asked Amy.

"I'm in the first group of testees," Guppy grinned, "after the mice."

"Why would you *do* that?" Jillian said.

"Hey, it's a public service," Guppy told her. "New drugs can't go to market until they're thoroughly tested. On human beings."

"You don't care about public service," Alice teased.

Guppy spread his hands and grinned. "Is it a bad thing," he asked, "if I save the world while I'm making a living?"

"What's the drug?" asked Tad.

"It's an anticholinergic. Don't you like the sound of that?"

"I thought you were already doing a drug trial," Alice said.

"I'm doing *two* others," said Guppy with a certain pride.

"Shit! You're doing three drug trials at the same time? Dude," said Tad.

"But you tell them, right?" said Jillian.

"No, I don't tell them. They wouldn't let me do more than one at a time."

"But what if the drugs interfere with each other…?" asked Jillian.

"Man, that is just crazy," Tad said with relish. "You are

crazy."

The three women were alarmed. "I wouldn't be so cavalier if I were you," said Jillian.

"Yeah, dude, you've obviously already damaged your mental health," Tad put in.

"*Adspicere oportet quicquid possīs perdere,*" said Alice with theatrical solemnity. "'You should keep an eye on things you could lose.'"

Guppy laughed. "You know what I just realized? One way or another, all five of us are selling our bodies."

It was true: Tad sold his semen; Amy sold her hair; Jillian was renting out her womb. Alice of course had been working at Cootchie-Coo for a while now, and Guppy was paying his way through college by offering short-term leases on his central nervous system.

"You don't have to put it like that," Jillian said.

"Better this than the debt vortex," Alice said.

Guppy turned to Jillian, still grinning. "So, how much are they paying you to pop out a kid?"

"Excuse me?"

"No offense. I just wondered."

Jillian remained silent.

"They pay your health insurance?"

"There are a lot of medical expenses involved in having a child. I have a check-up every three weeks, and there are ultrasounds, amniocentesis." Jillian speared her salad greens with violence. The other housemates looked at one another.

Guppy scratched at the roots of his hair-thatch and continued, "Yeah, but I mean, if you had to have a mole removed, or something like that, they'd pay for that, too?"

"A mole."

"It'd be sweet to have health insurance," Guppy said. He stabbed an enormous pile of mizuna and chicken and stuffed it into his mouth. "I wish I could get pregnant for money."

"It's not a day at the spa," Jillian snapped. "There are all the hormone changes, you have to pee all the time, you're sore, you have weeks of morning sickness."

"Yeah, but you don't have to go to work."

"You don't sleep well. You have to be super careful about what you eat for the health of the baby. For the last two months you can't tie your shoes or get in and out of armchairs by yourself. Not to mention childbirth."

"Yeah, but still," Guppy said.

"You can't drink." Jillian gestured at Guppy's beer.

"Oh, that is a good point," Guppy conceded. "So, how did it work? They use a turkey baster?"

"And you have to suffer endless questions from fools," Jillian said. She pushed her plate away and left the table.

Guppy stuffed another hearty forkful of food into his mouth. "She's kinda touchy," he said to his other housemates through a jumble of chicken bits and greens. "Probably the hormones, huh?"

Chapter Thirty-Two

ELSA

Elsa's stay was the best possible antidote to Dori's woeful performance on the fencing *piste*.

"Guess what?" the sixth-grader said to Dori as they pulled away from the airplane hangar and turned toward Bridges. "I learned to French braid. I'll show you." She fixed her hair as they drove to Dori's condo. "See?"

"I see," said Dori, smiling. When they got home, Elsa, an enthusiast of Dori's condo, slipped her arm under Dori's and skipped up the walk with her.

"I thought we could take a bike ride tomorrow," Dori said, "if it's not raining. And that thing is out. In the sky. What's it called? It's been gone so long I can't remember."

Elsa was in on the joke right away. She scrunched up her face in mockery of hard thought. "That round thing? Yellow?"

"That's the one," said Dori as they climbed the stairs. "Emits warmth."

"The sun?"

Dori smacked herself on the forehead. "The sun! That's

it!" She unlocked the door and they went inside.

Elsa bounced once or twice on the yellow loveseat and sprang up again. "Guess what else? I got my ears pierced." She turned her head this way and that so Dori could admire the prim gold studs in both earlobes. "The left one got infected and got all oozy and red and I had to wipe it with rubbing alcohol three times a day."

"Did it hurt?"

Elsa shrugged. "Yeah," she said. "But it was interesting." She twisted her earrings in their holes.

"You never have been squeamish, have you?"

"Nuh-unh."

"That'll come in handy when you take biology."

"I can't wait to take biology! I want to dissect frogs," Elsa told her.

"I enjoyed dissecting frogs," Dori mused. "Except for the pithing."

"What's the pithing?"

"Sticking a needle in the frog's brain to kill it before you dissect it."

Elsa looked disconsolate. "They make you do that?"

"Sometimes."

"Why can't they just use frogs that are already dead?"

Dori said, "I imagine they're too hard to find."

"Well. That can be something I'll do when I'm older. I'll go through the forest finding dead frogs and I'll sell them to schools and laboratories so they don't have to kill perfectly good ones."

"I think that's a fine idea."

"Or I could raise them myself and donate the ones that have died of old age."

"Even better," Dori said. "Do you want to put your stuff in your room?" Elsa would sleep in Dori's office on an armchair that folded out into a slim twin bed.

"Yes. I love my room!" Elsa told her.

After a supper of macaroni and cheese, Dori and Elsa went to a movie, a spooky little PG-rated ghost story. Dori couldn't help but think of Linnea. She wondered if she should try to get some insight from Elsa about her situation. If anyone would have some, it would be Elsa. But she didn't want to tell her niece the truth, and she didn't want to lie.

Luckily, after the movie, Elsa volunteered her perspective on her own. "Do you believe in ghosts? I do. Only," she continued, not letting Dori respond, "I don't think they're all bad like in the movie."

They were sharing a roll of SweeTarts as they crossed the parking lot. Dori handed a purple one to Elsa, who liked the purple ones best. "Why is that?"

"It just makes sense to me. The ancient Romans believed there were three kinds of ghosts—good ones, bad ones and neutral ones."

Dori was startled. "The ancient Romans? Are you kidding me?"

"No," said Elsa, jutting out her chin a little as though affronted. "We studied six ancient civilizations and their ideas about the afterlife. The Romans had the best ones. Good ghosts were *Lāres*, neutral ghosts were *Manēs*, and bad ghosts were *Lemures* and they haunted Roman houses."

"Lemurs?" said Dori. "Ring-tailed tropical primates?"

"No, *Lemures*. The *Lemures* were bad people or they were people who had died prematurely or been murdered."

Dori nearly choked on a SweeTart.

Elsa continued, "They had a festival to make the *Lemures* go away."

"Really?" They had reached the Prius. Dori was listening

very carefully. She unlocked the doors and they got in, but she didn't start her engine yet. "How did they do that?" she asked.

"They walked around the house nine times in their bare feet spitting out black beans and chanting, 'With these beans I redeem me and mine,' and then they went inside and banged all their pots and pans together to scare the ghosts away."

The homeowners' association would love that, Dori thought. "Did they really?" she said. "You're not making this up?"

"No!" Elsa was insulted. "Why would I?"

"I'm sorry. It's just kind of funny, that's all."

"It *is* funny. I like the part with the beans," Elsa said, and they both started to giggle.

"I like the pots and pans," Dori said.

"I like the chant."

"I like that the ghosts are lemurs."

In the morning Dori awoke to Elsa bouncing at the foot of her bed and asking, "Are we going bike riding now?"

Dori rubbed her face. "Well," she smiled, "I thought we could start by making pancakes. And then I have a proposal, which I'll explain to you over breakfast. You tell me what you think."

After pancakes they went to visit the downstairs neighbors to borrow a bicycle and, if Dori were in luck, to draw them into her conspiracy.

The Pheasants were no taller than Dori, and were round like gnomes. Chesterfield had tufts of white hair growing from his ears, and though Frannie didn't, they might have suited her. Frannie said, "You'd better come in and have some orange juice. I've just squeezed it, and it's divine."

The Pheasants won Elsa over right away by dispensing with questions about what grade she was in and how she liked school, choosing instead to get right to the good stuff: "Elsa, can you yodel?"

She couldn't, so Chesterfield commenced a yodeling lesson and they practiced there in the dining room until Elsa produced a passable yodeleheehoo. Then, as if Elsa hadn't charmed the Pheasants already by being so game, she captivated them by announcing that today was Lemūria, the day of chasing out *lemures*, and explaining in detail how it was done.

"Aunt Dori and I are going to observe Lemūria," Elsa told them.

"And we wondered if you'd care to join us," Dori said.

"Heavens, yes," said Frannie without hesitation.

"It sounds as though we'd better," Chesterfield put in. "We don't want lemurs prowling around. The raccoons are bad enough."

"Do they get into the garbage, do you suppose?" Frannie asked.

Dori had reasoned in her own mind that the only way to undertake the ritual without drawing undue attention from the neighbors was to include them, and make it appear that they were indulging a child's whims. Dori felt a little bad not coming clean to Elsa. But they would all have fun, and the ritual just might have the effect of laying Linnea to rest, even without her heart.

So they got out some pots and pans and took off their shoes, and Frannie found a jar of dried black beans and counted out nine for each of them. "Careful not to swallow them, now," warned Frannie. "They'll give you a bellyache."

They went marching round the periphery of the condo, spitting black beans into the azalea bushes. It was a little hard to chant with beans in one's mouth, and the resulting mumbles and pursed lips amused them all. After they'd made their rounds they sent up a great clatter by banging on pans with spoons.

"There!" said Chesterfield with satisfaction. "That should do the job. No ancient Romans tipping over *our* garbage."

When Elsa and Dori left, the Pheasants sent a bicycle with them.

"Are we going for our ride right now?" asked Elsa.

"If you want. Do you need anything to eat or drink first?"

"Nuh-unh."

"Okay. Well, get a layer, in case it goes behind the clouds. That thing... What's it called?"

"The sun?"

"The sun."

Elsa was wearing a T-shirt that read *Sans souci*—a gift from Dori—and flare-legged pants printed with blue horses. She grabbed a jacket from the apartment and they headed for a nearby city park, pedaling down Dori's street and turning onto Catullus, a quiet street with a bike lane that led them through some of Bridges' quainter neighborhoods. Once in a while they stopped to look at something: a funny bumper sticker, an unusual tree. The last block of the street leading to the park ran steeply downhill. At the bottom it narrowed to a dirt lane that went right into the park itself. It was a fine place to bike, because you could fly down the hill as fast as you wanted without worrying about having to stop for oncoming traffic.

"Race ya to the bottom," Elsa said.

"You're on." Dori began to pedal as fast as she could, wind singing in her ears. Elsa did, too, weaving in front of Dori and leaning over her handlebars for aerodynamic efficiency. They were going at top speed when the flared leg of Elsa's pants got caught in her chain and she flew right over the handlebars and skidded across the asphalt.

"Shit!" Dori swerved, slammed on her brakes and leaped off her own bike. "Are you okay? Oh, honey."

Elsa had scraped the skin off both elbows and both palms, which were darkening as blood rose to the surface beneath ragged bits of epidermis. Dori turned Elsa's arms gently and examined her wounds. "Ouch," she said with empathy. "I'm so sorry, Elsa."

"I I I I'm okay," Elsa said in breathy little near-sobs. "I'm okay."

"Did you hurt anything else?"

"Just my chin. And my knees," said Elsa. She'd gotten a hard knock on the chin and would have a purple spot there later. "And my elbows and my hands. I'm okay. I mean,"— she wiped her nose on the shoulder of her T-shirt—"I'll be okay in a minute."

"We should try to wash these scrapes so they don't get infected," Dori said. "Do you think you can walk your bike a little ways?"

On the other side of the park was a Shell station, and they made their way, Elsa hobbling, through the grass and across the street to get there. They tended Elsa's wounds with soap-dispenser soap and paper towels in the women's room, and then Dori went into the station and found some band-aids for sale.

"I have to tell you," she said to Elsa as she bandaged the last of her niece's skid marks, "that was a first-rate accident. One of the most spectacular wipe-outs I've ever seen."

Elsa laughed.

Dori continued, "I was going to suggest we do this after lunch so we wouldn't spoil our appetites, but I think under the circumstances we need to go have some ice cream right now. What do you think?"

They walked their bicycles down the street to Bovine Divine. After a few licks of her treat of choice, Elsa became her chatty self again.

"My friend Nancy can't eat ice cream," she said in the hushed, sympathetic tone of someone witnessing another's great loss. "She's allergic to cow's milk. At home she drinks goat milk,"—she paused to stick out her tongue—"but they don't make goat ice cream."

"I wonder why not," Dori said. "They make goat cheese and goat yogurt."

"That's foul," said Elsa.

"They make water buffalo yogurt."

Elsa giggled. "They do not."

"They do! I've seen it in the food co-op. I suppose," Dori continued, "you could make yogurt from the milk of any mammal."

"Any mammal that would let you milk it," Elsa said astutely. That led to a discussion of dairy products they were unlikely to find on the shelves of the co-op. Badger Bars. Cheetah Cheddar. Wolverine Whipping Cream.

In the late afternoon, Dori showed Elsa some cat's cradle, and Elsa taught Dori some hand-clapping games. They turned on the radio and danced around the living room singing into hairbrushes. They attempted to French braid, with ridiculous results, Dori's soap-bubble hair. Elsa's folks came to get her after dinner, and Dori waved good-bye from her window, sorry that anyone ever had to grow up.

Chapter Thirty-Three

ALICE'S PARTY

Alice and Tad lay on the floor in the living room, a little stoned, staring at the textured ceiling of the house on Baudelaire. It was the tail end of Alice's birthday party.

She'd been out all day, trying to keep herself busy so she wouldn't brood, and had come home to find that the living room window—the only way into the house—was locked. She'd banged on it, and after a time Guppy had appeared. He did not undo the locks, but instead pressed his mouth to the glass, cupping his hands at his face, and shouted to her.

"We're not using the window any more!"

"Why?"

"Jillian is too pregnant! She can't get in and out!"

"What are we supposed to do?"

"The landlord's coming over to fix the door!" Guppy shouted. "He said to stop using the window!"

"When? Right now?"

"I think so."

Alice had to pee. "I need to get in. Just unlock the

window!"

"I can't."

"Why?"

Guppy disappeared, then reappeared shortly. "Never mind," he said, undoing the latches. He slid the window open and reached a hand into the yard, although Alice was perfectly capable of hopping up and through the window by herself.

It was all a ruse. Friends jumped out from behind the couch, hollering "Surprise!" They'd brought pizza and cake and beer and pot and presents, which were piled on the old hospital gurney in the center of the room. They'd fashioned an enormous "20" out of discarded flotation devices and tacked it to the wall.

"Did you organize all this?" Alice asked Tad.

"Gremlins came and did it in the night," he said, pulling her to him with his lanky arm and giving her a big wet kiss.

Guppy was the first to step up with a gift. "I brought you this," he said, handing Alice a program from the Division III college basketball tournament, "in honor of the illustrious anniversary of your birth." Guppy tapped the back page. "There's the schedule for next season," he told her. "Bear it in mind."

Alice had little interest in glossy pictures of lay-ups and bios of the players, but she noticed that the schedule included upcoming dates for dance team tryouts. She'd forgotten all about the Marmettes, and the schedule got her attention for a moment, until other friends stepped over to Alice with their own gifts: origami paper, *The Pocket Marcuse,* a plastic shower cap to put over the seat of her parked bike when it was raining, soap for blowing bubbles, a holographic Julius Caesar refrigerator magnet. Jillian had baked oatmeal cookies for her (Alice did wonder about Jillian being able to get in and out of the house through the window, but she never got a chance to ask her about it). Amy gave her a pair of elbow-length purple velvet gloves, and Tad a calligraphy pen "for writing on bathroom walls," he said. "You should carry it with you at all times."

"Okay. Good idea," Alice said. She did like to write on walls—especially in Latin—and would like it even better if she could do it in fine calligraphy. Tad passed the pen in a fancy case to her and promised some cunnilingus as well.

Tad was obviously pleased with the fête, which he'd probably gone to a lot of trouble to arrange. Alice hung close by him over the course of the evening, enjoying the heft of his arm slung over her shoulders, dancing with him from time to time.

Later, lying on the floor next to her boyfriend and floating about six inches outside herself, she thought, This is how it's supposed to be—this companionship that's so comfortable and at the same time so unfettered, free. When Tad had taken up with Amy, Alice had disappointed herself with her own dismay. Wasn't this arrangement exactly what they'd envisioned? Their relationship, they had always said, would not be in a cage. Like happy chickens, their love would be organic and free-ranging. If she loved Tad, she shouldn't want to own him, to restrict him, and vice versa. As they lay on the floor together, their shoulders lightly touching, Alice felt herself relax into acceptance. Yes. This had been their vision. They had what they had always wanted. The very reality of it confirmed the strength of their arrangement.

She didn't say any of this to Tad. Instead, she studied the ceiling for a long time, watching the patterns in the cheap texturing anthropomorphize themselves. She said, "I never appreciated this ceiling before. I always thought it was tacky."

"No, no indeed," said Tad expansively. "It's a whole fairy

kingdom. Look. See the castle?" He pointed at one particularly elaborate formation. "It's inhabited by the tiny upside-down people."

They giggled at the ceiling for a while, holding hands and spinning out stories about it, until Jillian came down the stairs in her nightgown and ordered them to shut up.

Chapter Thirty-Four

DISHEARTENED

Dori was flossing her teeth a few minutes after Elsa left when Linnea said to her, "Dori. How could you?"

Dori's head jerked up.

Linnea was standing in the bathtub. "I'm sorry, but I'm very offended," she continued. "What were you trying to pull with the Lemuria?"

"Hi. Oh. The Lemuria." Dori took a few steps back. "I thought it might allow you to—rest in peace." A piece of floss was dangling from between her teeth.

"You're trying to get rid of me."

"No, no," Dori protested. "It's just that—since I haven't managed to get the heart yet—I thought it might help."

"That business with the beans. You know what they're for, don't you?"

"Um. Not exactly."

"The *Lemures* accept beans in lieu of the souls of people in the family. I'm hardly after anybody's *soul*, Dori, for crying out loud."

"Oh." Dori didn't know what to say. She pulled the floss from between her molars. "I'm sorry."

"I'm not *haunting* you. Is that what you think? Are we not understanding one another?"

Dori had backed away to the point that the towel hook on the door was poking her in the back of the head. "No, I understand," she said miserably. "I mean, I don't understand, but I *am* trying to get the heart. I just keep running into dead ends." Dori started to tell her about sneaking into the forensics building, but Linnea didn't seem to want to hear the details.

"Four days," she was all she said, and she pulled the shower curtain closed before her.

Dori sat down on the toilet seat to think. She could not do this alone. It was time to fess up to Pablo. She would need to tell him everything and try to enlist his help, as desperate a gesture as that seemed. And she'd need to do it on their getaway, as soon as they had time alone together. He was coming to take her to the airport in an hour.

The hotel in San Diego was spendy. It was silly to shell out that kind of money on a lover you weren't in love with, but the price of their room was an ant among the elephants of Dori's problems. She spent the whole night not telling Pablo about Linnea and the heart. Instead, she started undressing him as soon as they'd set their bags down.

She could have told him in the morning, but instead, she claimed to be starving, and they went to the breakfast buffet downstairs. Dori took her time at the fruit bowl, picking up one berry at a time with the serving tongs. Not only had she failed to tell Pablo what she needed to tell him, but she'd reinforced his view that she was really into him.

As they took their seats with their laden plates, Pablo said,

"You know my mother lives here."

Dori's heart dropped into her pointy shoes. She'd been afraid of this moment since Pablo had brought up San Diego. He must want to take her to meet his mother, because he thought Dori was Somebody Special. This was a bad, bad idea. When she finally ended their affair, he was going to get his heart broken.

"I have a couple things I'd like to do for her today," Pablo continued. "But you don't have to tag along, unless you want to. You can do your own thing, and we could meet back up in a couple hours. Would that be okay?"

Dori nodded with more cheer than necessary. She'd been granted a reprieve—and an excuse to delay the inevitable for a little while longer.

Breakfast behind them, they walked a few blocks to the Embarcadero and watched little tongues of water lick the yachts docked up and down the bay. Dori waited a polite number of minutes after their meal to bring up dead bodies.

"So Linnea's brother," she said.

"The one who refuses to manage her estate."

"Yes. He'll still have to deal with funeral arrangements and all that, won't he?"

"No. He could decline to pay for the disposal of her remains."

"He can do that?"

"Sure."

"Well—what happens then? Does Linnea become a ward of the state?"

"Of the county, actually. If the deceased or the family has no money to cover the costs, the taxpayers pick up the tab," Pablo explained. "Or sometimes the funeral homes do the work pro bono."

"But Linnea had means."

"In cases like hers, the estate will eventually pay the costs of her cremation or burial, but it will have to go through the courts."

"Really! Doesn't that take forever?"

"It can take months. She'll probably stay at the funeral home for a good long time."

Dori opened her mouth to tell Pablo about her strange errand, but she chickened out. Instead she said, "And what about the heart? I guess it went with her to whatever funeral home..."

"The heart's still with us," Pablo said. "The investigators wanted to hang on to it a little longer." His eyebrows drew together in sympathy. "You're still looking for closure, huh?"

Pablo took a trolley north of downtown to visit his mom and Dori stayed in the city center, content to have time alone among the refreshing distractions of a tourist destination. It was 74 degrees and cloudless, the sky an insouciant chalk-blue. Dori hadn't been able to go about in short sleeves for six months, and now she felt as though she'd been lifted into someone else's life. How could the sky be so blue if one's best friend had been murdered? Then again, how could one be weighed down by worry if the sun were so brassy and bold?

She met Pablo in Little Italy for a late lunch. An Italian restaurant might be dangerously romantic, but Dori decided she could regard the meal not as encouragement to her lover but as simple professional development. Besides, they were the only patrons here. She should use the opportunity to reveal her quest.

The waiter approached, and Dori asked him, "*Di dov'è?*"

"*Di Napoli.*" He smiled like one who smiles for a living—

friendly enough to ensure good tips, but not genuinely delighted to have a tourist practice her Italian on him. But Dori's Italian was better than most tourists', and soon she was chatting away with their dark-eyed server.

Dori was aware of talking a little too long. Courtesy demanded that she turn her attention back to Pablo. Maybe if he finds me rude, she thought, he won't like me so much. Then she scolded herself for being passive-aggressive.

The waiter said to Pablo, "Your companion is quite an Italian speaker!"

Pablo responded, "*È tutto pepe!*" She's all pepper—that is, she's quite something; she's a live wire.

Dori turned with new eyes to Pablo. "*Parlai Italiano tu?*"

"Not a lot," Pablo told her. "But I understand it pretty well. It sounds like Spanish with a funny accent."

The realization hit Dori like a falling safe.

Pablo wasn't boring at *all*. Foolish Dori! She'd been resisting emotional involvement, telling herself Pablo was dull, but look—he was *trilingual*! He was funny, he was kind, he was well-read and musical, he spoke two romance languages—he was perfect. He was wonderful! Oh, my God, Dori thought.

Her heart sank almost as soon as it had leaped. Now she couldn't tell him about Linnea's request. He'd think she was delusional, and that would pretty much put the kibosh on his amorous intentions.

But if she didn't enlist his help, she'd be letting Linnea down, abandoning her to ancient Roman authorities. She didn't know exactly what that meant, but she was getting the impression it was something pretty bad. Would she have to choose between them? If she remained loyal to Linnea, would that dash all hope she had for this thing with Pablo?

Even if she could somehow avoid letting him in on the

business of the heart, her secret was keeping her from being her best self with him. He could grow weary of her anxiety, her cageyness, her obsession with Linnea's corpse. She started imagining multiple ways in which things with Pablo could fall apart, and she saw the dreadful truth: if it didn't work out, she would be crushed.

Chapter Thirty-Five

THE PSYCHIC

As her time ticked away, Linnea wondered if she had any loose ends from being alive to tie up. If she did, she'd better take care of them soon. She let her mind rove over the trappings of her days on Earth. She'd been to campus; she'd been to her house; she'd been relieved of all her possessions relating to both. Oh—there was one meaningful task she'd left undone. She remembered that her student Alice had asked her for a letter of recommendation for the Millicent Vena Cava Award. Alice's request had come the week before Linnea's murder, and Linnea hadn't written the letter before she was killed. She felt bad about it and thought now that maybe she could perform one last service for a favorite student before she left this plane for good. She knew how much these letters meant to students, for whom a solid scholarship application often made the difference between being able to stay in school or not.

If she could weft into the computer lab at Middlebridge, she could probably compose the letter quietly at a computer in a back row and print it on the networked printer without anyone noticing. She had never tried to weft such a distance before, but Vergil had said it could be done. Linnea took a breath and called forth an image of the computer lab. The image appeared, but so did others from Middlebridge: Dean Budgie, Linnea's dog-eared copy of *De Bellō Gallicō*, the copper beeches on the green, Ned Callow. These mental pictures came at her with such rapid fire she could not control them. Before she'd blinked, she found herself standing between a urinal and Ned Callow, who was at that very moment unzipping his fly.

Linnea let out a cry when she saw him. Callow staggered backward, his fly undone. "I didn't mean it!" he gurgled. "I'm sorry! I didn't mean it!"

Linnea squeezed her eyes shut and thought very hard about the back row of the college computer lab. When she opened her eyes, she was there.

Panting, Linnea took a seat at a computer and ran her hands through her dark hair. Of all the things Ned Callow might have blurted out, Linnea hadn't expected him to say what he did. Clearly he thought she was haunting him, and just as clearly, he had a guilty conscience. Was he confessing to her murder? It was the only thing that made sense.

Linnea drew a deep breath and forced herself to quell her thoughts. She needed to think carefully about the issue, but she was afraid that if she dwelled on the feckless substitute Latin teacher she would pop back into the men's room again. The last thing she wanted was to get peed on by Ned Callow.

She would have to set the matter aside for now. After quieting her mind, Linnea turned to Alice's letter. She praised the young woman's intellectual curiosity, her creative spirit, her hard work and gumption and her passion for Latin, and made the argument that it would be a frightful shame if Alice could not afford to stay in school. Linnea spent an hour or so on the letter, read it over a few times for final edits, and printed it off. She slipped it out of the printer when no one was looking and tried to conjure up the faculty mail room.

She didn't know how she went awry so badly, but Linnea not only overshot the mail room but sent herself clean off campus. She landed on the other side of the river in the industrial district. Linnea frowned at her dismal wefting skills. At least she hadn't plunked herself right into the water. She looked around. She wasn't exactly sure where in Bridges she was.

A set of old railroad tracks, no longer in use, crossed the road. To her east and west lay warehouses, their great doors open to loading docks, wooden pallets piled outside each one. This end of the city was a little seedy and forlorn. Rent was low out here and business not brisk. Linnea saw a lifeless form in the street and cringed, thinking it was a dead animal, but as she drew nearer she saw that it was only a dead plastic bag.

She picked her way down the block, mindful of buckles in the sidewalk. She was hoping to spot some obvious landmark when she encountered an old Airstream trailer flying a purple flag. It sat on an otherwise empty lot. A hand-lettered sign in the window offered psychic readings. Linnea stopped to consider whether a psychic could be of any use to her. Given that the Buddhists and the Christians didn't want her, Linnea supposed the likelihood of some other hereafter opening its doors to her was remote. There seemed little point in visiting the heavens of additional traditions, if she could even locate them. Besides, it would take all of eternity to explore all the eternities, and she was running out of time. In just three days, Evil Claws and Evil Tail would be coming after her, puncturing and squeezing and lacerating her and then hauling her away to a lake of liquid nitrogen or flaming shit. If Dori hadn't procured Linnea's heart for her by then, Linnea had better have come up with a good solid alternative. She had some doubts about the authenticity of a psychic's services, but she was getting desperate.

She approached the Airstream and tapped on its aluminum door. Lights were on in the little trailer and through the small window Linnea could see a medium at a pull-down table. Thankfully, the woman did not wear a turban, nor did she have a crystal ball. She wore jeans and flip flops and had red hair braided into two long pigtails.

The psychic opened the door. Her mouth opened wide. "Jesus and the Twelve Disciples!" she said. "You're the real deal." She scrambled to get behind her chair, barricading herself.

"I guess maybe I am," said Linnea, embarrassed. "I'm sorry to alarm you."

The psychic gripped the back of her chair.

"I was hoping to get a reading from you."

"You were?"

"I need some guidance," Linnea said, "either from you, or,"—she gestured at the air around them, as though it might be full of dearly departed—"or whoever."

The psychic stared at Linnea, then relaxed her grip on the chair. "You're not here to avenge someone?" she asked. "The thing with the fish? You're not upset about the thing with the fish?"

Linnea shook her head.

Without taking her eyes off Linnea, the psychic moved out from behind her chair. "Okay," she said. "Okay. Come in. Leave the door open, would you?"

Linnea stepped into the tiny trailer. The air inside was close. Two small windows afforded little natural light, and the space was cluttered with a medium's instruments and a lot of skin-care products. Linnea squeezed into the trailer's only other chair with her back to the open door.

"Okay," said the psychic. "Tell me."

"First things first," Linnea said. "I don't have any money. I can't pay you. But I need your help."

The redheaded woman considered. "I'm open to barter," she said. "Would you be willing to run an errand for me after we finish?"

"Of course."

"So, how can I help you?"

"I'm stuck," Linnea explained. "I keep getting rejected by different afterlives, and the one that *will* take me I don't want. I need to know: are there any religious traditions that accept non-members after death, and how do I get in touch with them? Or is there somewhere else I can go to spend eternity— some neutral territory?"

The psychic took one end of a long braid and began to play with it, thinking. "I have to tell you," she said, "I've never been faced with exactly this request before."

"I'm not surprised."

"I'll see what I can do," said the psychic. She stretched her arms out, gripping the edges of her table, and shut her eyes. Her eyelids fluttered, and she said aloud, "No... no...no... I'm striking out here... no... no... Bingo." Her eyes flew open. "I found one for you," she told Linnea. "Grab that pen and paper, would you?"

Linnea searched a cluttered shelf beside her for something to write on.

"It's not exactly a religion," the psychic said. "They can guarantee you 39 hours a week of work, and as long as your performance is satisfactory, the other authorities will leave you alone." She scribbled on the paper.

Linnea took it, eager to see. "Wal-Mart?" she read.

"Honestly, it's kind of like Hell, only not as hot," the psychic said. "But they'll take you, no questions asked."

Linnea slumped back in her chair. "That's it? That's all you've got?"

"Pretty much," the psychic said. "The afterlives tend to be pretty exclusive. Even the crummy ones. You have to pay your dues while you're alive."

"I see." Linnea looked down, tracing a design on her thigh with one finger.

"So about that errand," the psychic said.

Linnea looked up.

"I had a client try to exorcise a demon," the psychic said, "by putting a dead fish in the demon's bed. But I'm having second thoughts about it. Would you mind running over to her house and getting rid of the fish?"

Linnea wasn't sure about that. "What if I get caught?"

"The demon has a day job," the psychic said. "It's probably safe to go over to her house during business hours."

"Okay," said Linnea against her own better judgment. "What should I do with the fish?"

The fortune-teller fiddled with the hairband at the tail of one of her braids. "You will need to dispose of it properly," she said. "Otherwise you might rile up all the demons in the neighborhood."

That didn't sound good. "What is 'properly'?" Linnea said.

"Best-case scenario would be if it were consumed."

"I have to *eat* it? How long has it been unrefrigerated?"

"It needs to be transformed," the psychic said.

Linnea found this advice unhelpful, but she was stuck with the problem now.

"I'm sorry about my little freak-out earlier," the psychic

told her. "I commune with spirits, but I don't usually see them in the flesh. You kind of caught me by surprise."

Linnea decided to take advantage of the psychic's contrition. "There's something else," Linnea told her. She hoped to milk at least a little wisdom out of this visit, especially since she'd agreed to do the psychic an unappetizing favor. "I have a colleague. His name is Ned Callow. He took my job after I was killed, and I need to know—did he murder me?"

The psychic jotted down a few details about the oafish Callow and then closed her eyes and consulted the spirits. Her eyelids fluttered. "I'm not getting any hint of that," she said. She kept her eyes shut a while longer. "No," she said finally. "No. It doesn't look like he was involved."

"Hunh." Linnea was surprised—not because she had really thought Ned Callow had it in him to cut her heart out, but because she couldn't imagine what else he could have been confessing to. She thought hard.

"Did he pass secrets about union organizing to Management?" she asked.

The psychic closed her eyes again. She frowned; she rolled her head toward the ceiling. "Mmmmm," she said, and then, finally, "No. Not getting anything like that."

Linnea was frustrated. "Well, he did something he thought I wouldn't like. Can you find out what it is?"

The psychic glanced at the clock. "I'll make one more ask."

Her eyelids dropped and she stretched her arms out, trembling slightly. "Oh," she said aloud after a moment. "Yes, I see. Thank you, spirits."

Her eyes sprang open. She fixed Linnea with her gaze and told the erstwhile professor, "He fucked up your Latin class."

Chapter Thirty-Six

THE LARRIES

Alice was distracted by recurring thoughts of the conversation she'd overheard between Guppy and Dexter. At the time, she'd dismissed it, but lately it had been nagging at her, as if some nugget of crucial information had passed between those two, and she'd just missed understanding what it was. She kept replaying the incident in her head, and she was still thinking about it as she approached the tip rail after her first set.

A patron in a trench coat and whose hair was hitting his collar asked her, "What's your name, baby?"

"Baby," she repeated. Baby was not her stage name. She'd just had a moment of distraction-induced echolalia. Many of Alice's co-workers took alcoholic beverages as their stripper names—Sherry, Brandy, Absinthe. Others picked something edible—Cinnamon, Sugar—or something tantalizing and out of reach—Mystery, No-no. Diminutives went over well, given patrons' propensity to infantilize the dancers, especially if the name doubled as a sexual euphemism. Alice worked with two

Cherries, two Candies and one Lollipop. At Cootchie-Coo, she herself went by "Jalapeña." But the name "Baby" apparently went over well with this patron.

"I like your goo-goo ga-ga, Baby," he told her.

Alice leaned over the rail and put the tip of her finger in her mouth with a childish pout.

"Does Baby want to sit in my lap?"

Lap dancing was against state law. "I'm not allowed to," she said in a toddler's voice. The patron pulled out a bill and handed it to her.

"Goodie!" she exclaimed, and the man in need of a haircut laughed.

Alice noticed the two Larries watching the interaction, and she skirted them as she moved on to collect other tips.

Back in the dressing room, Alice pulled out her homework, but she couldn't focus on calculus. She kept thinking that the conversation she'd overheard between Guppy and Dexter Beet was related in some way she couldn't fathom to Dr. Nil's murder. And when she'd exhausted her ruminations in that regard, worry about murder do-si-do'ed itself to worry about money. She'd realized that Cootchie-Coo might not have extra hours to offer her. She might have to work two jobs. Until now she had only worked nights, keeping her daytime hours safe for classes. If she loaded up all her classes on two or three days a week, she could dance mornings and afternoons the other days. But when would she study?

Alice danced until midnight this night, and then, because she needed every dollar of her tip money to pay for her share of rent and groceries, she did something she'd never done before—she set out for home on foot. She'd pulled on sweat pants and a rain jacket over her fishnets and slung her school backpack over one shoulder. It wasn't a sufficient camouflage. As she crossed the parking lot, two men fell into step beside her, one on either side.

"Where you headed, 'Baby'?" said one Larry.

Alice said nothing—*nē timōrem exhibeam,* she thought; lest I show fear—but her mind whirled, trying to think how to shake the men. She turned, not too quickly, and headed back toward the club door.

"I thought her name was Banana Split. With whipped cream and a cherry," said the other.

"Let's split her open and find out," said the first Larry.

There was no one else on the street. The fast-food joint next door was closed for the night. Across the way, a car wash stood empty and gray in shadow. Each of the Larries grabbed one of Alice's upper arms and began to steer her toward the rows of cars parked behind Cootchie-Coo.

"Hey!" She yelled as loudly as she could and struggled to free herself.

Alice had heard about the surge of strength that could come with fear—ordinary people suddenly being able to lift Volkswagens, for example, in a dire emergency. Though she tried not to take risks, Alice had always thought she'd be able to hold her own in a struggle. She had faith in her adrenaline.

So she was surprised and very dismayed when her writhing and kicking did not deter the Larries. She might be motivated, but they were bigger than she was, and there were two of them. Even after a little struggle she began to feel her energy flag, and she realized they could just wait her out.

One of the Larries was digging his fingers into the flesh of her upper arm. She turned her head and bit his hand. He yelled, and the other Larry laughed. They corralled her into the shadow of the building. Alice was breathing hard. Her heart was jackhammering.

The back door of the club opened and three of Alice's co-workers stepped out of the light and began to cross the parking lot together. When the Larries saw them, they dropped Alice's arms and soon shuffled away toward their cars. Alice hurled a few epithets at their backs before joining her friends.

"What was that about?" said one dancer. "Were they hassling you?"

"*Semper idem*," Alice muttered.

"What?"

"Always the same old shit," Alice translated. She turned and went back into the club to have a word with her manager.

Chapter Thirty-Seven

PERSEVERANCE IS A VIRTUE

When she got back to Bridges from San Diego the following day, Dori called Kristin. "Okay, I just realized," she told her sister without preamble. "He's not boring. He's perfect."

"Well, good," Kristin replied, noncommittal. "That settles that."

"No! Not good!" Dori cried. "Are you hearing me? He's perfect! Sooner or later he's going to realize how *not*-perfect I am and get disgusted with me."

"Don't be daft," her sister snapped. "He saw your performance at the fencing tournament, didn't he?"

"Yes." Dori shuddered to remember.

"Well? Did he make any unpleasant remarks about it afterward?"

"No."

"Did he offer unsolicited advice on your technique?"

"No. How could he? He doesn't fence."

"That doesn't stop some people. Was he snide? Was he condescending?"

"No, of course not. He was great."

"Well, there you go. He already knows you're not perfect. And he's okay with it."

"Really?"

"Dori. Your flaws aren't all that well hidden. If he was going to dump you for being flawed, he would have done it by now."

Dori was in her office, and she should have been getting work done, but after ending her phone consultation with Kristin, she instead did an on-line search for funeral homes. Eleven were listed for the greater Bridges area. She started calling them, and nine dreary conversations later she located Linnea. The Latin professor was in storage at Peaceful Departures across town. Absent consent from Linnea's brother, who, they said, had not responded to repeated attempts at communication, the body was going nowhere. That was probably good news from Dori's point of view. But she still didn't have a plan.

Midterms were coming up, and Dori checked over her grade book. She thought for a moment and then descended to the student lounge in the basement, looking for Tad, who had been cutting class. She thought he might be down there practicing again with the band. No such luck. As Dori headed toward the stair she heard a familiar voice. Her veins flushed cold. The back stairs were too far—she wouldn't be able to escape that way. She looked around and ducked behind the big boiler—pulling a Linnea—to hide from the Dean of Allocations. If Fiercey caught sight of her, she would pin Dori like an insect to a mounting board and demand the list of expendable French faculty.

The dean's booming voice preceded her in the stairwell, followed by her great bosom like the prow of a ship, and finally by Dean Eleanor Fiercey herself. She was accompanied by a workman. "It wouldn't be expensive," he was telling her. "We'd just need your signature on the work order. This is it here."

The two of them stopped at the out-of-order electrical outlet, the one with the hand-written sign taped to it, on the wall near the staircase. "This is the student lounge," Dean Fiercey said with distaste.

"Yeah. You can see it's a simple—"

"I don't trust them. The students. Given the privilege of electricity, they abuse it. They've already proven they aren't to be trusted."

Dori peeked around the side of the boiler. The workman laughed uneasily, uncertain if the dean were joking. She wasn't.

After teaching, Dori headed for a café a few blocks from the college to meet with the union organizers. Isabelle Grenouille had told Dori on the phone she had important news. Of course she couldn't go into detail on the phone. They would meet at Two Lumps, Please.

As a precautionary measure, the organizers arrived from different directions and parked in a scattered way in a three- or four-block radius around the café. Grenouille, Ian Elf, Bleistift and a few others trickled in over a 45-minute period, careful to not arrive all at once. Over monstrously strong coffee, the faculty who were key to the unionizing efforts leaned in close to each other so they could hear above the din from the kitchen.

Ian Elf was new to Middlebridge and not well known outside the English department, so he had been chosen to do some espionage for the union effort the previous night. He'd posed as a member of the organization Indignant Taxpayers.

Ostensibly a local grassroots organization, the group had funding from big out-of-state corporate sponsors. Its *raison d'être* was the contention that taxes in any form were unconstitutional, and it especially loathed the burden of public education. Organization lobbyists had convinced the state legislature to lop even more funding from state colleges and universities. They'd also found a special friend in Eleanor Fiercey.

In his guise as an Indignant Taxpayer, Elf had infiltrated a meeting of the budget subcommittee of the Board of Regents in the faculty lounge of Verizon Wireless Hall, and he wanted to share with his colleagues what he'd learned there.

At the board meeting, Dean Fiercey had unveiled a new budget initiative presenting a fresh idea for cutting the cost of instruction and saving the taxpayers money. Universities had long stayed in the black by denying instructors tenure— keeping turnover high to keep salaries low—and by giving more and more classes to part-time faculty, who taught the same classes as their full-time colleagues but for half the wages and without benefits. They also farmed out lower-division classes to graduate teaching assistants, who earned only a stipend and were even less likely to unionize than part-time instructors.

But no one else had hit on a cost-cutting idea as far-reaching as Dean Fiercey's. There among the mauve suede furniture of the faculty lounge, the dean had turned to a fresh page on her flip chart, beamed at the regents, and said, "Work-study students!"

The members of the board had raised their eyebrows and lowered their lips in expressions of appreciative thought.

Certain students took jobs on campus to earn money while they attended school, and the funds for these positions came not from the college's coffers, but from the federal government. Most work-study students were library pages and errand runners, but Fiercey didn't see any reason why their job descriptions couldn't be expanded. As for the requirements that professors have doctorates, well, they'd been bending that rule for years. A college must, after all, have flexibility.

The easiest department to staff in this new way, Fiercey went on to explain with vigor, would be the English department. Most work-study students were English speakers; why not have them take on the English classes?

In the faculty lounge, the members of the board reclined on the beautifully upholstered couches and murmured among themselves as they considered the possibilities.

"I thought I was going to have an aneurysm," Elf said. "But I didn't break character. I barked, 'hear, hear,' and one of the board members clapped me on the back."

"Did she say anything about foreign languages?" Dori asked.

"Actually, one of the board members suggested that international students on work-study teach them. But Fiercey intimated that the foreign languages departments were already being—how did she put it?—*rendered*," Elf said.

Of course Elf and the others asked Dori if she'd come up with Linnea's notes, and she had to admit that she had not, and that she'd run out of places to look for them.

Dori returned to campus to finish up some paperwork. As she crossed the green toward Verizon Wireless Hall, she saw Dean Budgie stepping out from behind a copper beech, almost as though he'd been lying in wait. He stopped Dori in her tracks.

"Dr. Amore," he said simply. "The Mid-Year Assessment."

"Yes! Yes, I'm nearly finished with it," Dori lied. She wished she had some pastel mints to offer him.

Dean Budgie fixed her with a cold eye for a moment, as though he didn't believe her. Then he said, "There are some additional items that need to be appended, due to an upcoming accreditation team visit. I have a list here." The MADCAP already demanded documentation of program improvement in a multitude of areas. Middlebridge expected its faculty, over time, to produce a continuous increase in enrollment, retention, number of graduates, average starting salaries of alumni, and cumulative grade-point averages, as well as student IQs, height, and ratio of good to bad cholesterol.

Dean Budgie reached into an inner suit coat pocket and pulled out a handful of items. "This isn't it," he said, impassive, returning them to that pocket and reaching for the other side. Dori tried to keep a poker face while her mind whirled like a slot machine. In that first suit coat pocket, among Budgie's glasses and other papers, was a small flowered notebook. Linnea's flowered notebook. The flowered notebook with all her union notes inside.

Dori was certain that the notebook contained minutes from all the organizing meetings, including the all-important meeting that occurred a few hours before Linnea's murder, as well as an outline of the plan to call for a vote, documentation of decanal behavior and management abuses, and, of course, the names of everyone involved in the unionization effort.

Budgie pulled a list from the other side of his jacket and began enumerating points that Dori needed to include in the Classics MADCAP.

She nodded with each thing he said, but she couldn't take in his words at all.

"When did you say I can expect it?" Budgie asked at last.

Dori hadn't said, but she plucked an arbitrary date from the near future and scurried away as quickly as she could without—she hoped—looking frightened. Or at least not more frightened than was merited by the MADCAP.

Chapter Thirty-Eight

MISS LONELYHEARTS

The medium had scribbled down an address for her, but Linnea didn't know the street, so she couldn't just weft there. She'd have to find a map. She hurried down the road to the nearest gas station. Among sticks of beef jerky and bags of chips she found a rack of maps and began turning it. The cashier looked up sharply at the sound of the rack squeaking and frowned to see it turning by itself. Linnea stopped, chiding herself for her carelessness. She idled, waiting until the cashier had to leave the building to help someone unjam a bathroom door. She was still not used to invisibility. Even in a mostly solitary life, Linnea had never felt so hollow and bereft as when she wandered the streets of Bridges unseen.

She plucked a map from the rack and unfolded it, studying the streets until she located the one she was looking for. The house was in the college district—Linnea wondered briefly if the demon's day job was as Dean of Allocations for Middlebridge—so it would be easy to locate. She refolded the map and placed it back in the rack just as the cashier returned to the store. The cashier eyed the map rack with suspicion.

Linnea closed her eyes and concentrated on the intersection of E. Gorey and Jane Austen Row, a neighborhood she could picture well. She wavered out of the gas station, wavered into the street near the college, and then lost her target, coming to rest about a block away. She didn't want to wear herself out, so she walked the remaining distance.

The demon's house was a pretty brick home with a colonnaded porch. No car stood in the driveway. Linnea double-checked the address and formulated a plan. She had to be careful when wefting not to collide with furniture. It was always best to weft to a place she could see, or that she already knew and could see in her mind, but the demon's living room drapes were closed. Linnea followed a walkway around the side of the house and through a latched gate to the backyard. Like the front, it was a uniform carpet where dandelions feared to tread: mowed, edged, doused in Round-Up and fertilized to a green that does not occur in nature. A box hedge lined the back fence. Linnea peered in each of the windows at the back of the house, but the shades were drawn. On the other side of the house was nothing but a trash bin and a recycling container. A tight-lipped fence separated these from the compost bins and jungly garden of the next-door neighbors.

Linnea would have to weft blind. She closed her eyes and willed herself to the other side of the front door.

An overwhelming stench of rotten fish hit her. Linnea opened her eyes. She was standing in a spacious living room, and from there she could see a formal dining room, uncluttered, table polished. The decorative style of the house was tasteful and bland. Linnea understood why a dead fish would be a good way to drive out this demon, who was obviously a fastidious housekeeper. She tiptoed into the kitchen to check the clock. 2 p.m. She should have plenty of time to do her deed.

Linnea crossed the living room, her feet making no sound on white plush carpet. She moved past a sideboard and into a hall. Two doors on the left, and two on the right—a bathroom, an office, two bedrooms. The fish smell was so strong here that she had to pull a corner of her fleece jacket up over her nose. She opened one bedroom door. The bed was made smooth. She pulled it shut again and turned to approach the second bedroom when she heard what sounded like a car pulling into the driveway. Linnea stood stock still. She had given very little thought to demons during her lifetime. It occurred to her now that she should perhaps have been more afraid of this assignment.

Would the demon be able to see her, or would Linnea appear invisible as she did to the living? Would a demon be likely to hurt her? Were demons opportunists who tormented anyone if given the chance, or did they only pursue certain people? A car door opened and shut outside. Linnea crossed the hall and opened the door to the master suite. A wave of rotten-fish stench crashed over her. The bed, a queen, had a duvet and dust ruffle with matching pillowcases and flounces. The duvet had been disturbed, and Linnea could see the faint lump of something under the bedding. That must be the fish.

She could dash into the master bathroom and hide behind the shower curtain, or she could crawl under the bed, but if the demon were to find her in one of those places, Linnea would have nowhere to run. The front door opened, and she heard a surprised and angry sound from the person at the door, who must have caught her first whiff of fish. Angry footsteps now crossed the carpeted living room and clacked into the kitchen. Linnea heard the sounds of cupboard doors opening, rustling, thumping—the demon was probably inspecting the garbage can for the offender.

Linnea pressed herself up against the far side of the armoire, hoping the demon would not enter the bedroom, or if she did, that she would not come far enough into the room to see Linnea huddled there. She remembered hiding behind the pop dispenser from Dean Budgie a few days before. She'd always been good at disappearing on college administrators. With luck, she could make herself scarce in the presence of even more diabolical forces.

Why did I agree to this? she thought. Why had the psychic "thought better" of leaving a dead fish in the demon's bed? Was it because the demon was dangerous and vengeful? What if it wasn't a coincidence that Linnea had landed this job? What if—what if—Linnea's mind began to poke around the one thing she knew of demons. What if this devil was *her* demon, her own hidden monster, her worst fear?

At the back of the house a door opened and shut, and then Linnea heard banging around on the side—probably the demon was taking out the garbage.

Linnea began to feel certain she was right. She was going to have to face her demon. And she had no idea what that expression meant, really. She was completely unprepared.

The back door opened again. The demon was in the house, ready to sniff out other sources of bad smells.

What was her demon? Linnea's thoughts darted around a possibility. This loneliness, which she'd held at bay in life but which had become quite acute in death—this could be her demon. She leaned her head against the armoire, thinking. She had long suspected that no one in her life really cared for her. In death she was already ancient history. Her union organizing efforts, her teaching, her research, her work as Department Chair—ashes and fables. Her professional relationships, her family ties, her friendships—it came to nothing. Nil. In the end she was unloved, unredeemed. Damned to the near shore of the Acheron.

Linnea could hear irritated footfalls in the bathroom, the office, the guest bedroom. In minutes she'd be facing her demon. But what then? What happened in the moments after you confronted your dark side?

Linnea, you imbecile! she thought. What are you doing? Weft! Weft out of here!

She scrunched her eyes shut and tried to think very hard of the green lawn outside. She could sense herself move. She opened her eyes and found herself on the other side of the queen bed, next to the window that looked out on the lawn, just as the demon threw open the bedroom door.

"Why... are... you... in... my... house?" said the demon. Her voice was low and deliberate and gripped Linnea like a fist.

The demon was a woman who resembled Linnea: early forties, dark-haired, 5'9" or 5'10," carrying a few extra pounds.

"I know who you are," Linnea said, though she could hardly breathe.

The demon removed her glasses. Linnea could see her eyes flash. "I don't know who you are," the demon said, in a voice that seemed to squeeze out the last of Linnea's breath.

"I acknowledge you!" Linnea cried, acting purely on instinct. "You exist! You have been with me a long time, unacknowledged! I acknowledge you now!"

The demon breathed out hard through her nose and took a step toward Linnea. Two trails of black smoke drifted from her nostrils.

"I am ready to bring you into the light!" Linnea yelped, hardly knowing what she was saying, but letting a lifetime's accumulation of self-help literature speak through her.

The demon rushed toward Linnea. Linnea hurled herself at the bed. She seized the duvet with both hands and pulled it back. There on the bed lay the dead fish. She grabbed it up by the tail and thrust it at her pursuer. "Out, demon!" she cried.

The demon recoiled, put off by the odiferous bane.

At the same time, Linnea got a good look at what she held in her hand. It was a slender fish, about seven inches long with a classic fish-shape. Its pungent rottenness included briny, smoky notes and its flesh was the color of dried blood. Linnea recognized it as a common European breakfast item. A herring. She gave it a little shake in the direction of the demon, who now was looking more puzzled than angry. Linnea drew her gaze to the fish again. She, too, was puzzled. The fish was a red herring.

Linnea glanced at the demon, who had her head cocked at a quizzical angle. They looked at one another as though to say oh—very strange—all some sort of misunderstanding—and then Linnea squeezed shut her eyes and willed herself to weft, weft anywhere, she didn't care where.

Chapter Thirty-Nine

MORE MURDERS

Dori must have been in the shower after fencing when the evacuation call came.

She and Jaspar had trained for an hour. A workout with him was the only way to break the awful spell cast over her mood by the deans, the legislators, the Indignant Taxpayers, the Board of Regents and their nefarious plans for the college. Then, because she also needed to break the spell of her dismal performance at the tournament, she had stayed in the gym and worked on her technique alone. She'd heard nothing while in the dressing room but had dried off, frowned in the mirror— her hair was going every which way—and dressed. FEAR was empty and strangely silent when she emerged.

From the gymnasium lobby she could see that the sky was darker than it should have been at that time of day, and the grass was dark, too. Her skin prickled. Dori left the building and was engulfed in sound, and she pressed her fingers in her ears. Crows. The campus was covered with them. A huge flock—a *murder*, she thought with a cringe—of crows. They made the lawn a sea of black. They tucked themselves into ivy, turning the green pods of the campus buildings into dark lumps. They huddled in trees and on rooftops and darkened the sky itself, flying, flapping, calling to one another in their hoarse voices. They cackled, cawed and croaked. They rattled like maracas. Crows, Dori had read, were capable of more than 20 distinct vocalizations, and now they seemed to be exercising them all at the same time.

Dori paused on the steps of the gymnasium, wondering what to do. She was pretty sure the crows posed no threat to her, and the humanities building wasn't far. She didn't see another human soul on campus. Everyone must have fled. Dori hadn't driven to school that day. If she wanted to go home, she'd have to wait with the crows at the bus stop for 20 minutes—if buses were even running now in this strange emergency. She opted to return to Verizon Wireless Hall.

Dori picked up the bag holding her fencing gear and made her way through the birds in the grass, the heels of her Fun Shoes stabbing the wet earth with each step. The crows tended to wait until the last instant to move out of her way, ruffling their feathers as though insulted, turning and eyeing her with their shiny eyes. Dori wasn't afraid, but the noise was overwhelming. She moved as quickly as she could diagonally across the quadrangle and into her own office building.

Dori unlocked the doors to Verizon Wireless. Inside, her footsteps made spooky taps in the empty hall. Someone had turned the lights off on the way out, and she had a long journey in the gloom to the far end of the hall to reach the stairs to the second story. As she approached, a voice said, "Hi."

Dori's heart jumped. Squinting, she could see a figure on the bottom step of the staircase.

"Who's that?"

"It's Mary Ellen."

"Oh! Mary Ellen! Well, good," Dori said to the French major who often frequented the humanities building. She was relieved that the figure was a small young woman with whom she was personally acquainted. "I didn't really want to be alone with the crows," she said cheerfully. "Come on up to my office."

The student dutifully followed Dori upstairs without a word. Mary Ellen always had been a shy little thing, requiring extra effort on Dori's part to draw her out during class. "So how did you manage to get left behind?" Dori asked. They trooped down the hall toward Dori's office, the younger woman a step or two behind Dori.

"I didn't want to leave campus," Mary Ellen said in a tight voice. "I'd rather be here, even with the crows." Mary Ellen tucked a strand of her long, straight brown hair behind her ear.

"Oh." Seemed like an odd choice, but Mary Ellen was kind of an oddity.

They got to Dori's office and Dori ushered her former student inside.

"I'm going to see if Campus Security has an update for us or any advice," Dori said. She picked up the phone and keyed in a number, but no one answered. The campus was deserted. Dori's scalp tingled. She placed the phone in its cradle quietly and said, "Well! It looks like we're on our own. I'll check on line and see if there are any postings."

She tap-tapped away and found several breaking news reports about the crows, which she read to Mary Ellen. Bridgesians were told not to be alarmed but advised to stay indoors. There was no word from the college.

Mary Ellen was quiet and contained. Dori asked her what she was taking this term and how her classes were going, and she received telegraphic responses. When she had exhausted the avenues of conversation that occurred to her, Dori said, "Do you have anything with you to read?"

"Always," Mary Ellen told her.

So by mutual agreement the two women tackled their own work. Dori sat at Linnea's old desk and set Mary Ellen up at her own. The young woman pulled a tome from her immense backpack and drew her legs to her chest in Dori's office chair.

Apparently Mary Ellen and Dori were the only homo sapiens on campus. No one knew where Dori was. And if the taciturn French student were a psychopathic killer? Should Mary Ellen pull a Sawzall out of that enormous backpack right now, Dori would have no recourse except to trust her own wits.

Knock it off, Amore, Dori thought. She wondered how long they'd be stuck here. She checked her email and then looked again for news updates about the crows. Electricity was out in a few places around town where the weight of perching crows had brought down power lines. Residents were told to wear ear protection when going outdoors because the avian cacophony could reach 100 decibels or more.

Since she had the time, Dori thought she might try to hack Linnea's computer. If she was lucky, she'd unearth some backup copies of the documents the union organizers wanted.

Dori glanced Mary Ellen's way. The student was sucking on a length of her hair and seemed to be completely engrossed in a biography of Victor Hugo.

Dori went to Linnea's email first. She entered Linnea's name and pondered what her friend's password might be. It seemed she had heard it at one time or should be able to deduce it. She thought a second and then typed "Roma." Linnea's e-mailbox popped open. It was full to overflowing, of course. Email had continued to pour in during the days since Linnea's death. It was only due to the slipshod Middlebridge way, Dori guessed, that Linnea's account hadn't yet been canceled.

It was wrong to pry into someone else's mail, even if that someone was dead. What if she uncovered some business Linnea wouldn't have wanted her to know of? Dori did not suspect her friend of any dirty doings, but Linnea might have been having a little fun on the side that she'd kept mum about. The idea made Dori a bit giddy. But as she scrolled through the mail, she saw only work correspondence. There were messages here from Classics faculty, from students, from deans. She found two messages from other union organizers, but they were written so cryptically that Dori did not know what they meant.

She looked in the "sent" folder, too, and there she found attempts on Linnea's part to initiate contact with her estranged brother. The brother, from what Dori could gather, had not responded.

Dori shifted in her chair. She scrolled through messages about the Classics conference Linnea had been planning to attend. She found a couple emails offering to enlarge Linnea's penis and another from a Cameroonian prince asking permission to deposit a million dollars into Linnea's bank account.

But there was nothing from friends or lovers. Dori checked Linnea's search history and found one web page about Italy and one about dressing to flatter your figure. Linnea's life had been every bit as staid and respectable on the inside as it had appeared from the outside. She had had no secret goings-on, no hidden romances, no hush-hush plans to run off to the Antilles with someone. She was not writing a screenplay or taking a skydiving class that no one knew about. Dori was disappointed on Linnea's behalf. She had always wished for a little sizzle for her friend. Now it occurred to her that being dead might be the greatest adventure of Linnea's life.

"I've had enough," Dori said finally. "How about you?" Mary Ellen whispered yes. Dori wished she'd gotten stranded with someone more sociable, or at least someone who didn't set off images of homicidal butchery in her imagination. "Let's go to the faculty lounge," Dori said. "We'll be a lot more comfortable there. They have couches. There might even be some cookies and coffee left over from a meeting. I don't know about you, but I'm starving."

Mary Ellen looked uncomfortable but didn't say anything. She wedged the biography into her full pack and tucked her hair behind her ear again.

"You okay?"

Mary Ellen nodded.

Up to the third floor they went, to the faculty lounge with its fireplace and cherry wood trim and mauve couches.

Dori buttoned up her jacket and rubbed her arms with her hands. "Is it cold in here?"

"It is cold," Mary Ellen concurred. "I'll build a fire."

With the ease of someone who made fires routinely, the young woman got one going in the lounge's big stone fireplace.

"You're a regular Girl Scout."

"Well," Mary Ellen said in a strained voice. "I hang out here a lot."

Students weren't supposed to use the faculty lounge, but Mary Ellen was so awkward that Dori didn't want to make her feel worse. Besides, Dori had seen the student lounge in the basement, and she couldn't blame anyone for preferring to be up here instead. "No cookies," she observed, looking around. "Too bad."

"Oh," said Mary Ellen. "I have food."

Dori thought her companion would pull something to eat out of the big back pack, but instead, Mary Ellen went to the closet at the back of the room and produced a turkey sandwich and a bag of chips, which the two of them split.

"Lucky you made a trip to the cafeteria before the crows came," Dori said, but wondered what the goodies had been doing in the closet.

Dori chatted for a while about this and that and Mary Ellen seemed, finally, to relax. She knew her French professor pretty well, after all, having taken three or four courses from her. The younger woman added wood to the fire, and then said, "Are you still cold? I have blankets."

"Blankets?"

Once again the student went to the closet, and this time, Dori followed her. The storage cubby was mostly empty, but contained a stack of bedding, a suitcase, and a milk crate full of what appeared to be EMT uniforms.

Mary Ellen lifted two blankets and two pillows from the pile.

"Um?" said Dori, not sure what to make of these things, and not sure how to ask for clarification. "This is handy. I guess."

"I keep a few things here," Mary Ellen said. "I guess I'm not the only one. That stuff's not mine." She indicated the milk crate.

"Yeah. Weird. The EMT program is clear across campus," Dori noted.

They returned to the couch and settled in with their respective pillows and blankets. Then Mary Ellen said, "Dr. Amore? I have a problem." She twisted a strand of her hair around her finger. "I've been living here. In Verizon Wireless

Hall. I've lived here for three years."

Dori sat up straight. "*Living* here? For three *years*?"

"I can't afford student housing. It's the only way I can to go to school at all."

"But—what do you mean? Where do you stay?"

"I'm on campus all day, in different buildings," Mary Ellen explained. "And then at night I come up to the faculty lounge and sleep on the couch here."

"Oh, my goodness, Mary Ellen."

"I wash up in the women's rooms and I have my stuff stashed in a few places. I carry most of it with me," she said, patting her big backpack. "It works out."

"Oh, Mary Ellen, I can't believe it."

"But now,"—the young woman's voice broke—"now they have this new curfew. At first I was hiding every night, but then I got caught, and now the Campus Security officer checks every nook and cranny, and I can't live here any more." Mary Ellen placed a thick strand of her own hair in her mouth. "I don't have anywhere to live."

"Mary Ellen, I sympathize, but you know what happened to Dr. Nil. It's not safe for you to be here alone at night." Dori remembered that they were alone here at night now. She crossed the room and checked the door, but it didn't have a lock. She returned to the mauve couch and sat facing Mary Ellen.

"I know." Mary Ellen was crying in earnest now, her shoulders shaking with sobs. "I know better than anybody." Mary Ellen pulled her palms across her wet cheeks. "I was there," she continued. "I was there, in the bathroom, right after it happened. It was about 11 p.m. I went into the restroom to take a sponge bath. I think he had just been in there."

Dori gasped. The young woman must be talking about

Linnea's murder.

"I didn't see him. But I thought I heard somebody in one of the stalls when I went in. I looked, and I didn't see any feet, so I thought I must be wrong. But there was blood on the floor in the stall." Mary Ellen hugged her knees. "I didn't know it was from a killing," she said, her voice breaking. "Women's rooms aren't always pretty places."

"But the heart?" Dori said. "Linnea's heart wasn't in the sink."

The young student shook her head. "I took my bath. I was in there a while. And then I came up here to the lounge and went to bed. He must have been somewhere in the building the whole time, with Dr. Nil already dead or wounded. I was here in the building when he killed her." Mary Ellen drew her shoulders up around her ears.

"Have you told the police?"

"I was afraid I'd get in trouble for living here."

"They need to know," Dori persisted. "It might be important."

"Okay," Mary Ellen said in a mouse voice.

"I'll advocate for you," Dori told her, "and make sure there aren't harsh consequences for you. It's important, Mary Ellen. Okay?"

The young woman dragged her palms across her cheeks again. "I know," she whispered. "Of course I want them to catch him. I've been so afraid."

"I can't believe you stayed here after what happened to Linnea."

"Well, I didn't. They won't let me. I've been staying in shelters. I only came tonight because nobody was around. I hid in the broom closet when the evacuation call came."

"Oh, dear heavens," Dori said. "Look. You can stay with me until you find a permanent place to live."

"Really?"

They talked a few minutes more, and then Dori suggested they push one of the couches up against the door of the faculty lounge. The student, having made her confession, went limp in one of the chairs and fell asleep quickly. Dori sat by the fireplace thinking about the offer she'd made and how she and Mary Ellen would work out their living arrangement. Dori's condo was small. Mary Ellen would have to take Dori's office. She hoped she wouldn't regret her impulse. She knew the young woman wouldn't be noisy. But what if she were emotionally needy? Or disinclined ever to move out? If she were sloppy—well, that wouldn't be much of a change, Dori had to admit. Anyway, sometimes compassion trumped convenience. They would work it out. Dori settled her head on a bolster and dozed fitfully the rest of the night.

Chapter Forty

IN THE DARK AGAIN

When she opened her eyes, Linnea found herself in the dark. She sat up and bumped her head on something. With puzzled fingers she felt around above. She seemed to be in a tight enclosure of some kind, and the floor was dirt. Short stripes of daylight shone in through what appeared to be a vent to one side. She supposed she was in a crawl space, perhaps under the demon's house. Linnea felt on all four sides and found she was walled in and with little room to move. The close darkness made her think of her time in the morgue.

Where had her wefting ineptitude deposited her now? She still had the herring in her hand and remembered the fortune teller's admonition that she would need to dispose of it if she did not want to draw attention from other diabolical forces.

Waves of unpleasant thoughts rose and crashed. Dori, the goon squad from Hades, and the demon-irritating fish all bobbed in the surf for her attention.

One thing at a time, Linnea, she said to herself. She had to put her larger difficulties out of her mind and focus on the task at hand, which was to get out of this space, wherever it was. But Linnea couldn't seem to get hold of herself.

At the very least she might find someplace to stash the fish. She was worried about its stench. Did she have a bag or a piece of plastic on her? She slid a hand into her pants pocket. She found nothing there to wrap a fish in, only the mantra in its cellophane sleeve given to her by the donkey in the Buddhist advising center. It was too dark to read, but Linnea remembered what the card said: "Always come back to the breath."

Breathing deeply would not present solutions to her problems, but it might put her in a frame of mind to solve them for herself. Linnea leaned back against the wall of wherever she was. She had confronted the demon on the supposition that her biggest hangup was fear of being alone and unloved. But the fish in the bed had turned out to be a symbol of meaningless distraction. Maybe, Linnea thought, I am not gone and forgotten. Maybe I'm not alone in this world. Linnea knew that Vergil was on her side. She still wasn't sure that Dori would come through for her, but surely she was doing her best? She thought about colleagues who had respected her, students who had prized her. Students like Alice, who at the end of LAT 101 had made her a thank-you card out of corn husks, her message of appreciation burned into the leaves with a matchstick. It could not be true that Linnea's life had meant nothing to others. Whether the loyalty of friends like Dori and the appreciation of young people like Alice could redeem her, Linnea did not know. But she began to suspect that her attack of fear had been misplaced, that the loneliness she'd thought she was fated to acknowledge was in fact a red herring. Linnea closed her eyes and began to breathe long, slow breaths, following with her attention the flow of air, until she felt calmer. When she started panicking again, she returned her attention to her breath, to the sensation of air going in and out and of her chest rising and falling, and to the smells in the air. The odor of ripe herring predominated. But as Linnea relaxed and breathed, she could perceive other smells, too—a humus-y earthiness, not unpleasant, and fresh lawn clippings.

Linnea's eyes sprang open. She knew where she was. She felt around her once again to verify. Yes; the enclosure was a perfect square, and she sat on a little hillock of dirt. She could not have wefted to a more appropriate spot after leaving the demon; this was a place better suited than anywhere else to transform the fish, as the psychic had advised.

Linnea used her hands to scrape away a little hole for the herring in the soft earth before her. Then she buried it in dirt and in cut grass and banana peels. It took little force for Linnea to push the lid of the compost bin open. She peered out, and then clambered over the side of the enclosure and hurried away, hardly pausing to shake the kitchen scraps out of her clothes.

Chapter Forty-One

THE 379TH NIGHT

Alice hurried back into the club. She went straight to Renee's office and asked to speak to her manager privately.

"Shut the door," Renee said.

Alice began to tell her what had just happened. Renee folded her manicured hands on her desk. She waited without expression while Alice described her struggle with the Larries. When she finished, Renee opened her hands. "And?"

Alice's legs were shaking. "And, I think you should ban the Larries from the club."

Renee had a salon coiffe, tinted auburn and styled to make the most of hair thinning with late middle age. She wore a tailored jacket and slacks, and her pink lipstick was always fresh. Renee *looked* like a woman. But she said to Alice, "If you can't stand the heat, stay out of the kitchen," and Alice saw now that Renee was management first and female second. Her loyalties lay with accounts receivable, not with the women in her employ.

"What does that mean?"

Renee was impassive. "You know perfectly well what the occupational hazards of this job are. If you don't like them, you should choose a different line of work." She opened her office door to see Alice out.

"If I don't *like* them. Like some people *like* getting jumped."

The faintest smirk crossed Renee's face. "That's spreading it on a little thick," she said. "I'm sure you realize that your actions on stage invite a certain kind of attention."

"It's a *job*," said Alice. She had to struggle to keep her voice civil. "When I leave the building, I'm no longer on the job."

Renee shrugged. "Some girls don't clock out when they finish dancing," she said. "You can understand why the patrons might be confused."

"I don't accept that."

"We have nothing more to discuss," Renee said.

"So Cootchie-Coo has no responsibility to ensure the basic safety of its workers?"

"If the establishment were to get involved in what goes on outside the premises, it might appear that we condone or permit prostitution, which of course we do not," Renee said firmly. "What happens outside our doors has to remain a girl's own business. It is our policy not to get involved."

"So 'getting involved' in protecting dancers from rape would be bad for business." Alice's face and neck were hot.

"A lot of girls dance for fun," Renee continued. "If they want to continue their fun after hours, that's their business. I'm not in a position to second-guess what a girl's motives are and interfere."

"For fun," Alice repeated. She thought of the 379 nights she'd put in, nights of boredom, nights of aching feet. She thought about the careful accounting she'd done for a year and a half, squirreling away every dollar, squirreling her precious minutes of study between sets. She thought about the patrons who called her ugly names; the patrons who withheld tips on caprice; the laundry to be done after every shift; the infection she'd gotten from a dirty pole. 379 nights.

Alice took a cab home, tipped the driver well, and went straight upstairs to Amy's room. Amy was lying in bed with a cracked and faded copy of *Anne of Green Gables*.

Alice sat on the end of her housemate's bed. "Look," she said. "You don't want to work at Cootchie-Coo. I made a mistake introducing you to it."

Amy's eyebrows jumped. She put down her book. "Did something happen?"

"I got assaulted," Alice said, her voice calm. "I'm okay," she added, seeing Amy's eyes get big. She did not want to go into detail. "There's no guarantee it won't happen again. You should quit. I'm sorry I ever got you into this. If you want, I'll turn in your resignation for you."

"What about you?" Amy asked. "What will you do?"

"I already quit," Alice told her. "Just now. I told Renee I was done." Alice didn't feel like telling her housemate the rest of her plan. Tomorrow she would go down to the Student Data Intake Center and drop out of school. There was no way she would be able to keep paying for it now. The four years of Latin and two of Greek she'd planned, the Western Civ, the Art History and all the other beautiful degree requirements, the B.A. in Classical Studies, the master's and the doctorate she was contemplating were all dribbling through her fingers. She might move back in with her parents, go to community college, find a waitressing job.

Leaving Bridges meant leaving the band, too. And leaving Tad.

Alice perched on the edge of Amy's mattress, unable to find the breath to tell Amy what quitting her job meant to her life.

But Amy wasn't thinking about Alice. She had danced just the one time at Cootchie-Coo, the afternoon that Renee had hired her. She turned her baby blues to Alice and told her, "You have no idea how relieved I am."

Chapter Forty-Two

SUB UMBRAS

As soon as Vergil saw Linnea at the foot of his stairwell, he clapped his hands. "Come up!" he cried. "Come up! Sit! I'll make tea. Sit, sit, sit, sit! *Mi casa es su casa!*"

Linnea climbed the stairs and kissed the old man's cheek.

"Tell me what you've been up to," Vergil said. "Tell me everything."

Linnea filled him in on her excursions to the Buddhist outlet of the great beyond. She told him about having visited her house and campus and about the psychic and the demon. Vergil listened with his chin in his hands. Linnea wished she had better news for him. Instead, she admitted she was exhausting her resources and was no closer to a happily-ever-after. "Can I ask you something?"

"Of course. Ask away."

Linnea voiced the question she'd held at bay for almost two weeks. "Can *you* redeem me?" Her voice was small.

Vergil gazed at Linnea with fond sadness. He took her hands. "If only I could, dear heart," he told her. "But your redeemer will have to come from the ranks of the living."

Linnea said, "I suspected as much." She sighed. "I don't think redemption is going to pan out for me."

"Isn't your friend working on it?"

"I guess so. But it's only a matter of hours now. I don't think she's going to make the deadline." Linnea's eyes puddled up. "If she's even trying."

"My dear girl! Why wouldn't she be trying?"

Linnea didn't want to confess that she was losing faith in Dori. Maybe their friendship did not merit the kind of effort, the kind of sacrifice, required. It was her own fault. Linnea should have given more to the friendship while she'd had the chance. She could have been more enthusiastic about Dori's personals-ad finds, more available to make the rounds with her to shoe shops, more often present at Dori's fencing tournaments.

"Come. This will make you feel better," Vergil said. He hunted and pecked on his laptop until he found an Elvis impersonator singing "Love Me Tender" in Latin on YouTube. Linnea couldn't help smiling.

When they finished listening, Vergil said, "Now I have a favor to ask you."

"Me?"

"Will you read something I've written?" he asked. "And tell me what you think?"

"Of course," Linnea said.

Vergil rummaged through a pile of papers on his nightstand and pulled out a sheet of verse. It was written in Latin, in dactylic hexameter. Linnea adjusted the light beside her and settled in to read.

" ...*fūgit indignāta sub umbrās*." Goosebumps traveled up her arms and neck. She recognized the prose, even though most of the passage was new to her. She was holding in her hands fresh verses for the *Aeneid*. Vergil must have been working on the missing ending to his famous book.

She read to the end of the page before she realized she'd been holding her breath. "Vergil!" she told him. "It's marvelous! You've overcome your writer's block!"

"Ssshhh," Vergil said in mock-seriousness. "Don't jinx it. It's only just a start. But I think—I think I'm onto something. I think it has promise."

"I do, too," said Linnea. "It's the ending you can't quite envision before you've read it, and then when you read it, it feels like the only ending possible."

"Yes, yes!" Vergil cried. "That's how it feels to me, too. I'm so glad you perceive it that way. I'm so glad you understand." He patted her hand.

"This page is perfect, Vergil. It's flawless." Linnea wasn't being flattering. She meant it, and she was awed to be the first mortal to read words that had died to the world with the great poet.

Vergil beamed at his friend.

"Do you have far to go? Are you close to the end?"

"Not far," Vergil told her. He tapped his skull. "A lot of it is already written up here. The problem I'm having now is my arthritis. I can only write a few lines at a time and then my hands ache. But I'll get there."

"I'm very happy for you."

It was Vergil's bedtime, so Linnea rose to leave. Her two-week grace period would be up at around 11 the following night. She promised to come over the next afternoon to say good-bye. She was disappointed that she wouldn't get to see the finished *Aeneid*. Vergil was disappointed, too, but he offered to make her a meal to send her off. "Unless you're already redeemed by dinnertime, of course," he said, with what seemed to Linnea like forced optimism. "If you don't show up, I'll understand, and I'll know it's for the best!"

Chapter Forty-Three

A HARDENED HEART

Tad liked French class okay, but he didn't have Alice's language lust, so even though Alice didn't know French, she sometimes helped him with his homework.

"Tell me again what 'articles' are?" he said to her the next afternoon. They were sitting on the peeling front porch steps, drinking green tea and doing Tad's French homework together. As the weather had dried out, so had the front door, and they were able to open it once again. They left it open, letting what passed for springtime warmth waft though the screen door. "Dr. Amore told us, but I forgot."

Alice had just returned from dropping out of school. She hadn't told Tad yet—not about school, not about the Larries, not about Cootchie-Coo, nothing. She figured she would fall apart as soon as she started talking about it, and she wanted to wait until the right moment. "*The* and *a*," she said.

"Oh. I remember now. In French they have more than we do. Too many."

"In Latin they don't have any."

"They don't have a word for 'the'?"

"Nope."

"That's weird."

Tad toiled at his homework for a few minutes. Alice peered over his shoulder. "What's that cute little carrot?" she asked, pointing at a letter wearing a kind of pointed cap. "I've always wondered."

"That's a circumflex," Tad said.

"What's it for?"

"I happen to have an answer to that question," Tad said with mock self-importance, flourishing a pencil. On the cover of his notebook he wrote a letter *û*. "In the Middle Ages, certain words had 's'es in them." Tad wrote *aoust* in his lovely, leggy Tad-handwriting. "Monks would leave out the 's'es and write a circumflex over the letter that came before. It saved space when they copied out manuscripts." *Août*, he wrote.

"It's a thing of beauty," said Alice. Alice favored diacritical marks of all sorts.

"The French government is trying to take it away from us."

"What? Why would they do that?"

"Because the 's' is silent now." Tad tapped *août* with his pen and said the word aloud: "Oot!" He stretched his neck and jutted his head forward like some kind of long-necked bird: "Oot!" They laughed and ooted together. Then Tad adopted a professorial tone. "Strictly speaking, the circumflex is no longer necessary."

"But it preserves the history of the language," Alice protested.

"I know. I thought you'd feel that way."

"No good can come of this."

"True," said Tad gravely.

"It's an outrage."

"Yes, it is."

"If I spoke French," Alice said, "I would rebel. I would refuse to participate in any circumflex omission."

"I know," Tad said. "I think a lot of French people feel that way too."

"I'm going to start using the circumflex in *English* words," Alice declared, "in solidarity."

"And the German es-set too," said Tad.

"What's that?"

"That big B thing in German words. They're trying to banish it." Tad wrote ß on his notebook.

"What? I love that thing."

"It's pronounced 'ss' so they're trying to replace it with a double 's.'"

"If I were German I would riot in the streets," said Alice.

"That's my girl," Tad said, and Alice was foolishly pleased. For a moment, she felt almost happy.

Tad worked on his exercises for a few minutes more and then clapped his French book shut. He said, "So, Amy applied for a job as a receptionist at an eye doctor's."

"Yeah, I heard," Alice said. She took a swig of tea. "I convinced her to quit skin dancing."

"You did, really?"

It was time. Tad was finished with his homework, undistracted by articles and circumflexes. No one else was home. Alice drew a breath to tell him about almost being raped, about Renee's blunt refusal to help her, about quitting work and quitting school, about having to leave Bridges and everything she loved. She could feel the tears, suppressed all day, rising like a warm tide.

"I have to say I'm glad," Tad continued.

"You are?" He hadn't even heard her story yet.

"I didn't really like her working there," Tad told Alice. "It's weird. It made me feel kind of jealous."

The j-word struck Alice like a slap. "I thought jealousy was the by-product of a consumerist economy."

The sardonic edge to her voice escaped Tad. "Yeah, I know, I'm such a hypocrite." He laughed, releasing two years' worth of underclassman ideological fervor in a single comment. "I don't like to think about other guys looking at her that way."

Alice had a hard time finding her voice. "You never minded other guys looking at *me* that way."

"Yeah, but that's different. You're *Alice*." Tad drained his tea and pulled Alice to his chest. "Come on, don't be that way. You know it's different with us."

Alice held herself stiff as a mannequin as Tad wrapped his arms around her. She tried to feel the old comfort, the old Tad-warmth, but she couldn't breathe.

Tad ran his fingers through Alice's hair. "Is something up?" he said. "Tell me. We never really talk any more."

"Yeah, well," Alice said. She loosed her head from under his hand and sat up. "*Adspicere oportet quicquid possīs perdere.*"

You should keep an eye on the things you could lose. Alice stood and went back into the house, letting the screen door fall shut with a slam behind her. She didn't bother translating for Tad.

Chapter Forty-Four

HEARTFELT

A river bisected Bridges, and public parks ran the length of both banks, excellent for strolls. It was possible to start at the northernmost of the town's five bridges, walk along the water to the southernmost bridge, cross, and walk back up to one's starting place in about an hour. Pablo had asked Dori to meet him at the north bridge.

Dori was glad to get out of the house. Mary Ellen had moved into her condo first thing in the morning. The young woman owned very little and was quiet as a spider. Still, it was a small space. There was no way Dori and Pablo were going to have a personal conversation at home.

Dori walked down to the waterfront and hailed Pablo when she saw his form approaching.

"Thanks for meeting me. There's something I need to talk to you about," Pablo said.

He was breaking up with her. He must be. I'm too flawed, Dori thought. My fencing practice is a joke, my hair is made of soapsuds, I'm perimenopausally crazed, I'm incapable of being a good partner because I'm all tied in knots over my dead friend. And I haven't even told him about the heart yet.

Pablo moved in for an awkward hug, stiff with whatever he had come to tell her.

"Dori, there's something I need you to know about me."

"About you?"

They began to walk. Did he have herpes? Was he bisexual? Epileptic? Bipolar? A communist? Planning to move to Cleveland? Dori had no idea. She couldn't come up with anything she thought she'd be unable to live with.

Pablo seemed to be having trouble moving on to the next part of what he had to say. He cleared his throat and clasped his hands behind his back, gazed at the slate-gray waters of the river, drew a breath, hesitated. Maybe he was about to tell her that it was he who had left a saw blade and a set of Canadian quarters on the windowsill of her office, and why. Maybe he was going to confess to Linnea's murder. Maybe, Dori thought, *maybe* he suspects *me* of Linnea's murder, because of my unhealthy obsession with her heart. Oh my God! He's been working for the FBI and has been investigating me when all this time I thought he was falling in love with me. Dori had to stop herself from staring.

"I have obsessive-compulsive disorder," Pablo said. "Do you know very much about it?"

So many worries were going swirling down the drain of Dori's imagination that she couldn't answer. She needed to stop walking. She put her hand over her heart.

Seeing her expression, Pablo asked, "Are you upset?"

Dori shook her head hard. "I'm relieved."

"Oh! Really? Oh, good," Pablo said. They began to walk again. He smiled. "Maybe you won't be when you hear more about it."

"Tell me."

"Well, OCD can take many different forms. For me it means that I have to vacuum. Every day. Well, several times a day. I can't stand for there to be a speck of anything on a floor."

He's not breaking up with me! Dori thought. He's not breaking up with me! "That's it? Vacuuming?"

"That's it. Sooner or later you were going to see it happen, and I didn't want to alarm you."

Dori set her hand on Pablo's arm. "It's not very alarming."

"Oh, it's pretty weird. It can inconvenience people who end up waiting for me to vacuum when we have someplace to go."

Dori remembered the night they missed the Fellini film.

"I budget time for it," Pablo continued. "We've been spending more time together and, well, I just wanted you to know. Daily vacuuming is part of my life. It's probably not something that's ever going to go away."

Dori smiled. "Is that your darkest secret?"

Pablo considered. "Maybe," he told her. "Yes. I think it most likely is."

Dori let out her breath. Pablo wasn't an undercover cop. He wasn't a homicidal maniac. He wasn't fatally ill or a watcher of FOX news. But the best part was that he had a flaw. He had a flaw! He had a weirdness, an irrational, incurable something that sometimes bothered other people, and he knew it. Dori turned to Pablo and threw her arms around his neck. If he had a flaw, it meant it was probably okay for Dori to be a little flawed, too.

The sound of sirens rose from Dori's coat pocket. She had already received a desperate message from Ian Elf about an announcement for Middlebridge faculty from Dean Fiercey. Undoubtedly it was him again. And so instead of saying to Pablo, "I have something to tell you, too," and asking him outright for his help in getting Linnea's heart, Dori said, "Shit. I've got to get to campus." She kissed Pablo and promised they'd speak soon. She hated to admit how relieved she was to slip away without sharing her own dark secret.

Chapter Forty-Five

CLEARHEADED

Her decisions made and her mind free of clutter about money, school, skin dancing, and Tad, Alice now found her intellect sharper. As she lay on her futon, her thoughts returned to the conversation she'd stumbled into the other day between Guppy and Dexter.

Alice had not prevented Dr. Nil's murder that night in Verizon Wireless Hall. She understood that she could not have done so. But the urgency to do *something* for Dr. Nil remained, and it was now becoming clear to her that that *something* was solving the murder. She felt sure that the exchange between Guppy and Dexter contained information she needed, and she was going to find out what it was.

Alice jumped up. Guppy wasn't in the living room. He wasn't on his landing or in the moldy basement. Well, if she couldn't get an answer from Guppy, she would track down Dexter Beet. *Aut viam inveniam.* She knew she could intimidate the truth from one or the other of them.

Chapter Forty-Six

REVELATIONS

Dean Fiercey, Ian Elf had told Dori in that morning's voicemail message, had announced a plan to restructure the college's class offerings. She dubbed the new curriculum "modular." Rather than scheduling whole courses, which, Fiercey argued, were often too expansive and complex, each faculty member would now specialize in a single function—say, the construction of topic sentences, or the factoring of polynomials. They would teach self-contained units, which would be offered weekly throughout the school year and could be taken in any order. Faculty would be paid by the half-hour for each unit. Middlebridge would become the very model of educational efficiency.

In addition, as a cost-cutting measure, instructors would now be required to pay for their own office supplies, including photocopies and printer paper, ink, staples, markers and whatever else they might use. The supplies must be bought at the campus bookstore. Purchases would be automatically deducted from employee paychecks.

Dori texted Ian Elf as soon as she got to campus, but he didn't respond. After checking his office and classroom, she hurried to the third floor of Verizon Wireless Hall and pushed open the door of the faculty lounge. In an instant she clapped her hands over her eyes as though she had seen an unspeakable horror, and she backed out of the room.

Dean Eleanor Fiercey was sitting on the back of the faculty couch with no pants on. Her white bottom was a pair of vast twin moons against the mauve suede. Clutching that pale flesh and also bare from the waist down was Hank, the handsome registration clerk. He was thrusting fast like a rutting dog.

Dori was still flustered when, minutes later, a student of Latin appeared at her office door.

A steady stream of Linnea's students had been knocking on Dori's door for two weeks. Ned Callow had been inviting them to speak to Dori instead of interpreting Linnea's grade records himself. He'd left Linnea's grade book in Dori's mailbox with a little note saying he couldn't make sense of it, but he was sure she could.

"Name?" Dori said.

"Dexter Beet." The young man had pale, soft flesh and a cowed look about him.

Linnea's grade book lay open on her old desk where Dori could refer to it for these hapless students. She dug the heels of her Fun Shoes into the carpet to move her chair across the floor and found *Beet, Dexter* on Linnea's LAT 102 spreadsheet. The name rings a cliché, she thought, but she couldn't remember why she would have heard of him. "You weren't doing very well," she observed.

"I know."

"It looks like you got two D's and an F on quizzes and a C

for attendance and participation."

"I know." Dexter didn't move.

"You need to be writing this down." Dori felt her patience shriveling.

Dexter said, "That isn't why I came."

Dori looked up. "Oh."

She scooted back to make space for the student. "Come inside, then." She gestured at Linnea's chair. Dexter stepped into the room and pulled the door closed behind him. He dropped his worn book bag on the floor, sat, and pushed his glasses up over the bridge of his nose before telling Dori, "I know who killed Doctor Nil."

Chapter Forty-Seven

THE BOOK OF CHANGES

Linnea had one last, desperate notion left. After leaving Vergil, she hopped on a trolley to the Bridges public library. There was something there she thought was worth a try.

Linnea remembered having thrown the *I Ching* once or twice in college. So far as she knew, the *I Ching* did not require fidelity to Taoism. It was simply a tool. She couldn't remember just how it was done. But she could find out.

She hopped off the trolley at 4th and Melville and walked two blocks to the library. With a little concentration, she willed herself into the lobby and was pleased to find she'd wefted where she wanted on the first try.

She checked the on-line catalog and took the stairs to another storey, found the volume she wanted and knelt on the floor between two rows of bookshelves to skim it. Ah, yes, she remembered now. You tossed objects, either coins or yarrow roots, six times, and you took note of the way they fell. Then you looked in the book for that hexagram—the pattern of the way the objects had landed—for an interpretation.

Linnea thought about what objects she might throw. She'd given all her change to Charon for her ferry crossings, so coins were not an option. Yarrow roots? She thought for a moment. Why not use those dear little library pencils? They seemed symbolically appropriate for an academic, and she could readily lay her hands on them.

So Linnea gathered up six baby pencils and tossed them on the carpet, out of sight of other library patrons and as quietly as she could, and she drew her hexagram on a piece of scratch paper and looked up its meaning in the book. *Hexagram Five: Hsu: (Waiting)*, she read. Waiting, Linnea thought. Well, she'd been doing a good deal of that. But what about it?

It furthers one to cross the water, the *I Ching* told her. Linnea swallowed. That message could hardly be more clear. She read on. The hexagram then spoke of *waiting in the meadow*. Crap, thought Linnea.

She read the poem-like text again and then turned the page, looking for a modern interpretation and desperately hoping that the *I Ching* was not really advising her to ferry over the Acheron and patiently take her place in the Asphodel Meadows.

Wait in this place until success is sure, stated the interpretation in a footnote at the bottom of the page. *Accept things as they are. Through acceptance, the way will become clear to you.*

Linnea snapped the book shut and replaced it on the shelf. How did you make yourself let go of fear and embrace your fate? Dratted Eastern religions always made such steep demands.

She had half a day left on Earth. Should she pop in on

Dori once again? Look in the underworld hallway for yet more afterlives? Linnea thought she'd keep her date with Vergil and brainstorm with him one last time.

Normally in the afternoons when Linnea visited, Vergil was just rising from his mid-day nap and fixing himself a cup of tea. But when Linnea opened the downstairs door to call up the stairwell to her friend, he was crouched at the foot of the stairs, hiding in the dark.

"Come in!" he hissed, grabbing her by the wrist and tugging. "Quick!"

Linnea stepped into the shadowy entryway and pulled the door shut behind her.

"What's going on?" she said.

"They're coming for you," Vergil said, very low. "They've already been here looking."

Linnea felt the blood drain out of her face. "Who?" she asked, though in her heart, or in the place where her heart should have been, she already knew.

"The goons from Hades, of course. They ransacked the place looking for evidence you'd been here."

Linnea bounded up the staircase and into Vergil's little apartment. His papers were strewn everywhere. Books, kitchen utensils and bedding were flung on the floor, and Vergil's armchair had been overturned. "I'm so sorry," she whispered, though she knew he couldn't hear her. Linnea set the chair aright and gathered up the pages of Vergil's precious manuscript.

"Ssst!" The old man was summoning her from below. "There's no time for that now."

Linnea went back downstairs. "I don't understand what's going on," she said. "I'm supposed to have until tonight!"

Vergil raised his gnarled hands to quiet her. "Don't imagine that they care about fair play. They're searching for you right now, and you've got to go into hiding."

Linnea sank down to sitting on the bottom stair. "So it's too late to get in anywhere?"

"It's too late."

She wondered if the demon in the herring house had put the authorities onto her. "Where should I go?"

Vergil struggled to seat himself beside her. "You know where," said the old man. "The only place they can't get to you."

"That's what I thought," said Linnea in a strained voice, remembering the terrible cold of the refrigeration unit. Her skin was clammy. "So that's it then. That's where I have to be for the rest of forever."

"Better there than the place they'd take you."

Linnea swallowed. Why hadn't she just gone directly from the library to the Asphodel Meadows? Why had she so stubbornly held out for something better? Now it was too late even to follow the *I Ching*'s sorry-ass recommendation. "Can you deliver a letter for me?" she asked. She reached into the inner pocket of her fleece and pulled out the letter of recommendation she'd written for Alice.

"Of course."

"Do you have a stamp and envelope?"

"Yes, yes. I promise. You need to get going," Vergil said. "They could be anywhere."

Linnea hoped the task wouldn't slip the old man's mind. Queasy and lightheaded, she tried to think if there were any last thing she could do to avoid her fate.

"Don't go overland," said Vergil. "Weft."

"I don't know how to thank you," she told Vergil. This wasn't how she'd wanted to say good-bye.

He waved one hand in the air as though to say "it was nothing."

Linnea leaned down and kissed the tiny old man's wrinkled cheek. "Dearest Vergil," she said. "Are you going to be all right? Are you in danger on my account?"

"I'll be fine," he assured her. "I bend with the wind."

"Please take care," Linnea said.

"You too, my friend. I shall miss you." Vergil clasped Linnea's hands in his for a moment, and then said, "Now go! Go go!" And Linnea wavered out of his apartment, hoping she'd get the wefting right this time.

Chapter Forty-Eight

TAKE ANOTHER PIECE OF MY HEART

The days were getting longer, but it was dark by the time Dexter Beet left Dori's office. Dori would need to go straight to the police. She should be taking Dexter with her, but he had wriggled away before she'd collected her thoughts. Dexter had expressed mortification at not having come forward sooner, and he had wanted to escape her office almost as soon as he'd arrived. After he'd said his piece, he'd grabbed his things and hurried away before Dori really had time to grasp what he'd told her.

The phone rang and she jumped.

"Hi, Dori. Tim Fimbria here. I didn't know if I'd catch you in your office. I just wanted to let you know I'm thinking of you. How are you faring? Are you sleeping any better?"

"Oh. Hi. Yes, I am."

"No more disturbing dreams?"

Dori hesitated. "No," she said, managing to tell the truth while evading the question. She hadn't had any more "dreams" because Linnea's apparition was real. It was a problem Tim Fimbria wouldn't be able to help her with.

"And how are you managing otherwise?"

Tim Fimbria really was the kindest man. If things didn't work out with Pablo, she might think twice about the school counselor. It was probably just projection or counter-transference or whatever they called it. Patients were always half in love with their therapists. All that empathy and understanding. "To tell you the truth," she faltered, "I'm in kind of a state of shock right now."

"What happened? Do you have time to talk?"

"Not much." Dori summarized the news she'd learned from Dexter. "I'm still stunned," she told the psychiatrist.

"My God, yes," he said. "I suppose you'll report all this to the police. The sooner, the better."

"I'm on my way there now."

"I'll let you go then. Dori, if you want to process this, please do make an appointment to come see me. I imagine this has stirred up some complicated feelings."

"Yes. All right."

That was thoughtful of him, Dori said to herself. She hung up, then called Campus Security to escort her to her car. Verizon Wireless had grown quiet. Dori knew she was alone in the building. Although faculty were allowed to stay and work into the evening, students these days had to be out by 6. Dori opened her office door. The overheads in the hall were already off.

She turned off her computer and pulled her Stylin' Jacket on. Here was her escort now, waiting outside her office door for her.

"That was fast," Dori said by way of greeting.

"Dori Amore," the campus security officer responded in a soft voice. He hung back in the shadow of the hall, broad-shouldered, a metal case of some kind in his hand.

"Hang on. I just have to find my keys."

"You shared this office with Linnea Nil," the officer said. Dori glanced up. She didn't like the sound of his voice.

The officer knelt on the floor in the hall, opening his case. What in heaven's name was he doing? He continued, "Linnea Nil. Whose heart was cut out in a grisly murder in this very building. On this very floor, in fact."

Cold fear flushed through Dori.

"Are you afraid of knives, Dori Amore? Many people are."

Dori couldn't see what he was fiddling with in that metal case. He was kneeling between her and the wide-open door; she couldn't close it and lock herself in. He remained in shadow, but she could see his dark ponytail now. It was Hank, the handsome registration clerk.

Dori felt all the blood drain from her face.

"Are you afraid of power tools, Dori Amore?" Hank's voice was syrupy smooth. "You should be." There was a brief sound like an angry bee. Hank held what appeared to be a cordless jigsaw in his left hand, and he'd just pressed the trigger. Dori thought of the detachable blade she'd found on her windowsill.

"Let's talk this over," Dori said, trembling, her voice like sandpaper. She stepped closer to him, as though showing that they could be chummy. She sounded foolish to her own ears. "Maybe we can strike a deal." Her mind revved, but she couldn't think of anything she had that Hank might want. She held perfectly still in the narrow space between her desk and her office door.

Hank remained in the shadow just beyond the puddle of light from her desk lamp, but his eyes gleamed. For a moment Dori imagined that he had thought of some bargain, but then she realized he was only taking his time, toying with her fear.

"All I want," Hank said, "is for you to be completely and permanently quiet."

"I know how to be quiet," Dori said in a very soft, still voice, as though to demonstrate how good she could be. She said it just before she lunged and met his jigsaw blade with the ivy-clearing broom handle Alice had given her. She jerked her arm and sent the saw clean out of Hank's hand. It landed with a clunk in the empty hallway a few feet away. For an ill-advised second Hank's gaze followed his flying saw, and Dori brought the broom handle down a second time across his temple with a sickening crack.

Then she ran down the hall as fast as her pointy-heeled shoes could carry her. She gripped the banister so she could take the stairs four at a time. Hank was right behind her and much longer-legged than she. She didn't dare turn to look, but his footfall was close behind and she could feel his energy. She saw little, only vague shapes in the dim light, the angles of the stairs and the landing and the banister flying into her field of vision and out again. After several terrible seconds Dori reached the bottom of the stairs. She was on the first floor of the humanities building and within sight of the exit. Then she felt Hank's hand on her back. He had her jacket in his grasp—had her like a cat by the scruff of its neck. Dori shrugged her shoulders together and wriggled out of her sleeves as she hurtled herself forward, leaving him holding only the jacket. She nearly collided with the wall. Pushing away, she kept moving, but she was turned around. She should have been running down the hall to the front doors. Instead, she pitched headlong down the next flight of stairs to the basement. Dori threw her hands out in front of her blindly and found the banister and, more falling than running, kept going down.

It was black as tar below. Dori had to slow to feel her way

into the student lounge. She didn't hear Hank. He must be creeping after her. Now, at least, he wouldn't be able to see her. The tapping heels of her Fun Shoes would give her away if she let them. She paused long enough to pull them off and continued in her stocking feet. Hank must be right behind her. She could feel his presence but couldn't hear him at all. With the greatest gingerness she crept along the wall, desperately afraid of making noise, desperately afraid that with each inch forward her fingers would find not brick or metal but Hank's face.

She encountered the big old boiler and slipped behind it. Now she had her bearings. Having just visited this room a day or two before, she had a mental map of everything in it. When she emerged on the other side of the boiler, she bumped soundlessly into something square. She studied it with her fingers. Watery Discharge's amp. Dori felt around until she found something else she thought might be of use, and she set out again with the amp's extension cord in her hand. She inched in the dark alongside the wall, traveling as quietly as she could. When she reached the opposite wall, she felt with careful fingers for the outlet, the one that bore a "do not use" sign, and she plugged in the amp. Now the cord stretched taut across the way. With a little luck, it would trip Hank up.

Dori knew that if she kept walking along the northern wall she would come to the far stair, the head of which lay immediately to one side of the front entrance to Verizon Wireless Hall. She only had to manage about seventy-five blind, silent feet, one after another. Hank must be in the basement with her by now. She still had her Fun Shoes in her hands. To throw Hank off her scent, she jettisoned one shoe in the direction she wasn't walking. It clattered at the opposite end of the hall. Dori held her breath, hoping Hank would follow the sound, and tiptoed forward, holding tight to her second shoe.

After an eternity she felt a faint movement of air that told her she must have reached the stairwell. She found the first step with her toes and began to creep up. When she came to the landing and rounded the corner, the front doors of the building were in view, rectangles of paler black against the dark indoors. She heard Hank behind her encountering the amp's cord. It sounded as though he went down on one knee, grunted, and recovered. Dori broke into a run. So did Hank. She was on the penultimate step, the front doors of the building in full view, when Hank hurled himself forward from below and seized her by the calf, pulling her down the stairs toward him. Dori still had her footwear in her hand. With the full force of her 103 pounds, she twisted and sank the sharp pointy heel of her Fun Shoe into Hank's eye.

Chapter Forty-Nine

TAKING CARE OF BUSINESS

The silhouette at the top of the stair looked strangely familiar. When Dori first looked up and saw another human being towering above her, a second wave of panic crashed over her. Hank must have an accomplice. But a voice said, "Dr. Amore?"

It was Alice.

They were both drained when they left the police station two hours later. They'd been there long enough for officers to let them know that Hank had been captured on campus and taken into custody.

"So, what made you go to Verizon Wireless after curfew?" Dori asked as they headed to Alice's house.

Alice explained that she had come to suspect Dexter Beet of having some knowledge about Linnea's murder. She had tracked down him on campus and made him tell her what was going on.

Dexter had spilled the clichés readily—"He's afraid of

me," Alice told Dori—and Alice had demanded that he talk to Dori then and there. She'd started for home then but decided she didn't trust Dexter to do the job right, so she returned to Verizon Wireless to speak with Dori—and found her on the stair with the wailing Hank coiled at the foot of the steps below her.

As they rolled past the campus on their way to Baudelaire Street, big tears began to run down Alice's face.

"This is all very stressful," Dori told her. "But it's over now."

"It's not that," said Alice. She told Dori that she had dropped out of school because of financial troubles. "I applied for the Millicent Vena Cava Award," she said in a despairing voice, "but Dr. Nil was my main reference, and she died before she could write me a letter."

Dori almost exclaimed, "I'm on that committee!" but checked herself, since the deadline for application was past. There was little she could do for the Latin student.

They drove on in defeated silence. Despite what she'd said to comfort Alice, Dori reflected that this ordeal was not, in fact, behind her. The murderer was caught, but she was down to a few hours before her heart-delivery deadline. She cringed to think of the cowardice with which she had wriggled away from Pablo that morning, using the faculty's woes as an excuse to avoid coming clean with him. Then a thought struck her, and she smacked her forehead.

It was Alice, not Pablo, she needed to come clean to.

"Listen," she said. "I have a favor to ask you. A big favor. But I'll make it worth your while."

Instead of turning on Baudelaire, Dori made a U-turn, cruised back onto campus and pulled into the parking lot of the humanities building. Both women shuddered as they approached. Police had cordoned off the main entrance with yellow tape, but no one was about, so Dori and Alice slipped in through the doors at the opposite end of the building and hurried upstairs to the third floor to get what they needed. Then they headed to the county forensics building, stopping briefly at Alice's house on their way.

At the morgue, Dori let the Prius idle in the driveway at the back. She and Alice pulled the old gurney, courtesy of the living room at 636 Baudelaire, out of the trunk and unfolded it together. Alice hopped onto it and Dori covered her with a sheet. The doors opened automatically as she wheeled the gurney toward them. She and the supine student entered the hall at the back of the building, and Dori shouted, "Incoming!"

A lab tech met her in the refrigeration unit. Dori hoped he wouldn't ask her anything, since she didn't know her lines, but that he would simply accept her in the EMT uniform she'd borrowed from Alice's costume collection.

The tech said nothing. He wheeled the gurney away into the autopsy room and closed the stainless steel door behind him. Dori sprinted to the freezer case and had the box containing Linnea's heart in her hands by the time she heard Alice's voice from the side room saying, "I'm not dead."

There was a yelp of surprise and a clatter of instruments. Dori didn't stick around to find out what happened next. She ran back down the hall to her idling Prius and sped off, leaving a stripe of rubber on the concrete drive behind her.

Chapter Fifty

LE DENOUEMENT DE MON PROFESSEUR

"You will forever be my hero," Jaspar said, his hand to his heart with characteristic melodrama.

"Jaspar, I owe it all to you and our many hours of training." She described for them how she'd redeemed her sloppy saber work by re-enacting it in the hall with Hank and his power saw.

Jaspar and Antoine were treating Dori to dinner to celebrate her feat of the night before. And because they wanted to hear every last detail of her sordid story.

"You just had such balls. I'm so proud of you."

"Ovaries, honey."

Antoine raised his wine glass. "To Dori's ovaries," he said.

"To a Middlebridge safe from Hank," Dori said.

"To a Middlebridge safe from Fiercey!" Jaspar added.

"Cheers."

"But now, back up," Antoine said after they drank. "Last I heard, Hank and Fiercey were just canoodling, unsavory a sight as that was. How did all that lead to murder?"

"Well!" Dori said, trying to pull together everything she'd learned from police detectives and from Alice. "It looks like Hank was part of a black-market organ ring that runs all down the west coast and up into British Columbia. Big international business. Hank and his cohorts set up shop near the college knowing they could get desperate students to sell their kidneys to pay for tuition."

"His job in Registration gave him access to lots of students," Antoine mused.

Dori said, "He'd arrange for the surgery and tell the students that the proceeds from their kidneys would cover tuition. But when he sold the kidneys he'd pocket the money himself and simply enter the students' tuition as 'paid' in the system."

Jaspar cried, "That's why so many students are on record as paying for tuition in cash!"

"And that's how he got himself into trouble, because when Fiercey was hired as Dean of Allocations, she started going through the college's financial records with a delousing comb. It couldn't have taken her very long to find the discrepancy. She must have traced it to him."

"I don't see how that led to them jumping in the sack together," said Jaspar. "Ew! No." He clapped his hand over his mouth, suddenly understanding.

Dori said, "Apparently he was exactly to her taste, so in exchange for keeping quiet about his financial shenanigans—"

"That's revolting," Antoine said, pulling a face.

A waiter came to the table with bread and butter.

"So, Dori, you haven't told us why Hank came after *you*," said Antoine.

"This poor guy, Dexter Beet, a student of Linnea's, came

to see me early yesterday evening. He had had one of Hank's back-alley operations in the fall, and they'd botched it," Dori explained. "He'd been sicker than a dog all school year. He was failing all his classes—Linnea thought he might not be so bright, poor kid, but it turned out he was really ill. And he had this terrible secret. Finally another student convinced him he had to come forward with the information. He approached me, because, I guess, I was Linnea's friend and I had cred among the Latin students."

Jaspar buttered himself a round of bread. "Why didn't you go straight to the police?"

"I intended to," Dori said, "but Hank got to me first."

"How?"

"Fimbria. He was in on it, too."

"Fimbria! The school counselor?"

Dori told them about the phone call she'd gotten from Tim Fimbria just before Hank appeared, and how she'd told Fimbria what Dexter had confided in her. "He already knew about my suspicions, because I had told him everything I conjectured about the case when I went to him for a counseling session."

"That scoundrel," said Antoine.

"Fimbria must have tipped Hank off. They knew there was no time to waste, because I was on my way to the police. I told Fimbria what I knew, and minutes later, there was Hank, jigsaw in hand," Dori told them.

"Oh, sweetheart!" Jaspar cried.

Dori refilled her wine glass.

"And what was Fimbria's involvement?" asked Antoine.

"Well, he is an MD, of course, so he must have some basic surgery skills. I suppose kidney removal isn't 'basic,' but then, Dexter is proof that the surgeon was no expert."

"But how did they go from kidneys to hearts? Seems

awfully risky," said Jaspar.

"I think they got greedy," said Dori. "If you kill people, you can take *all* their organs."

"So Linnea became a victim when Hank decided to expand his business," Jaspar surmised.

"Exactly. He worked on campus, so he had opportunities to watch who came and went and at what hours. He probably knew Linnea worked late a lot. Our office window looks right out onto the registration building. He would have seen her silhouette."

"Imagine him right there in Registration, plotting a murder!" Jaspar exclaimed.

"I spoke with the investigator again this morning. He told me they found a stash of Hank's stuff behind a hedge alongside the back of Student Intake. A big canvas bag holding scalpels, disinfectant, syringes—all kinds of stuff. Not only that, but when they found it, there was a crow sitting on it. The same crow that's been visiting my office window for weeks."

"You told me about that crow," Jaspar said, refilling his glass.

"Evidently the crow would pull on the zipper with its beak and fish out shiny items. I was able to produce a whole collection of things the crow had left on my windowsill. Including the detachable jigsaw blade Hank used on Linnea. They're going to run tests and see if it has her DNA on it to be sure, but right now it looks like it's the one."

"Good Lord," murmured Antoine. "And why did Hank leave Linnea's heart in the sink?"

"Turned out Linnea wasn't alone in the building that night. One of my French students, Mary Ellen, was there, and she went to use the restroom. Hank must have heard her coming and he ducked into a stall with Linnea's body. We think he stood on the toilet seat with her body in his arms. This young woman, the French student, was actually living in the building at the time, and she bathed at night. So she spent about half an hour at the sink, giving herself a sponge bath, while Hank was hiding in the stall." The bread basket was empty, and Dori looked around for the waiter and held the basket up for him to see. "By the time she finished and left, he was running out of time. He left the heart in the sink— probably intending to come back and get it—and went to ditch the body in the kiln. But then there was an electrical fire—you remember, set off accidentally by some punk rockers—and by the time the hubbub was over the heart was no longer viable."

"But why did he put the body in the kiln?"

"The detectives think he was planning to cremate Linnea's remains there," Dori explained. "You remember that student who disappeared fall semester, don't you? I have a terrible feeling that his organs were harvested and his body turned to ash right on campus. He became the raw material the art students used to make all that beautiful ash-glazed pottery."

Antoine pushed his plate away.

Dori continued, "The fire alarm in Verizon went off while Hank was over at the Art department. By the time the firefighters had come and dealt with it, the early-bird workers were already starting to show up on campus—custodial staff, landscapers. Hank couldn't have fired up the kiln without drawing attention to himself, so he just left Linnea there."

"Your French student was incredibly lucky he didn't kill her, too."

"Yes, she was," Dori said. "I suppose he might have considered it and figured he wouldn't be able to dispose of two bodies in one night."

"So Hank and Fimbria are under arrest," Antoine said.

"And Fiercey. Maybe the union vote can move forward now," said Jaspar.

"Oh! I forgot to tell you. Turns out Dean Budgie actually *supports* unionization," Dori told her friends. Ian Elf had called Dori with the news that morning. So much had happened in a few hours' time that her head was dog-paddling. The waiter arrived with more bread, and Dori continued, "That's one reason he'd been pressing so hard for the MADCAP—it documents how hard faculty work, how many hours they put in, and all the projects they complete. It shows that part-time faculty actually end up with an hourly pay of less than minimum wage. So it makes a strong case for the union organizers' efforts." Dori shook her head with disbelief. "I looked all over for a secret memo from Fiercey that Linnea had gotten her hands on. The reason I never found it is that Budgie had gotten hold of it first." Dori told her friends about the day she'd seen Linnea's flowered notebook in Budgie's breast pocket. "He put it together with a few other pieces of damning evidence and gave it all to the union organizers. They're preparing a public statement and announcing a vote to unionize."

"That's astonishing," Jaspar said.

"Now if he would just lose the yellow suit…"

"A faculty union will be a great tribute to Linnea," Antoine said.

"And now Linnea can finally rest in peace," Jaspar added.

"Indeed." Dori lifted her glass to Linnea but said no more. Her role in Linnea's final journey was a part of the story she was keeping to herself.

Chapter Fifty-One

THE HEART OF THE MATTER

Dori had left the county forensics building the night before at something over the speed limit. She was giddy thinking what would happen if she were caught impersonating an EMT, an ersatz corpse in her wake and a stolen heart in the trunk of her car. She hoped Alice would be able to improvise her way out of the autopsy room with grace.

Dori took back streets to get to the funeral home and pulled crookedly into a dimly lit lot a block from Peaceful Departures. Hands trembling, she retrieved her gym bag from the trunk. It contained her fencing saber as well as the frozen organ.

A fencing saber, even if she couldn't wield it competently on the *piste*, was still a useful thing. Dori relieved the weapon of its rubber safety tip and used the blade to pick the lock of the funeral home's door.

There were fewer bodies in storage here than at the county morgue, and Dori found Linnea readily on a table in a freezer unit at the back of the building. She removed the heart from her gym bag and placed it on the table beside her dead friend.

"All right, now what?" she said aloud.

Nothing happened.

"Linnea?"

The shape under the white sheet may as well have been a statue. Dori sighed. "I've gone to a lot of trouble to get this for you."

Silence.

"Look, I don't know what else I'm supposed to do. I need a little guidance here." The heart was beginning to thaw, pale blood pooling underneath it.

Linnea did not stir, but Dori thought she heard a sound from the other end of the room. Her own heart froze momentarily. There was no place to hide. Dori tiptoed to the far end of the space. She waited there for the better part of a minute, holding her breath, listening at the door through which she'd entered. Again she heard the sound. It was only the wall clock, pushing its minute hand to the next number with a hollow tock. Dori released her breath.

Linnea's clear, firm voice said, "*At amīcitiā nullō locō excluditur. Friendship finds its way into every place.*"

Dori turned. Linnea was sitting up on the table, the sheet pushed aside. She held the heart in her lap.

Dori flushed with a mixture of relief and trepidation. She took a few steps toward the dead woman. She wanted to ask Linnea to explain everything, but she couldn't think how. Instead, she said, "Are you okay?"

"Yes, thanks. You?"

"It's been a hard couple weeks," Dori admitted. "But the good news is that your murderer is in custody. Thanks in no small part to yours truly." Dori made a little curtsey.

"Tell me all about it," Linnea said, so Dori did. She explained how and why Linnea had been murdered and how

Dori had thwarted the killer. She told Linnea about her various botched attempts to get the heart and the way she and Alice had finally managed it.

"I'm sorry I ever doubted you," Linnea said when she was finished. "I admit I was a little worried."

Dori flushed, ashamed that she had made Linnea wait until the last minute, ashamed that doubt and self-doubt—and her feelings for Pablo—had interfered with her loyalty to Linnea. She leaned against the wall. "No, *I'm* sorry," she said. "I could have been a better friend."

"No worries," Linnea said. "You've carried out a redemptive act."

"A what?"

Linnea explained.

"Do you mean," Dori said when Linnea had elaborated on redemption, "the heart itself wasn't all that important—it was the *effort* that mattered?" Dori wished Linnea could have asked for a favor that didn't involve breaking the law.

"That's probably a fair assessment."

"So now you're free to do as you like?"

"I am."

"Are you coming home?" Dori put her hand over her own heart. For two weeks she'd thought she'd been robbed of her best friend, and now it appeared that might not be the case.

Linnea said, "I'm not coming back to Bridges."

"No?"

"I've had a lot of time to think things through. Bridges was never the right place for me. I shouldn't have settled for a life in which I wanted to disappear all the time."

"I guess you have a point," Dori said. It was hard—having her friend taken away, then given back, then taken away again. "The important thing is that you're safe. I'm relieved I made the deadline," she said.

Linnea smiled a little. "Actually, you missed it."

"What?"

"It's not your fault. They came for me early." Linnea explained the rules of the afterlife and described a pair of Dantesque goons who'd been on her trail.

"So—what does this mean?" Dori asked.

"Well, technically, I am banned from all afterlives, and I'm supposed to stay here in my corpse from now on. But it's okay."

"What? Oh my God," Dori said. It didn't sound okay in the slightest.

"No, it really is, because now I have a sop for Cerberus." Linnea patted the heart. "I think he'll find it very tasty."

Dori felt her eyes grow wide. "I see," she said with slow understanding. It was a lot to take in, and Dori was having a hard time finding words. "And once you get past Cerberus, what will you do?" she said.

"Go to Rome."

"Oh. Of course."

Linnea must have seen the sadness in Dori's face, for she tried some levity: "Maybe I'll finally develop some fashion sense." She set her heart aside and slid off the table to her feet. "I can't thank you enough, my old friend, and I'm going to miss you." She approached Dori for a hug.

Putting her arms around Linnea was like embracing a side of frozen beef, and to override her squeamishness, Dori said, "*Buon viaggio. Bon voyage.*"

Linnea stepped back and picked up her heart. Dori had to admit that, even two weeks dead, her friend appeared more relaxed and cheerful than she'd looked in a long time. Dori smiled. Linnea waved good-bye as she began to vanish, her merrily wiggling fingers the last of her to disappear.

Chapter Fifty-Two

LIGHTHEARTED

Alice drew a small bottle of liquid soap from her bike basket and began to blow bubbles as she pedaled, look-ma-no-hands style, down Poe Avenue. It was a fine day, and a fine task lay before her—registering for summer semester at Middlebridge.

Alice sent out a silent thank-you to Dori Amore as she approached the college district.

In exchange for her hijinks at the morgue—which Alice had secretly enjoyed—the French professor had landed a Millicent Vena Cava award for Alice. Alice hadn't inquired how—mysterious political connections? An ability to hack into the scholarship database?—and she'd felt guilty all day about taking an unearned award. But then Dr. Nil's letter of recommendation had turned up in her mailbox, mailed by whom, Alice would never know. The letter was so full of praise that Alice understood she deserved the scholarship, even if she had snagged it in an unconventional way.

Alice passed the site—a charmingly decrepit apartment

building on a side street near campus—of her new part-time job. She'd landed a little gig as an assistant to a very old poet who wrote, of all things, in Latin. She liked him. He was funny and flirtatious, in a nonagenarian way. He dictated lines of verse and she keyed them into his laptop, since he was too arthritic to type them himself. Alice figured her job assisting the poet would be a healthy addition to her eventual applications to grad school. And of course the extra cash was welcome.

Change had come to Alice's life not gradually but in a tsunami. A few days earlier, Alice had told Tad that Amy could have him all to herself, and she'd asked Tad to move his stuff up into Amy's room. He'd agreed to the new arrangement with painfully little objection.

Then Alice realized she didn't want to go on living at 636 Baudelaire at all—not with the post-partum but still hormonally uneven Jillian; not with the experimental-drug-addled Guppy; and most of all not with an ex-boyfriend and his newly full-time girlfriend.

According to Dr. Amore, Linnea Nil's house had been standing empty since her death. Apparently the late professor's brother lived on the east coast and had little interest in dealing with the house, at least for now. And Dr. Amore knew a French major who needed a place to live, who could room with Alice and share expenses. "I can't officially condone this," she had told Alice, "and if you get caught, I had nothing to do with it, right? But I have a feeling the house is just going to sit there unlived-in for a long time. It might as well serve a purpose. As long as you look after it, I feel Linnea would approve."

So Alice and this other chick, Mary Ellen, would be squatting in Dr. Nil's old place. Alice held the house in reverence, and the idea of a room of her own felt absurdly luxurious. Mary Ellen seemed like she would be a mellow housemate. The two had met briefly that morning. Mary Ellen had showed Alice the stack of French books she was reading. Alice had encouraged Mary Ellen in circumflex rebellion.

Alice guided her bike up onto the sidewalk and rolled past the notions shop and, on a whim, she stopped to check out the stock. Her last visit to the shop had been a sad one, and she thought this would be an auspicious time to pick up a new notion or two.

Alice was locking her bike when she caught sight of Guppy shambling across the street. She hailed him. "Wanna see my new tat?" she asked, pulling up her sleeve. "It's in honor of Dr. Nil."

Her old housemate looked over the tattoo. *Cor unum*, it read, in Roman-style capital letters across a red heart. "What does it mean?"

"One heart."

"Oh, yeah. Obviously." Guppy nodded in appreciation.

"I owe you a thank-you."

"Why's that?"

"Because if it weren't for you, I never would have known about the Marmettes," Alice explained. "And if you hadn't given me a basketball schedule for my birthday, I would not have known that tryouts were today."

"You tried out?"

"And made the team," Alice said. "Rehearsals start next week. There's a lot of choreography to learn before basketball season."

"Oh. Sweet," Guppy said. "Well, hey, I need to scoot. I slept through my Chem final and I have to go talk to the prof."

"Oops."

"Yeah, I was asleep for six days. New drug trial." Guppy grinned.

Alice waved goodbye and pushed open the door of the notions shop. The little bell above the door tinkled.

The clerk looked up. "Haven't seen you in a while," he said. "Take a look around. We just got a new shipment."

Alice picked an aisle and began flipping through notions. She came across an old one of her own, "Monogamy is inherently oppressive," which she'd sold back to the shop a few weeks earlier. Right behind it in the rack, since the notions were organized alphabetically, she found "Monogamy is the deepest expression of real love." This latter notion was a dark mahogany color, polished and almost antique-looking, very classy, and Alice was drawn to it. She pulled it out of the rack and looked at it for a long time. She set it aside to think about it while she continued browsing, once in a while returning to it, fingering it and considering.

Alice checked out the crochet hooks and darning needles and considered whether she could use them as musical instruments. After she'd broken up with Tad, she realized she couldn't stand to go on playing music with him, especially with Amy following them around to every gig and every practice like a devoted puppy. Anyway, Alice had been wanting to take her music in another direction for a while. She was experimenting with sounds that could be coaxed from a bass by playing it with something other than her fingers—spoons, for example, and oil dipsticks.

She had decided to start her own band, and Brian had defected with her. They called themselves Day Shift Werewolf, and they would perform at the student government picnic on the last day of the term.

Alice carried the monogamy notion in both hands—it was

hefty—to the counter. She stroked the notion with one finger. She took some bills out of a pouch, counted them, and pushed the money across the counter toward the clerk. Then, at the last instant, she snatched up the notion, took it back to its rack, and left the store instead with "Manicured lawns are an instrument of social control."

Then she hopped astride her bike and pedaled off to campus.

Author's Note

Writing a novel is like getting pregnant: if you understood at the beginning what you were in for, you'd never agree to it. This book, which was supposed to be a quick project, turned into a labor of six years. Many midwives helped me move the baby out. I would like to thank the following people for holding my hand when I was screaming and for gently coaching me to "push": Kate Carney and Charles Grey, who commented on an early draft (you were both right); Michael Cannarella, who helped me understand how unions work; Scott Prahl, David Levant and the kind folks at the Fencing Center Salle Trois Armes, who gave me fencing pointers (and yes, I'm aware that I bent the rules, both of tournaments and of physics, for my purposes); Deborah Hobbie, Bridget Benton, Tamara Sorella and Jill Kelly, who commented on a middle draft; Zan Kocher, who helped me fine-tune my Latin and French and who found typos with his eagle eye; Melissa Edwards, who offered advice about the publishing world; Izettta Irwin and Mary Eastman, from whom I filched good lines; Rick Craycraft, who chauffeured me to countless writing retreats and who fixed my faulty sports and power tool references, among other things; Sam Underwood, who taught me about role playing games and the French Revolution, and who offered insights into the last draft; Jerry Underwood, who beautifully copy-edited the final manuscript; and all the wonderful women of Writing Friday, without whose constant presence I might still be stuck at nine centimeters.

The author with the poet Vergil, Naples, Italy

Jan Underwood lives and writes in Portland, Oregon. She has
taught for more than 20 years at Portland Community College,
which, thankfully, does not much resemble Middlebridge.
Utterly Heartless is her second novel.

Proof

Made in the USA
Charleston, SC
13 August 2013